Praise for One Drop . . .

"People who are from New Orleans, and those that call it home, understand that it is a special and unique place. Alice Wilson-Fried's novel, *One Drop*, captures the spirit and essence of New Orleans with its entertaining and colorful characters. Having hurricane Katrina as a foreboding backdrop, adds to the suspense as the main characters weave in and out of danger." — Dr. Calvin Mackie, New Orleans, LA

"I enjoyed reading Alice Wilson-Fried's impressive latest mystery, *One Drop*, set in New Orleans. It is a fast-paced satisfying story with clever humor, a dead billionaire, a family's drama, complex and secret race relations and one tropical storm about to become a hurricane named Katrina. Everything is riding on Ladonis Washington, the first Black PR director of a steamboat company, with aspirations to become the first woman Vice President. The price of failure could be tragic for Ladonis and her innocent co-worker, for family members who rely on Ladonis, and for the survival of the Floating Palace Steamboat Company. I feel 100% positive about the excellence of this mystery." — Elizabeth Lyon, Book Editor and Best Selling Author of *The Sell Your Novel Tool Kit* and *Manuscript Makeover*

I'd follow Ladonis Washington, the 'accidental' detective from *Outside Child*, anywhere! In *One Drop*, she takes on another New Orleans mystery, and shares her thoughts, and the wry comments of her brother, HeartTrouble, as they contend with race relations, corruption, hurricane Katrina and, of course, murder. Alice's insights about interracial attitudes are as compelling as the plot. — Marilee Scholl, Retired Teacher, Turning Pages Book Club, Vacaville, CA

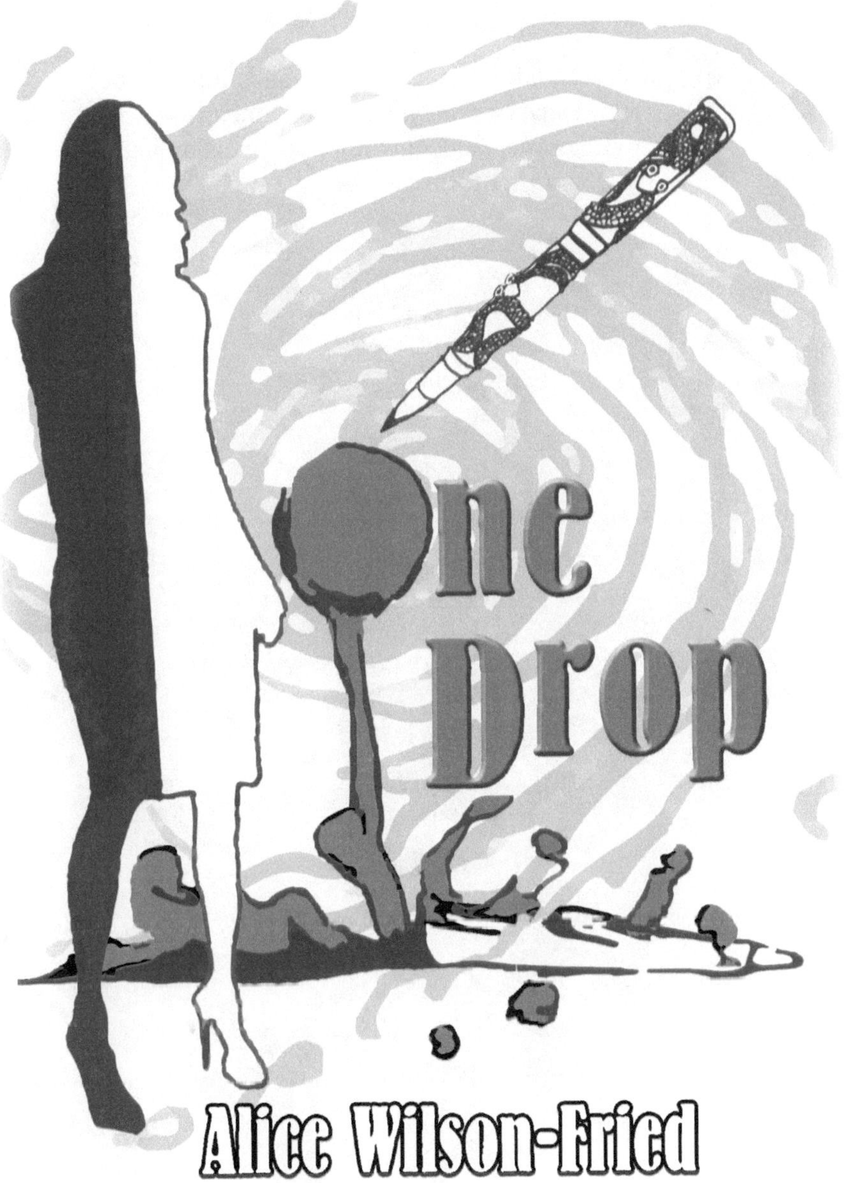

One Drop

Alice Wilson-Fried

Bink Books
Bedazzled Ink Publishing Company • Fairfield, California

978-1-949290-48-6 paperback

Cover Art
by
Russell Weber

Cover Design
by

Bink Books
a division of
Bedazzled Ink Publishing Company
Fairfield, California
http://www.bedazzledink.com

For my children, grandchildren and nieces and nephews.
You fill my life with joy and pride.

Acknowledgements

Special thanks to my grandson, Alex, who read pages written before the passing of my husband and sister. He made me promise to finish even though my creative energy was overwhelmed by sadness and grief. He reminded me of my words of encouragement to him, never give up on your dreams.

Thanks, Alex.

Prologue
Clicking Beetle

LADONIS WASHINGTON SAT in the passenger seat of a rented Toyota Solara convertible, top down. "These mountains sure are so pretty," she observed, awed by the desert's beauty cast through the glow of the setting Arizona sun. "But there are no trees."

Bunnie Sinclair, Ladonis' co-worker and nemesis at the Floating Palace Steamboat Company, gripped the steering wheel while leaning forward to read the street signs as she drove through the Ahwatuakee district of the Phoenix mountainside. Bunnie had been a thorn in Ladonis's side since the day they'd met—when the company that operated the country's only two overnight paddle wheelers, relocated its headquarters to New Orleans from Cincinnati. Yet, here she was, on her way to a high-society soiree invited by the bane of her career existence.

Bret Collins, FPSC's CEO, had arranged for Bunnie, Director of Charter Sales, to give a presentation at a meeting of a newly formed organization of female corporate executives. The board had directed him to encourage them to charter one FPSC's paddle wheelers for their first conference next year. He'd strongly suggested that the company would have a better chance of booking that charter if the black female Director of Publicity was on hand to help with the pitch. And since Ladonis had an executive corporate position on the brain, she'd jumped at the opportunity. However, hanging out with Bunnie after they'd completed their task was not part of the plan.

"Fifteen Warpaint Road," Ladonis exclaimed. "Turn. We're here."

Bunnie mumbled something incoherent and drove onto the circular drive. She stopped the car behind a sleek shiny black BMW in front of the four-car garage attached to the two-story house. Ladonis got out of the convertible and cast a wide-eyed stare onto the sprawling home and its landscaping—red geraniums bordered by the bright white flowers of sweet alyssums with rock mulch.

"A palace," Ladonis whispered, hoping to hide the fact that outside of pictures, she'd never seen anything like this structure, let alone enter one.

Bunnie nudged her out of her stupor.

Ladonis frowned. How humiliating if Bunnie suspected she hadn't made it far enough up the ladder to get invited to a place like this before. "Are you sure you have the right address for this party?" She smoothed out her knee-length, blood-red, figure-hugging cocktail dress.

"Auction," Bunnie said. "It's a charity auction where rich and famous people bid on and purchase collectibles and other expensive items to benefit a charity. Not a party."

"Auction, party, whatever. I don't hear any music. You said there'd be a live band."

"The music probably hasn't started yet." Bunnie retrieved her briefcase from the back seat. "I was asked to get here early with my mother's jade. I am a last-minute contributor and my stuff has to be catalogued or something, then put on display before the guests arrive."

"Well, I'm just saying it's a little quiet for a party. I mean auction." She still wasn't convinced that Bunnie's recently deceased mother had known the richest man in Louisiana, let alone extend her daughter an invitation to some swanky party in Arizona. "I hope the Sun's basketball players show up like you promised. I'd hate to think I changed my flight just so you could attend a wealthy flea market. I was supposed to get home in time to take my mama grocery shopping. I've already missed her choir's concert to help you out."

Bunnie walked up to Ladonis. "What's that noise?"

Ladonis trembled, the sound eerily familiar and frightening.

Bunnie looked down. "See that?" She pointed to an elongated shaped, brownish colored insect making a clicking sound as it struggled to flip back on its legs before joining the caravan of bugs making haste to a boulder. "That's a beetle. It's called a clicking beetle because it makes that noise."

Ladonis headed up the steps to the front door after Bunnie who raised her hand to ring the bell. The door flung open followed by a stronger, louder click. Ladonis gasped. Bunnie's briefcase fell to the ground.

"Heard that," Ladonis said, staring into the barrel of a nine-millimeter.

"Turn around," the masked man holding the gun ordered, picking up the briefcase.

"Oh, my God. Are you thieves?" Bunnie turned to face the masked men. "Give me back my briefcase."

Ladonis almost tripped down the steps, but caught herself. That crazy white girl held out her hand as if she expected the masked man to respond. The men looked at each other and snickered, then grabbed her shoulders, and shoved her forward. Bunnie, her eyes and mouth opened wide with terror, glanced at Ladonis.

"Where's the host? Where are you taking us?" Ladonis asked.

"The garage," one of the men said.

Were they being kidnapped? Killed? Ladonis wanted to cry out, to run, to protect herself. Her vocal chords froze in panic mode.

Inside the garage, the two men tied Ladonis's and Bunnie's hands behind their backs, covered their mouths with duct tape then pushed them inside a Bentley. Or was it a BMW?

Chapter One
Arresting Developments

"SLOW DOWN, BUNNIE." Ladonis tripped backward in her half-inch-high sling-backs on the wet, slick brick pathway to the New Orleans Police Department (NOPD). She rubbed her tongue back and forth across her teeth. Disgusting after-flight breath. Only thirty minutes since she and Bunnie Sinclair had debarked a plane at New Orleans International Airport from Phoenix, Arizona following the business trip from hell.

"I want the NOPD on this right away." Bunnie climbed the steps two at a time of the converted 1826 Greek mansion on Conti at Royal Street. On the top step, she turned to face Ladonis. "Those two thugs who jumped us?" Her voice cracked. Distress lines bunched up around her eyes. "They knew exactly who I was and what I was hauling. They knew because Jarvis Maynard arranged it so that I'd be there."

"What do you think NOPD can do?"

"Arrest him, that's what." Bunnie yanked open the plexiglass door and stormed inside.

"Arrest Jarvis Maynard?" Ladonis glared after Bunnie. "Are you kidding?"

Ladonis sucked in a quick breath. Didn't she know that the Maynards owned as much of New Orleans as the DeBeers owned diamonds in the world. Just as sure as the clouds circled the moon and the light drizzle that misted the air forecast a heavy rain, she had a pretty good idea what was in store if Bunnie stormed into this French Quarter police precinct and accused the richest man in Louisiana of robbery. She flapped her hands and rushed to catch up to Bunnie.

A boat-sized cop stood behind the tall counter desk. He was so large, his fat belly struggled to stay inside his shirt. And he had a scowl on his face designed to make anyone feel that if there was a problem communicating with him, the problem was theirs, not his.

Why was this woman willing to go this distance to accuse Mr. Money Bags USA of instigating a plan to steal from the likes of her? Then again, who would've thought that she, Ladonis Washington, a descendant of slaves and former inhabitant of the Magnolia Housing Project, would skirt the lines between right and wrong to score a window office in corporate America?

"Can I help you?" the desk cop said to Bunnie, continuing to look down at whatever he was reading.

"The bastard set me up." Bunnie placed both her hands on the counter, her head peeking over the top. "He had two crooks gag and tie me up at gunpoint and then leave me to suffocate in a garage."

Was this white girl for real? Ladonis couldn't take her eyes off Bunnie, caught up in her own drama. Did she forget that Ladonis and about twenty other people had been assaulted as well?

"And why would the bastard do that?" the desk cop asked, his head still lowered, his sarcasm as commanding as a drum roll.

"For my jade, that's why." The sheen of sweat on her cheeks and forehead glistened under the fluorescent lights. "He knew I would be there. He got me invited to that auction. So he paid two men to steal from me. I know he did."

Ladonis stepped forward just when the big man lifted his head. She didn't need eye contact to detect his smugness. Still, nothing jarred like the cool, condescending glare of a blue-eyed good old boy in a police uniform. Ladonis retreated.

"Who told who to steal what?" The policeman said.

"Jarvis Maynard told two thieves to steal my jade." Bunnie tugged at her torn, soiled, black, day-to-night dinner jersey mini dress, forcing it to slide back into place on her petite frame. "They stole it and left me for dead. I want him arrested."

"Jarvis Maynard?" the desk cop said, eyeballing Bunnie. "You want Jarvis Maynard arrested? *The* Jarvis Maynard?"

"Yes, *the* Jarvis Maynard," Bunnie said. No missing the emotion in the way she stressed "the." "He committed a crime against me, and I want him thrown in jail. The bastard set me up."

Ladonis inched her lean 24/Hour Fitness sculpted body backward to the bench near the entrance door. She took a seat and crouched down. Bunnie had the cop's attention. Time for her to be invisible.

The policeman's eyes widened as he took Bunnie into his sight. Was he surprised at how stunning and sophisticated Bunnie looked despite her disheveled appearance? Or was it her incredulous accusation against Jarvis Maynard? A mocking smile spread across his face. But at whom was he smiling? Himself for ogling a nutcase or at the nutcase herself?

Ladonis fanned the bodice of her dress away from her sweaty skin, wishing she'd had the good sense to go home and wash away her travel grit instead of following this woman. Thank goodness for the small breeze from the ceiling fan overhead. Too bad it squealed like the Aaron Neville wannabe sitting on the other end of the bench belting out "Tell It Like Is."

"Let me get a detective on this." The desk cop sounded as amused as Ladonis felt anxious.

"He has to pay." Bunnie's brow furrowed as she blew out a truckload of impatience. Every bit of her five-feet-three-inch body pulsated.

Ladonis couldn't tell by Bunnie's wounded tone if she was out for justice or revenge. And why was it so important to get either tonight? Didn't these things need time for a plan to come together? Besides everybody knew that when it came to the rich and connected, NOPD had a way of turning a blind eye to evidence and a deaf ear to witnesses. Accusing Jarvis Maynard of stealing will not fly. It didn't in Phoenix and won't in this town. His town.

An anybody-but-me expression crossed the cop's eyes. Ladonis recognized the put-off. A suspicious bank teller would've said, "I have to check the signature" or it's over my limit or under my limit or some other today-is-not-your-day corporate speak.

"Have a seat, Miss—?" He flung his hand in the direction of where Ladonis sat.

"Sinclair," Bunnie responded. "Bunnie Sinclair."

Who in their right mind would name their child Bunnie? Ladonis had chalked it up to a white thing. But right now, listening to Bunnie accuse Jarvis Maynard of robbery, her name added silly to the tone of her angst.

Bunnie paced up and down. Her heels clicked on the tiled floor, overpowering the sounds from the squeaky fan, the grumbling drunks crowded in the holding cell on the other end of the room, and even the Aaron Neville wannabe who wouldn't shut up.

"Girl," Ladonis scolded, "sit down. You're wearing out my ear drums."

"You see the way he looked at me?" Bunnie plopped down beside Ladonis, forcing Ladonis to move closer to the off-key crooner. "The way he talked to me? I'm not some lunatic, you know."

"Girl—" Ladonis gave the singer the evil eye. "The way you bust in here ranting and raving, even I think you're a lunatic. And I was in that car with you."

The desk cop re-entered the room followed by a man wearing a dark suit, his tie hanging around his neck. Bunnie jumped up and walked toward the two men. Ladonis slid down on the bench and lowered her head.

"That her?" the suited policeman said to the desk cop.

"Yeah," the desk cop said, shrugging.

"I'm Detective Shiloh," the man said to Bunnie. "What's your problem, lady?"

"The problem is Jarvis Maynard." Bunnie craned her neck up to look at him. She leaned onto one hip and placed her index finger on her chin. "He stole several thousand dollars' worth of jewelry from me. A jade necklace. Ah . . . ah . . . matching bracelet and earrings. Not to mention all of my identification and credit cards."

"Look, ma'am, I ain't got time for foolishness," the detective said.

Ladonis recognized the menace in his voice, the crease in his forehead. She had dealt with his kind before. Nothing short of murdering his mother's torturer would arouse empathy in this good old boy.

"The new weatherman on Channel 8 say a hurricane probably on the way," Detective Shiloh said. "Where did you say this robbery took place?"

"On a Saudi Arabian's estate in Phoenix," Bunnie informed him. "Night before tonight."

"Did you say Phoenix?" The detective passed the desk cop a this-woman-is-a-kook look. "As in Phoenix, Arizona?"

"That's right," Bunnie said, her head bobbing up and down. "Jarvis Maynard arranged for me to be at this private jewelry show there. But instead of telling my mother's clients to buy from me like he said he would, he sent two thugs to steal my jade." Her jawbones twitched.

Shiloh rubbed his chin, a grimace on his face. Clearly Bunnie made no sense to him. Perhaps Ladonis should interject how one's communicative skills became skewed when one's life was physically threatened at the point of a nine-millimeter. No, best she held her tongue. No need for the detective to think they were both nuts.

"Now why would Jarvis Maynard want to kill you?" The detective removed his tie.

"Because—" Bunnie folded her arms across her chest. "Why don't you ask him when you arrest him?"

The detective pivoted to look Ladonis's way. Oh, no. So far he hadn't acknowledged her hiding on the bench, hadn't put the two of them together. But how would he respond if Bunnie continued to be defiant and forced her to put in her two cents? She had not gone to Phoenix to become a character in Bunnie's life saga.

"Just how do you even know Mr. Maynard?" The desk cop slowed and softened his speech as if he believed Bunnie had difficulty understanding him. Could this be the voice of a so-called compassionate cop? "Ma'am?"

"My mama," Bunnie told him, also slowing her words. "My mama, who passed away last month, used to own an antique store. Jarvis Maynard is a collector and was one of her clients. He called me up after her funeral and offered to help me sell off some of her inventory. That's when he told me about this auction in Phoenix."

Ladonis recalled the day Bunnie told her that story after she'd buried her mother. Her jaws had twitched, and either she couldn't or wouldn't use makeup to cover the dark circles under her puffy eyes. She sounded crazy then and she sounds crazy now. No way was this cop going to believe that old man Maynard called Bunnie. Let alone offer to help her.

"And you told this to the Phoenix police, I take it." The detective looked at the desk cop standing at the end of the counter. The men shared a questioning stare and moved back, away from Bunnie.

"Yes," Bunnie said. "But they told me that there had been a rash of home invasions in that part of the city. So, they sent me here. Well, not here, specifically."

"Sounds like you were probably at the wrong place at the wrong time." The corners of the detective's mouth turned upward. Not into a smile, per se. More like a mean-spirited smirk signifying that he'd tricked her into making a fool of herself.

"It was not the wrong place." Bunnie raised her voice and rubbed the back of her neck. "It was not the wrong place."

Ladonis's skin tingled. Like hell it wasn't the wrong place. And she had red, tender skin around her mouth to prove it. She could still feel the stinging pain from when the guest who'd found them pulled that duct tape from her face.

"After my mom died," Bunnie explained, "the great Jarvis Maynard called and told me that he and my mother had been associates for years. That he knew for a fact several of her best clients would be at that auction. He set me up, I tell you."

Ladonis's eyes closed, weighted down by sadness. She understood how difficult it could be to process an assault on your life from personal experience. Perhaps someone should explain to the detective how violated, scary, and demoralizing it felt to be physically assaulted at gunpoint. But she said nothing.

"Look, lady," the detective said. "I mean, Ms. Sinclair. If the Phoenix police need us to get involved, they'll contact us. Then we'll contact you."

Ladonis's jaws clenched, set in resentment. If not for Bret's directive, she would not have gotten involved in a bi-state crime with this crazy white woman. And she wouldn't have been escorted through the airport security like a thing to be discarded with a condescending, "don't call us, we'll call you." Despite the free airline ticket home, she'd been humiliated enough by police because of Ms. Bunnie freakin' Sinclair.

"What?" Bunnie stomped up to the detective. "Are you telling me that you're not going to pick him up?"

The detective turned and walked through the swing door behind the counter. Bunnie just stood there staring at that door as if she expected the detective to come back and respond to her. Finally, she looked to the desk cop for an answer.

"Well—" She planted her hands on the counter and leaned forward.

"Like the detective said, we're not arresting anyone."

"But he's a thief," Bunnie cried, her lips and chin trembling. "And he's a—"

Ladonis tilted her head, a reflex reaction to the abrupt end to Bunnie's outburst. She waited to hear what else Bunnie had to say about Jarvis Maynard that might explain what was fueling her unreasonable attitude. Bunnie said nothing.

"Look, lady." The desk cop clicked his pen and tapped it on the counter. "We don't have jurisdiction. We don't have the authority to arrest anyone in this matter, especially not Jarvis Maynard."

Ladonis watched the anger, or was it pain, scroll up on Bunnie's face. What could Ladonis do? Nothing. Neither she nor Bunnie could say anything that would get through to this guy or anyone else in the NOPD.

"What do you mean? Maynard arranged a robbery. Paid someone to steal from me, for Christ sake. And he did it from right here." Bunnie pointed to the air. "Who cares about the Phoenix police?"

It was uncharacteristic for Bunnie to be irate, even under pressure. The girl was usually Miss Calm, Cool, and Calculating to a fault. What was really going on? Ladonis stood up, grabbed Bunnie's hand, and pulled her to the exit.

"Time to go. You can check in with the Phoenix police." Ladonis said in a low voice. "Let them take it from here."

"No." Bunnie snatched her hand away from Ladonis. "Jarvis Maynard set me up. I'm not going to let him get away with stealing from me just because he's some old southern aristocrat."

"He set you up how exactly?" Ladonis screeched through gritted teeth. She'd had enough of Bunnie's entitled, southern belle tantrum. "Pumping me up with lies about meeting basketball players and not telling me beforehand that you'd arranged for us to attend some swanky private auction to sell your mother's antique crap that got us robbed at gunpoint—now that's a set up."

"He has to pay, Ladonis." Bunnie's quivering lips pinched.

"Give yourself some time to calm yourself." Ladonis sucked in her cheeks. "I know I need time to get this duct-tape taste out of my mouth."

Bunnie backed away, cutting her eyes to the desk cop.

He stared back at her, shaking his head.

"Thanks for nothing," Bunnie called out to him. "I'll just have to take care of Jarvis Maynard myself."

"Girl, shut your mouth." Ladonis stepped behind Bunnie and shoved her out the door. "What are you trying to do? Get arrested?"

Chapter Two
Mo' White-Folk Shit

"DONNIE," LADONIS'S OLDEST friend, Evalena Matthews, called out. Housesitting, she had been behind closed doors in the guest room when Ladonis arrived home. Ladonis glanced at her bedside clock, inhaling the smell of cinnamon wafting its way upstairs. Now her house sitter was in the kitchen baking her favorite Pillsbury rolls.

Ladonis pulled the covers over her head. She'd been in bed for just an hour, unable to close out the memory of kicking and scratching at the door of a locked car until a couple from D.C. arrived for the auction, found her and Bunnie in the garage, the house ransacked, many of the auction items stolen and the owner and staff locked in a wine cellar. She wanted nothing more than to stay cuddled safely between the sheets.

"You heard me, Donnie? Get up. We gotta talk."

Ladonis didn't want to talk, even to her oldest friend. Evalena had taken her to task for going on the trip to Phoenix with Bunnie. Said that tokenism was just as degrading as racism and sexism, and that she should go to the New Hope Baptist Church Annual Gospel Concert to hear her own mother's solo performance instead. But Evalena only knew half the story. She was bound to go bat-shit nationalistic when she found out that Ladonis had also agreed to hang out with Bunnie at a private charity auction to hob-knob with professional basketball players.

She closed her eyes. Why in the world did she allow the likes of Bunnie Sinclair lure her to the Ahwataukee mountains? Now she had to face Evalena. She loved her bus-driver friend, but the girl had America's "isms" engrained in her mind, body, and soul and relished any and every opportunity to remind Ladonis how they fit into her life.

Ladonis yanked the covers off her face. If she wanted peace between her and her sisterfriend, she had to woman up and listen to Evalena rant about choosing work over family. She'd have to reveal her secret motive—her belief that the trip could be a step toward becoming the company's first female vice president. A personal goal she hadn't shared with anyone for fear of jinxing her prospect.

She dragged her long legs out of bed, snatched up a pair of black yoga trousers off the floor, and stumbled to the stairs. If she'd taken the scheduled red-eye flight home when negotiations with the female executives had wrapped up, she wouldn't be in this situation.

"Thanks for having my back and going to hear Mama sing," she rehearsed as she bounded down the steps, pulling an oversized black and gold Saints football tee shirt over her head. But when she arrived in the kitchen entrance, she knew she had to re-think her approach. There was no need to pussy foot around.

"Before you say anything, I know how you feel about Bunnie and how you call it, 'that slave boat' company I work for." FPSC owned and operated the only two overnight paddle wheelers, the *Bayou Queen* and *Magnolia Belle* still traveling America's rivers. "Was Mama real upset when you picked her up instead of me?"

"No." Evalena put the teakettle onto a lit burner. "We didn't go."

"Why?" Ladonis asked, her voice pitched low and scratchy. "Was Mama that mad? Oh, my God. Is she sick? She did say that she'd been feeling poorly the last few days."

"Well." Evalena said. Ladonis got the feeling her old friend didn't want to respond, or was afraid of the answer. "That's what we need to talk about."

What's wrong with Mama? Ladonis massaged the sharp twinge in her chest.

"The program's pianist had a stroke."

"A stroke? Gail had a stroke?" How old was the woman? Thirty? Thirty-five?

Ladonis sighed. She'd attended Sunday school with Gail. Too many of her peers had strokes these days. Was there something in the New Orleans air and food? Her mother surely thought so.

"The concert was cancelled." Evalena pulled the silk sleep cap from her head. Her dreads fell free to her shoulders. "But—"

The front door swung open. Evalena whirled around. Ladonis's younger brother, HeartTrouble, stormed in. He hurried past her and

Evalena in the kitchen into the cluttered, though stylish living room. His dark cocoa-colored skin, shiny from sweat.

Ladonis gave him an intense, fevered stare. "Boy." She marched over to confront him. "I didn't give you a key so you could bust your gangsta ass in here whenever you feel like it."

God forbid her six-foot-two, lanky sibling should ever change that vintage, neon-colored, rayon seventies Super Fly look. The look he'd adopted after watching reruns of Black exploitation movies.

"Did Mama send you to board the place up for the storm that is supposed to be coming?"

"You wish," HeartTrouble said, stepping over a stack of books and papers strewn about near the archway entrance to the living room.

"Mama needs to calm down," Ladonis said, ignoring his response. "According to Bob Breck, that storm is way out there in the Bahamas somewhere. Just because her weather God, Nash Roberts, didn't say it, doesn't mean Breck is wrong. Who knows, it may never get here."

Evalena made her way from the kitchen to the living room to join them. HeartTrouble's grasping hands found the remote control under the stack of vintage *True Romance* magazines she'd borrowed from the library, on the coffee table. Nothing she liked more than reading mystery novels and love stories. She'd discovered archived *True Romance* magazines while on an Internet hunt for short love stories. Turned out to be the reading breather that fit perfectly into her busy schedule.

HeartTrouble smiled when he noticed Evalena walking in. Ladonis squinted and frowned. Why was her brother always in combat mode with her and a gentle lamb with Evalena?

"Woodrow—" Except for their mother and schoolteachers, Evalena was the only other person who called HeartTrouble by his given name. "Somebody chasing you?"

HeartTrouble clicked the television on and held the remote out, scrolling through the channels until he found the news. "Why, Donnie?" His tone was pleading and condemning at the same time. He pointed to the television. "Why in the world you had to go and get mixed up in mo' white folk shit?"

Evalena stared wide-eyed at the television screen. "Hey, that's, that's—"

"Bunnie," Ladonis whispered.

"Yeah, her." HeartTrouble's soft voice did not match the glare of defiance in his eyes.

On the screen, the cuffed woman's makeup was smeared and spotty. Her expressions shifted from scared and scared to death. Ladonis shivered. The woman on television looked downright ghostly. Worse than when she wore the torn, soiled day-to-night black jersey dress for two days straight, before and after their Phoenix ordeal.

"Miss Thang don't look so good. Poor thing," Evalena said, tsk-tsking, pretending to be sympathetic.

"You wouldn't look good either," HeartTrouble told her, "if the cops thought you'd killed Jarvis Maynard."

Jarvis Maynard? Dead? Ladonis, her eyes glued to the television, envisioned the image of Bunnie the night before trying to explain to the cops why they should arrest the billionaire.

"Lord, today," Evalena said, shaking her head.

"How the girl even know Jarvis Maynard is what I wanna know?" Was HeartTrouble making an accusation or asking a question?

"She didn't," Ladonis whispered. "Her mama did."

Her body twitched. "According to Bunnie, her mama was an antiques dealer and old man Maynard was some kind of collector. He was the one who told Bunnie about that auction we went to in Phoenix."

Evalena's eyes lit up.

Uh-oh. Ladonis hadn't told her about the auction yet.

"Is that why you had to spend another day and night there? I thought you went to Phoenix to get women CEOs to cruise on them slave boats," Evalena said, taking a warrior woman stance.

"I did. But Bunnie needed to get rid of some of her mother's jade inventory to increase her cash flow. And since Jarvis Maynard was nice enough to tell her about this auction in Phoenix—and since we were there, we went." She neglected to mention that instead of selling Bunnie's mother's jade, they were robbed, gagged, and tied up with duct tape.

"Looks like Jarvis Maynard got knocked off for his trouble." HeartTrouble glared at his sister. "And the cops think someone you know done it."

She raised her middle finger fast in his face. That "someone you know" jab was the refrain she used on him every time one of his acquaintances got arrested and/or exposed on the news.

"Look." Evalena pointed to the television.

A picture of Jarvis Maynard popped onto the screen. Ladonis searched the crawl line below. She'd heard Whoopi Goldberg say once that the real news was on the crawl line. Could HeartTrouble be mistaken? Was Jarvis Maynard really dead? But, there it was in cold print tracking across her television screen. Jarvis Maynard was dead.

"Sweet Jesus," Ladonis groaned, shock, anger, and betrayal scrambling around in her head. Had Bunnie deliberately put her in a bad situation? Her knees slacked at the memory of her insisting that Jarvis Maynard be arrested.

"The man was shot through the heart." HeartTrouble walked through the archway into the kitchen toward the refrigerator.

"And the police think Bunnie did it?" Ladonis mumbled.

She blew air between her lips. Could Bunnie really have killed the man? How in the world did she even get to him that time of night? Didn't all the super-rich have guards or something?

"Don't you drink nothin' but wine?" HeartTrouble peered inside his sister's refrigerator. "I want a Dr. Pepper."

Ladonis ignored him and turned up the volume on the television.

"Miss Sinclair," the newscaster said, "accompanied by an unnamed black woman, filed a criminal complaint against Jarvis Maynard late last night."

"You hear that?" HeartTrouble said. "Unnamed black woman. They already talkin' 'bout how y'all was at the police station together."

"They wouldn't let her file the complaint," Ladonis said to the television. "Tell the story straight. That's why people never really know what the hell is going on."

"Sooner or later," HeartTrouble barked, "it's gonna cross somebody's mind that the unnamed black woman is you and ask if you was in on the killin' too."

"Boy, stop talking out the side of your neck. And get out my refrigerator. This is not Winn Dixie."

Ladonis had to do something. To find out what Bunnie did or didn't do after she'd dropped her off. She ran up the steps and grabbed her trusted, bad-hair-day Saints baseball cap and her walking Sketchers. Then she circled back and collected her keys from the kitchen counter, her purse from a chair in the living room, and headed for the door.

"Where are you goin'?" Evalena asked.

"To see Bunnie." Ladonis slid the black and gray sneakers onto her feet. "She must be beside herself by now."

"And just what do you think you can do?" Evalena's sentiment hovered between scorn and outright hostility.

"I don't exactly know what I can do." Ladonis hated how Evalena could make her feel like she was in a closed box being wheeled through a crowd just because her oldest friend was uncomfortable around anyone who wasn't black. "But it is my job to know what's going on. You know, so I can monitor what the press says about the company. Besides, the girl has no family here and maybe I can give her some support."

"Support?" HeartTrouble's voice hit a high note of disbelief. "You gonna support your ass straight into the penitentiary. Why did you go to the police with her anyhow?"

"I couldn't let her go alone," Ladonis murmured, unwilling to look at her brother. "Not in her condition."

"What condition?" Evalena said. "Whine-i-tis? That's not a condition. According to you, whining is her nature." She moved closer to Ladonis. "Don't fool yourself, Donnie. You ain't got what it takes to change nature."

"Yeah," HeartTrouble said. "And what makes you think them cops ain't gonna want to know if you went with her to kill Maynard?"

"Are you crazy?"

"No." HeartTrouble rolled his knuckles. "But you can believe that's what them cops is thinkin' on right now."

Ladonis glared at her brother. HeartTrouble glared back, but with a painful expression she couldn't ignore. His ghetto-sensitive analysis unnerved her, same as when she'd watched how unglued Bunnie became after the robbery. She'd never witnessed someone succumb to the power of their vulnerabilities that way. Made her think about her own susceptibilities and how strong she'd fare if they were exposed and manipulated. Moments like this made her feel as though she was the last person standing after fighting for her life in a war she didn't understand.

"Her jewelry had been stolen, for Christ sake," Ladonis said in a softer more reflective voice. "She was upset, but after we left the police, Bunnie drove me straight here. She ran through a red light. She said something about making him pay, but, I'm sure she didn't mean she'd kill him."

"Looks like she meant it all right." Evalena's voice oozed contempt. "She didn't get arrested for just complaining. The cops must have somethin' else on her."

"Yeah," HeartTrouble added. "Somethin' like she put a bullet straight through the old dude's ticker."

Hearing HeartTrouble mention the old man's ticker stirred Ladonis's sibling sensitivity. She'd longed believed that if not for her brother's heart murmur, he might've at least tried to live up to his potential. She heard the reporter's voice on television and her empathy left her as quickly as it arrived.

"Forecasters are saying that storm winds are continuing to pick up speed," Damon Singleton, a young meteorologist, droned on the television.

HeartTrouble pointed to the television. "If you got half a brain, which you act like you ain't sometimes, you'd go out and buy that plywood like I've been tellin' you to do and board up all these glass doors and windows you got in this place. That Katrina storm supposed to be the real deal. That means Katrina is more important than that white girl."

"Boy, move out my way. I have to find out what happened."

"Why?" Evalena griped. "Who died and left you in charge of white people?"

Ladonis stared at Evalena. How could she remind her nationalistic best friend that she was Director of Public Relations responsible for managing the spread of information about a company in corporate America, and that was a position of power that few women, especially black women had. She had to know what went down between Bunnie and Maynard. The information could heighten her chances to pull ahead, and increase her chance to become the next Vice President of Marketing and Sales when the current VP left next month. She desperately wanted that title and longed for the status of being the first female at the company to have it. Never mind that merely having that goal could expose her vulnerability to corporate failure.

The whistle on the teakettle blew. The sound hit her ears like a bugle. Ladonis could not continue to argue with her pissed-off friend or listen to her fool brother, neither of whom would understand her in a million years.

"I've got to go." She walked to the door. "It's my job."

Katrina had to wait. Hurricane Bunnie was about to hit. She had to lay down the sand bags.

Chapter Three
Voyeur

LADONIS DROVE ALONG Broad Street headed from the Mississippi River. The river flowed up and down and served as the city's compass, its never-get-lost landmark. Go toward the river and you'd end up out front of town. Ladonis maneuvered her way through traffic in the opposite direction to back-a-town. To where yelling from the tiny windows of Parish Prison was just as prevalent and pervasive as the exhaust fumes from old cars driving along, and where the mingled smells of Popeye's fried chicken and Dixie Brewery beer filled the air.

Ten minutes after passing the Whitney Bank on Canal at Broad Street and parking next to the Dixie Brewery on Tulane, Ladonis stepped inside the double doors of Central Lockup on Gravier and South White streets and it hit her. Someone might recognize her. In her role as the first black Director of Public Relations for FPSC, she'd been interviewed several times on television and radio. A baseball cap and her yoga pants-and-sneaker look might not hide her identity.

The back-a-town police headquarters burgeoned with cops. Hurricane warnings put every officer in the city on alert, yet there was no one behind the receptionist desk. Thinking fast, she rushed to catch up to two cops who'd entered the building holding up a dirty, smelly drunk and snuck through the double doors into the hub of the station close behind them.

Squeaking ceiling fans circulated the smell of old coffee with sweat and other body odors. Ladonis moseyed around, watching and listening, rubbing her moist, shaking hands on her trousers. The news reporter may have stated that the black woman who'd accompanied Bunnie to the police station the night before was unnamed. But, in reality, at least two NOPD detectives knew exactly who she was. She pivoted to the left and her thigh bumped into a folding table.

"Shit." Ladonis reached for a falling coffee pot.

Thank goodness the coffee container was lukewarm to the touch. She stepped away from the table, glancing around. She wanted to get a handle on the situation before the press and the cops had time to zero in on FPSC. She worried that the institutions of information and protection would go hog wild spinning the details of Bunnie's misfortune. She was still working with Sales to overcome the stigma of the drama that had surrounded the Chief Operating Officer, Tim Ganen's death by paddlewheel last year.

She sighed, hoping her disguise worked. Then again, it was not clear what she'd do if it did work. She lifted her chest, realizing that she would be recognized for sure if she didn't look confident, sure-footed. Preoccupied with the storm or not, NOPD officers smelled and reacted to fear like attack dogs.

Where the hell was Bunnie? She'd seen enough cop shows to know that a suspect could sit around for hours before being questioned and/or processed into the system. But wouldn't she be guarded?

She turned her head and poof, Bunnie appeared. From where, she couldn't determine. There were doors and hallways all along the path they walked. Two policewomen, one on either side of her, made their way past a row of three vending machines. One policewoman held a camera at her side. The other guided Bunnie into an office with picture windows overlooking the squad room. The interrogation room? In the movies, the interrogation room was always a space with a table and a couple of chairs and a two-way mirror. Well, at least it was starkly furnished like the room in the movies with only a table and four chairs.

Ladonis eased by more desks, ringing phones, and clacking keyboards than she could count until she had a clear view of Bunnie seated at a long table. Her clenched, cuffed hands rested in front of her. Her reddish-brown hair looked as if she'd forgotten to wear a helmet on a motorcycle ride. Sadness and desperation deepened the lines on her face.

The muscles in Ladonis's legs grew tense. *Now what?* Her plan didn't go beyond the disguise. Then she heard a loud banging noise followed by an irritated growl.

"God damn it," a male voice said.

Oh no. Ladonis looked in the direction of the sound. She eyed Detective Argus Travers pounding on a soda machine in the nook space next to the room where Bunnie sat. The detective's unshaved face and his wrinkled suit made her heartbeat run a marathon. To this man she was not nameless. She darted back toward the folding coffee table.

"Shit, shit, shit," she whispered, leaning against a wall. Trouble had to be coming her way now. The place was full of people trained to recognize anyone and anything out of the ordinary. What made her think she could nosy around without anyone noticing her? How could a mystery buff—a Tom Clancy purist like herself not consider a blatant detail like that?

Ladonis took one giant step forward, skipped in front of two women and a man, then headed for the exit. She had to re-think the situation; consider another way to find out what the police had on Bunnie. But when she got to the exit door, Travers stepped in front of her.

"Leaving?" His fake grin covered half his face. "Can't I help you?"

"No," Ladonis said, knees still wobbly.

Her grandmother, Lucille, had told her to look the enemy straight in the eyes no matter how scared you were. "Takes 'em off guard and makes 'em respect you," she'd said. Ladonis locked eyes with the detective bold as Joan of Arc while bolting her feet to the floor.

"Actually, it's good you're here." Travers had a way of looking and sounding like he was going to take you down right then and there. "You saved me a trip."

"Why is that?" Ladonis stuck out her chest, held up her head to mask how intimidated and frightened of him she felt.

"Why, she asks." Travers chuckled, waving his hands. "Because every time somebody from that river boat company gets into a jam, you're always hanging around. That's why." He moved forward, got so close, she could smell the Listerine on his breath.

"I do work there, you know." Ladonis inched back, away from his stare, his scent. "Director of Public Relations, remember?" She twisted her lips to avoid sounding too flip, her usual response when angered and fearful. "It's my job to know what's going on."

No way did she want the police prying into FPSC affairs. It would only rouse the scrutiny on how she handled the press from FPSC brass—namely the CEO, Bret Collins and Board President, Edward H. Velcroy. It bothered her that her PR duties had to evolve from creating ads and commercials to include running interference for a suspected murderer. But if she wanted to be even considered VP material, she had to demonstrate unequivocal loyalty to the company as well as its people. That meant having a media strategy to protect the company's image from Bunnie's upcoming tabloid hell ready to implement right away. To do that, she needed to know what had gone down between Bunnie and Jarvis Maynard. Bunnie's arrest was going to rile things up for her at FPSC most assuredly if she didn't have a plan ready to put into action.

"Is that why you're sneaking around here?" Travers said. "To find out what's going on?"

"I came out of concern for my co-worker." An inside voice warned her to be smart, not defensive. "And yes, I saw the news and decided that I should come here in my official PR capacity. Perhaps I can—"

"Help?" Travers sneered. "Did you help her last night too?" He took her arm. "Come with me."

Chapter Four
High Ground

"LADONIS WASHINGTON, ISN'T it? I'm Detective Wellsburg." Travers's well dressed, African-American partner walked up and stood in front of her. She was seated in a chair on the side of Travers' desk. Even in what some called the "NOPD Plantation," Danny Glover and Mel Gibson had started a diversity trend in the movies that transcended to real-world cop partnerships.

"That's me." Ladonis pushed back in the seat, then crossed her legs at the ankles, anchoring her trembling body. She blinked and exhaled, hoping the good cop of this duo would save her from the rude and confrontational Travers.

"Why are you here?" Wellsburg asked.

"Says she's here to see if she can help Bunnie Sinclair," Travers said to Wellsburg.

Ladonis could see the vein in his forehead vibrate. Was the cocky detective upset with her or with his partner?

Wellsburg glanced from Travers to her. "I'm afraid the only person who can help Ms. Sinclair now is an attorney."

Wellsburg's dark blue slacks and light blue and white pin stripped shirt with rolled-up sleeves softened his look but not his stern tone and all-business manner. Still, Ladonis trusted his professionalism. She had to if she was going to escape this situation on her terms.

"I see." Ladonis lowered her head, fending off her inclination to say something clever like what good is an attorney with you guys on her tail. Perhaps she should try that not-so-bright-female trick she'd seen Bunnie use in her dealings with men. No matter what she did, she had to heed the inner warnings urging her to tread lightly.

Bunnie would slip into her "I'm-just-a-know-nothing-female" mode until she'd aroused the man's protective sensibilities enough to gain the upper hand before pouncing to get what she wanted. Because of Bunnie's willingness to exploit her femininity that way boosted Ladonis's confidence. Assured her that having to depend solely on her own capabilities, unlike Bunnie, her move up would not be tainted with rumors, true or not, that she'd slept her way to corporate prominence. But would Bunnie's Victorian tactic work on these guys? One thing was certain. Acting like a modern-day smart-ass wouldn't. She glanced over at Bunnie. It was safe to say that at the moment, nothing was working for her.

"We have some questions to ask you." Travers' projected voice reinforced that he had the upper hand.

Her nerves swelled, but she concentrated on the Bunnie strategy. She was up to her eyeballs in Bunnie's mess. Why not mimic that ridiculous southern belle distress approach Bunnie used to get out of it?

"Questions?" she asked demurely. "Questions about what?"

"Come with me, Miss Washington."

Wellsburg took her arm and led her to another room. Ladonis eased into one of the black leather chairs as if moving in slow motion. Travers hung back a couple of steps. A few feet across the way, Bunnie sat in what Ladonis had decided had to be the interrogation room, clasping and unclasping her cuffed hands in front of her.

"We understand that you and Miss Sinclair were together last evening." Wellsburg leaned back onto the edge of a library table. "That's what we need to know about."

Wellsburg looked ten feet tall sitting on the edge of that table looking down at her. She shifted her body uncomfortably in the seat. She needed eye-to-eye contact to take away that feeling of being at a disadvantage and to perform that nauseating eye-batting routine of Bunnie's. No matter it went against every feminist instinct she'd ever had.

"Okay." Ladonis stared up at the detective. Yes, she'd be good. For now.

"We spoke to the Phoenix police. They informed us about the alleged assault at some auction you guys attended there," Wellsburg said.

Alleged? Ladonis frowned. What about the other guests at that auction who had been robbed and gagged? She felt certain they would object to being patronized and take issue with having their possessions stolen from them at gunpoint described simply as an alleged assault. She surely did. There was nothing alleged about it. They were assaulted, period.

"Did you accompany Miss Sinclair to Jarvis Maynard's place after returning from Phoenix?" Travers asked.

"No," Ladonis snapped. "And I don't know that she went there either." So much for treading lightly.

"Oh, she was there all right." Travers sat down hard on a chair on wheels and grabbed hold of the library table to keep from crashing into the wall behind him. He looked like an off-balanced, half-dirty drunk.

Ladonis held in a chuckle. "Well, I wouldn't know about that. I went with her to the police station. But you know that already."

"Yeah, we know that," Travers told her.

Ladonis detected the strain in his voice. Was he running out of patience? Or was impatience just another aspect of his contentious disposition and captivating personality?

"Bunnie tried to file a criminal complaint against Mr. Maynard," Ladonis revealed with all the female innocence she could muster. "But the officers practically laughed in her face."

"What time did you get home?" Wellsburg asked.

"Let's see—" She placed her index finger primly on her bottom lip. "We got off the plane around eleven-thirty, picked up Bunnie's car from airport parking. We arrived at the police station about forty minutes later. An hour after that I was home."

"And what time would that have been?" Travers inquired, his eyes cold and forbidding.

"One thirty in the morning or a little before." Ladonis cocked her head to one side.

"Can anybody verify that?" Travers asked.

"My friend, Evalena." Ladonis kept looking at Wellsburg. "She was house sitting for me."

Shit. Ladonis rubbed the muscle jumping in her thigh. If only she'd knocked on the guest room door and announced her presence. If Evalena hadn't heard her come in, she certainly was not going to say she did.

She'd telephoned Evalena from the airport in Phoenix on the police's dime to let her know she would be home soon. And she'd called out when she arrived, but breathed a sigh of relief when Evalena didn't respond. She had been in no mood to explain why she looked so beat-up.

"After I showered and changed into my pj's, I listened to Motown. I couldn't fall asleep."

No need to explain that she'd learned from Mama that listening to the upbeat Motown tunes was a good tranquillizer when stressed. And that the Phoenix trip as well as the tension she'd witnessed between the police and Bunnie had made her plenty stressed. She wished she could play those tunes right now.

Someone summoned Travers to a phone. The grubby-looking lawman stood and walked away. Ladonis opened her bag and dug around for nothing in particular, hiding her relief at his departure. But suppose he came back and questioned her again? That happened all the time in the mystery novels she loved to read. The detectives asked the same questions over and over until the suspect or the witness changed their response.

"Get me an unmarked squad car," Travers yelled into the receiver. "And put my Lexus in the garage. If Breck is right, I don't want my car to end up under a tree or an electricity pole during this storm. I want my ride safe and dry."

"Since I'm here," Ladonis said to Wellsburg in a soft voice, "do you think it's possible for me to speak with Bunnie." This was her seize-the-moment opportunity to find out from her co-worker what had happened after being dropped at her condo. "Just to let her know she's not alone."

Wellsburg gave her questioning look.

"Her mother recently passed away, and she doesn't have any family here."

Wellsburg tilted his head, his eyes narrowing as they bore into Ladonis. "Miss Sinclair is in a lot of trouble. What she needs is a lawyer."

"Has she contacted one?" Ladonis asked.

"She says she can't afford an attorney," Wellsburg said with a shrug. "So the judge will have to appoint her legal counsel at her arraignment."

Ladonis perceived a directive in the detective's words—that directive being—FPSC must get involved in Bunnie's defense. What better way to avoid stepping into a media provoked twist-and-spin public relations trap that might put FPSC, thereby, her professional acumen, into what was bound to become a sensational media frenzy? If FPSC was responsible for Bunnie's defense, it would require that she, working on behalf of the company, have access to the day-to-day developments, thereby, staying in front of the messaging.

"Perhaps she needs the company to help her," Ladonis suggested with all the feminine wile she could muster. "Can I speak to her about that?" She put her finger on her lip again and tried to look Bunnie-style perplexed.

Wellsburg's brows rose in contemplation for a second that felt like minutes. "Follow me." He led her to the room where Bunnie sat.

Holy shit. Bunnie's bullshit strategy worked. Ladonis looked around for Travers. The detective paced on the other side of his desk, still talking on the phone. She prayed he'd stay there until after she'd spoken to Bunnie and gotten the hell out of there.

"LADONIS," BUNNIE WAILED when Wellsburg opened the door and ushered Ladonis into the space. "You're here."

Wellsburg nodded at the guard and left. Ladonis paused to get a good look at Bunnie Sinclair, a frazzled shadow of the woman she knew. A woman who had it in her to be a calculating operator whether she was being all innocent and sweet or a hard-nosed negotiator. Could this Bunnie have killed Jarvis Maynard? Or was looking pitiful a part of her act?

"Girl." Ladonis rushed up to the table. "What in the world happened?"

"Beats me." Bunnie's watery eyes and rocking body showed the intense apprehension behind her forced smile.

Ladonis wanted to ask what in the world had Bunnie been thinking when she went to that man's house, but didn't when she saw the all-ears female guard sizing her up. The guard prompted her to sit in the gray, steel-leg leather chair across from Bunnie, and stood off to the side, staring ahead.

"They've photographed me and fingerprinted me." Bunnie wore a slack expression behind wet, dull eyes. "And Mr. Congeniality out there told me I was under arrest for murder." She gave a wan wave with her cuffed hands at the glass wall in the direction of Travers. He tried to make me tell him that you helped me. But I told him I'd driven you home before I decided to—"

"Listen, Bunnie." Ladonis had to stop motor mouth. It suddenly occurred to her that the window worked the same as a two-way mirror.

Suppose the detective had set her up to get Bunnie talking? The female guard, planted like a Secret Service agent, stared at a wall, but her ears weren't plugged. She could still hear. "The best thing you can do to protect yourself right now is keep quiet until you get a lawyer." For the time being, she was better off not encouraging Bunnie to recall any details.

"But I didn't do anything wrong," Bunnie whined. "Why do I need a lawyer? Doesn't the truth matter?"

"The police don't believe you didn't do anything wrong and you need a lawyer to prove it. It's the American way." Ladonis observed Mr. Bad Cop himself, now engaged in a finger-pointing, eye-glaring discussion with his partner.

"That's crazy." Bunnie shook her head. "They make the mistake, and I have to prove they're off base."

"Girl, how long have you lived in this city? In the world?" The girl had better not be using her to play one of her games. "You wouldn't be here if the police didn't think they could prove that you did it."

"Why? How?" Bunnie's face turned red. "Because they found the heel of my shoe on his walk? I told them about that. But will they listen to me? No. They want to tell me how it got there. They weren't even there."

Ladonis had heard enough. Bunnie Sinclair was in trouble, big time. Only one thing to do—call A. Tabor. Her old friend was one of the best criminal lawyers in the city. In fact, A. Tabor was the only person she knew who had the guts to go up against the Maynards. But would the self-proclaimed crusader for black justice want to get involved with a white girl accused of killing the richest man in the state?

She leaned forward. "I have this friend," she said in a soft tone. "He's a criminal lawyer."

"But I'm not a criminal," Bunnie shot back.

The door opened. Both Travers and Wellsburg entered. Bunnie grabbed Ladonis's hand. Ladonis winced at Bunnie's two-handed tight grip.

"I'm going to give him a call anyway and send him over," Ladonis whispered. "So, please, zip up until you talk to him."

Wellsburg walked up beside Ladonis and touched her shoulder. Travers hung back, arms crossed and glaring. Ladonis slumped.

"You're free to leave," Wellsburg told her. "We'll be in touch if we need you."

Ladonis rose to her feet. She turned and stood face-to-face with Travers. She made a side step and walked toward the door, glancing around. Travers made his way to the table and straddled the chair Ladonis had vacated like he was erasing her from having been there.

"Please." Bunnie cried out. "I shouldn't be here. I can't stay here."

Ladonis hesitated at the door, slapping away a lone tear that crawled down her cheek. Too bad the girl didn't have someone to comfort her. Everyone needed somebody when their world crashed.

"You have to." Travers bent his body forward, getting in Bunnie's face. "You won't be going anywhere until you're arraigned and the judge sets bail."

"Bail?" Bunnie cried. "I don't have money to pay bail. What am I supposed to do?"

"Ask your lawyer," Ladonis instructed, standing in the doorway. "Hold on, Bunnie."

"We'll be in touch, Miss Washington." Wellsburg's authoritative tone commanded her to get out. Now.

Ladonis nodded and rushed to exit the building. What should she do first? Contact Bret, or call A. Tabor?

"Tabor has a better chance of making sure Bunnie gets a fair shot," she whispered, thinking of the poor soul cornered in that room. "And I'll have a better shot at controlling what gets said in the media."

She dialed A. Tabor's number, glad that she'd had the good sense to recognize in a split second that her own phone was taken from her in Phoenix, and had picked up Evalena's cell phone sitting on the counter before rushing from her home. Tabor's phone rang and rang.

"Girl, why in the world did you go to that man's house?" she whispered, wondering how and when to tell Evalena she'd taken her phone.

Chapter Five
Another Job?

LADONIS'S HEART THUMPED. BRET, looking as dashing as ever in gray slacks and a light mauve, button-down shirt and suspenders, stood behind his massive oak desk, his blue eyes centered on her. She looked past her handsome boss out the wall of windows that overlooked the Mississippi River. Even though the port was not what it once was, it continued to nourish the city's bottom line. Paddle wheelers that once carried bales of cotton along the river, now carried groups of visitors assuring that the New Orleans waterfront remained one of the busiest in the country.

Since her breakup last year with her longtime boyfriend, Jack, after refusing to move to California with him, her romantic inclinations fell on Bret. Probably had more to do with him being tall, good looking, and always in her space than anything real. But to appear lusting after her white boss could end her climb up the corporate ladder and thwart any chance of her becoming the first woman vice president at FPSC.

She watched a red masthead light sitting atop the mainmast of a tugboat passing by before landing on the newspaper in Bret's hand. She exhaled. She suspected Bret's reaction to Bunnie's predicament would be explosive. The chairman of FPSC's board, Edward H. Velcroy, and other board members had invested a lot of time and money to court potential clients for Bunnie's charter idea without his input. He'd made no secret this snub had upset him.

"I, uh—" Ladonis clenched her fist. "I went to the police station to find out—"

"To find out what?" Bret interrupted. "To find out how the company might not break even this quarter if Bunnie's charter deals fall through while she's locked up?"

"No." Ladonis offered a fake smile. She didn't want that contemptuous attitude of his to set off the same in her. "To find out what can be done to help her so that we can keep FPSC out of it."

Certain that Bret would not be interested in being Bunnie's keeper, and despite the contest she'd internalized between her and Bunnie to become the first woman VP at FPSC, Ladonis believed helping the accused murderer was the best way to protect the integrity of FPSC as well as her career goals from the fallout of scandal. Neither of which is why she went into Public Relations in the first place.

When she started out with her hard-earned MBA, her plan was to take Wall Street by storm. But Wall Street was not impressed with her resume despite graduating at the top of her class. She was forced to take a job as an assistant to the Public Relations Vice President at FPSC to survive. However, she learned that public relations was not simply paying to have an ad placed in a newspaper, or a message in a television or radio spot. She discovered that she was good at spreading information that she'd created about FPSC and enjoyed the control it gave her over what people thought. It became a passion to build excitement and credibility in steamboatin', especially to a younger, more diverse audience, since nostalgia for the good old days is the basic product and appealed to more seniors.

"I need Alan Keyes and Bob Specter to sign on the dotted lines sooner rather than later." Bret placed two manila file folders in front of her. "If, or should I say, when Bunnie's troubles are sensationalized, and if she is imprisoned, it could not only nip these deals, but set back the company's future in the corporate charter business."

Ladonis let her shoulders drop. Bret wasn't focused on Bunnie's predicament, but on her two pending five-million-dollar charter contracts. If the latest financial stats were any indication, without those charters, steamboatin' at FPSC was headed for its second year-end financial shortfall.

"That's why I went to the jail." Ladonis softened her tone, sensing an opening to quell his anxiety and change his mind. "I went to find out what we should do to keep Bunnie out of jail and working on her own charters."

"I know what *you* can do." Bret's voice switched to calm. Too calm. "You can follow Bunnie's instructions and get those deals signed ASAP."

"Me?" Ladonis cried out. "Handling the press is going to be a tough enough job. Why not have the VP of Sales work on the charters?"

"Because personality has been a strategy in these deals." Bret's face showed surprising friendliness. "I've watched you and Bunnie interact. You understand how she operates. The VP of Sales is an outcome guy. Not interested in process."

Yeah, Ladonis surmised. She'd watched how Bunnie operated, all right. She had to keep tabs, convinced the girl had her cap set for the same window office that she wanted.

"Knowing how Bunnie operates and executing her deals are two different things." Ladonis dropped her chin to her chest.

No doubt Bunnie had batted her eyes, tossed her hair, and faked helplessness like crazy to get Keyes and Spector to host their Fortune 500 board retreats on a four-day, three-night Mississippi River cruise on a luxurious paddlewheel. And while Ladonis justified employing those southern belle tactics to avoid police harassment, using her so-called feminine wiles to succeed at her job—well, that, in her view, would undermine her business savvy as well as her perceived advantage.

Ladonis glanced at Bret, saw him doodling. If FPSC's bottom line continued downward under his watch, it would reflect on his record unless he had a viable "other person" to blame. The realization made her wonder whether or not he was looking out for the company or himself. As an aspiring CEO, she'd learned that in today's corporate environment, a cheating, thieving, lying CEO is inclined to keep the job over one who has vision, ethics, and works hard even if the company is losing money. Which was Bret?

Bret raised his head and his voice. "If you can't finalize a deal that has already been negotiated, you should find another job."

Ladonis had already fallen deep into Bunnie's mess thanks to him. Adding Bunnie's damn charters to her to-do list could become problematic during her quest to stay on top of the publicity storm headed their way. Besides, Bunnie had her friend and mentor, Chairman Edward H. Velcroy, and his board to wine and dine the billionaires, Keyes and Spector. She didn't expect to get any such support from Bret, especially after that personality as a strategy crack. It seemed to her that if the deals fell through, he wanted the failure to fall on her, another woman.

"What if Keyes and Specter object?" Ladonis asked. "What if they refuse to interact with me?" Southern white men often had issues about working with women executives, and she had the added complaint of being an assertive, ambitious, aka, aggressive, black woman.

"Get these contracts signed. Bunnie can't. You have to. We've been targeted for a takeover."

"A takeover?" Ladonis cast a long stare on the muscles tightening around Bret's cheeks, his downturned mouth.

"A couple of our board members aren't happy with the way gambling, or the lack thereof, is impacting our balance sheets. And with the costs of the new boat looming—well, I'm afraid that if those charters don't happen, and our stock continues to fall, the board will opt to guide the company in a different direction."

Instead of railing on him about his real motives for giving her the charters, she wanted to know if the company had some kind of poison-pill strategy to protect the company's share value, thereby his, hers, and everyone else's jobs. She'd learned in one of her economics classes that the main struggle in a takeover, or a merger for that matter, is how to safeguard shareholder investment without diluting the price of stock in the process. She also knew that so-called poison pill plans provided such defense tactics, but were used less and less these days, especially in big companies.

This would be her first experience with a takeover, and she had so many questions. Was the impending takeover hostile, or was there a buyer—a white knight bidder—already in place to acquire FPSC? Did the board plan to drive up the bids or discourage bids altogether? And what about a back-end plan? In other words, how could FPSC make the deal more expensive for bidders and lucrative for FPSC? There was no question, however, more pressing than how could this development advance her career.

Like so many of her interactions with Bret, she found herself asking what would she recommend if she was CEO. Poison pill plans were controversial these days and could present legal challenges that might not hold up under the company's economic infrastructure. If only she felt confident enough to compare strategy with Bret. But she couldn't ignore the feeling that whatever the action plan, the success or failure of Bunnie's charters would have an impact. If Bunnie's charters failed, she could be the scapegoat, giving Bret her career as leverage to keep his job. If she confronted him now, she ran the risk of being put on the defensive, making her even more vulnerable.

She needed time to find a way to respond instead of react to her fear that Bret planned to compromise her to hold his own position. With his words, *if you can't finalize a deal that has already been negotiated, you should find another job*, still ringing in her ears, she picked up the folders, blew out her frustration through unsmiling lips, and headed down the corridor. She clutched Bunnie's files to her chest, thinking, if—no, *when* she became a CEO, she would not behave like a jerk.

Chapter Six
Who Needs A Challenge?

LADONIS MADE A U-turn to her tiny, windowless office on the land side of the FPSC building located smack dab in the middle of a converted wharf on the Mississippi River pier. Posters and framed copies of articles by and about her plastered the walls that if it had windows, would overlook the unused train tracks along Tchoupitoulas Street. What loomed largest in her line of sight was a 5x7 photograph of her and Bunnie taken at the company's second annual office picnic on the tennis court at City Park.

Bunnie and her partner had beat Ladonis at tennis doubles that day, and the shellacking changed Bunnie from an aggravating, privileged white girl, to a rival. Bunnie was pint sized, but strutted around like a gallon jug full of herself. Determined to expose her vulnerabilities, Ladonis set out to become an FPSC first and prove that she had what it took to beat white privilege. Only now the impression of Bunnie she'd conjured up was nothing like the frightened, child-like woman sitting handcuffed in a police station charged with murder.

She laid Bunnie's files on top of a pile of accounting printouts on her desk. A pang of clarity fluttered in her chest. Showing Bunnie up was one thing, but horning in on the girl's hard work—well, that wasn't part of her game plan. Yet she couldn't ignore the fact that there was no way she could be denied a vice presidency if she completed those charter deals and kept up with the impending public relations nightmare Bunnie's arrest was bound to cause at the same time.

The unfairness of it all invaded her thoughts like ants on cake. She pictured the day in the eleventh grade, when she'd told her high school counselor that she did not want to take the recommended homemaking class. That she wanted to take a college prep class instead.

"College, huh?" Miss Foster, a short chubby white woman said to her. "Well, you've got good grades and you test well. But your only hope to have a career outside homemaking or cosmetology is to be a teacher. That's the only sure path for a black girl such as yourself. I think a good-looking gal like you should take the home economics class." Ladonis wasn't sure what she wanted to be at that time, but in that moment, she decided she wouldn't become a teacher or a hairdresser, and most assuredly not a homemaker.

She looked down at Bunnie's files. Her eyes prickled with tears. When had ambition taken hold in Bunnie's life? What obstacles did she have to overcome to get her career in Sales started? Had her high school counselor planted a seed of self-doubt that she'd have to uproot everyday of her life?

"Jesus," Ladonis groaned. Why couldn't she just knock instead of having to bulldoze her way through that door of opportunity and success? She stared up at the tennis photos on the wall, aggravated by the emotions running through her. "You," she said to Bunnie's image, "are a true pain-in-my-ass."

"Hello, Donnie."

She looked around. Tabor's dimpled chin caught her eye as he stood in her doorway. *Student Body*? She smiled. "Tabor."

"A.Tabor to you," Tabor said with a grin.

A. Tabor, aka "Student Body," handsome as could be, gave her the once over. She couldn't resist doing the same to him.

"You haven't changed a bit."

"Well, you've changed a lot," Ladonis said. It had been close to a year since she'd seen him. She walked over and embraced him.

Tabor was no longer the fat boy who had followed her and Evalena around the halls of Booker T. Washington High. In fact, decked out in a dark suit, his lean physique could be on the cover of *GQ Magazine*. *Sports Illustrated* even. She couldn't wait to tell Evalena that the always sweaty obese boy she'd nicknamed "Student Body" the year he'd run for student council president had turned into one lean fine-ass man.

"What are you doing here?" Ladonis pulled back from his hug. He smelled good, too. "I told you when I called that I'd meet you at your office."

"I was curious about where you work." Tabor's enthusiasm showed in his eyes. "When I see this place on television, it's hard to imagine you working here. Remember how you used to equate the port's demise with union busting and the downfall of hardworking black men?"

"That was Evalena's soapbox, remember. The port reminded me of *Gone With the Wind* times."

"Oh, yeah." Tabor rested a hand on her shoulder. "That's right. Now that I think about it, neither one of you had a clue back then."

"I object." She chuckled. How could he say that? Evalena's uncle was a laid-off longshoreman who'd fed his niece his union complaint. Ladonis had been a project born and bred, novel-reading straight-A student with a thing for history and romance. Sure, she and Evalena may have had issues with their teenage reality, and granted, they were idealistic, but clueless they were not.

"I was surprised to get your call." Tabor's voice had changed too, now deep and resonant. "It's been a while."

"I'm embarrassed I haven't been in touch." She offered him the big-striped, black and white wingback seat in front of her desk. "I should've contacted you sooner to congratulate you for proving that man innocent after he'd served forty years in prison. You've made quite a name for yourself, A. Tabor, Esquire."

Agibus Tabor preferred to be addressed by his last name after he discovered that slaves were not allowed to use their African names and were given the names of their owners instead. He also believed his mother had made up Agibus, convinced that she was probably unable to pronounce something else given her lack of formal education and the black proclivity to speak phonetically as a result. And after he learned that Tabor had Hebrew origins that meant center of the world, he legally became A. Tabor. "A man needs to know that his name stands for something," he'd said.

"You too. The first black PR Director at the fabulous Floating Palace Steamboat Company." Tabor rested his elbows on the chair's arms. "I've read your press."

"Thanks." She glanced away. Since she'd been identified as a black woman on the rise in the corporate world, she figured that becoming the first female vice president in a good ole' boy company like FPSC was a real reason to take the next step.

"Look, Tabor. I know you're into challenging legal obstacles for oppressed black folk, but this white girl really needs your help."

"Why me?" Tabor asked.

"She's an orphaned outsider for one thing." Ladonis took a breath, hoping not to come across as self-righteous. "And she's accused of killing Jarvis Maynard for another. She needs someone who champions underdogs who tend not to be viewed in the system as innocent-until-proven-guilty."

Ladonis had a hard time making the leap to guilty despite believing that Bunnie was sneaky and manipulative. She thought that even if Bunnie had been stupid enough to go to Maynard's house, the girl couldn't be dumb enough to kill him. She refused to believe that.

"Donnie, listen." Tabor leaned forward. "I know I agreed to meet with your co-worker, but like I told you when you called, I'm not in a position to go up against the Maynards."

His attitude had surprised her then, and it surprised her now. When they were in college, Tabor had gone on and on about the wealthy whites who controlled the city. Swore he'd never back away from a fight with them and the legal establishment they owned, including the NOPD, to see justice prevail.

"You mean you're not up to the challenge?" She tilted her head, lifted her chin upward.

"I'm always up to a challenge. But I'm no masochist. The Maynards can buy and sell every lawmaker and politician in this town."

"But not you, right?"

"Look." A frown made a circle of Tabor's mouth. "Maynard is considered royalty in this town. And he's been killed. Someone has to pay. The police have got your friend, Bunnie, dead to right."

"That's why she needs you." She frowned, concerned that he'd switched from old friend to an aloof attorney set on treating her like a client he didn't want in a matter of moments. "The cops are out to railroad this woman. And you're the best when it comes to being railroaded. I mean, that Detective Travers is no joke."

"Travers?" Tabor's relaxed voice separated from the grave look on his face. "I know the dude. His attitude problem is more personal than job related."

"What do you mean?"

"His wife is an heiress who was disowned when she married him. Only she acts like she's still rich." He ran his hand across his close-cut hair. "Even has their kid in that expensive Country Day School. If you put a guy with his issues in the real world with people on their worst behavior, you create a coldhearted hard-ass. But, like I told your co-worker, Bunnie, I understand the guy."

"You've seen Bunnie?" Ladonis asked in surprise.

"Yes." Tabor nodded. "I was curious, so I went to central lockup to find out who is this woman you're going to bat for." He lowered his head as well as his voice. "I gave her the name of a lawyer in Shreveport."

No. Tabor had to be Bunnie's attorney. She was counting on having access to information about the police investigation as it was happening instead of finding out things as a spectator in the courtroom.

"Shreveport? Another outsider?" Ladonis chastised. "Don't you know there isn't a judge around who is going to take kindly to someone coming here interfering in Big Easy justice?"

"He's a good attorney." Tabor batted his hand at her concerns like they were fruit flies in his face. "Besides, there isn't a lawyer in town willing to take on this case."

"Are you sure he has the moxie not to sell her out?" A snippet of sarcasm bled into Ladonis's words. "Not to help the cops take her to the tracks?"

"No." Tabor shook his head. "I'm not sure. But by reputation, he's a fair guy. What I do know is that this city's legal brand places high-profile cases such as this above the law. I'll be putting my entire career in jeopardy. Better for an outsider to take this one. I can't do it. Sorry, Donnie."

"What about the weapon?" Ladonis argued, desperate to change Tabor's mind. "Have they found a weapon? I lay you odds Bunnie Sinclair never held a gun in her life. She's a strange one, Tabor. That woman is so far removed from the ways of the world we live in, she actually believed the police had to let her go because she told them she didn't do it."

"Bunnie did say that she'd never fired a weapon before." Tabor leaned back in the chair and re-crossed his legs. "And agreed to be tested for gun residue without advice of counsel. But I've butted heads with enough lawyers, judges, as well as cops in this town to know that it will take a miracle to win this fight whether they have a gun or not."

"Yeah, but can they say she fired a gun if a scientific lab test says she didn't?"

"I can think of at least four experts who can testify that gunshot residue tests are unreliable."

A shadow blocked the light coming from the hallway. Ladonis looked up. *Uh-oh.* Her body twitched.

Bret hesitated in the doorway before strutting in, apprehension contracted his brow.

"Excuse me," Bret said, never looking away from Tabor.

"A. Tabor," Ladonis said. "Meet Bret Collins, Chief Executive Officer of the Floating Palace Steamboat Company, operators of the only overnight riverboat cruises on America's rivers. Bret, this is A. Tabor, an old friend, neighbor and classmate. He's also an attorney. Bunnie's attorney." She looked at Tabor. "Right?"

Tabor rose from his seat, showing no expression that assured Ladonis he was indeed Bunnie's lawyer. He and the six-foot-three Bret stood eye-to-eye. Neither of their broad-shouldered, powerful stances subdued the other.

"A, is it?" Bret extended his hand. "Nice to meet you."

"Yeah, me, too," Tabor said. "Just call me Tabor."

"Like Mount Tabor in Israel," Bret said.

Tabor nodded.

"Have you spoken to Bunnie?" Bret asked.

"Well . . ." Tabor sat down and leaned back into the chair. "She's scared and feels alone."

"Scared and alone, huh?" Bret moved closer to Ladonis's desk.

Ladonis didn't like his smug tone. Surely, he knew that Bunnie's legal matters needed attention even though their focus had to be on FPSC's bottom line. Especially since Bunnie's charters were the company's only money-making projects this quarter.

"How long will she be in jail?" Bret sat on the corner of Ladonis's desk facing Tabor.

"She says she didn't do it." Tabor's tone edged to match Bret's push for information. "But it will take as long as it takes to get justice."

Well, that didn't sound promising. Murder suspects rarely got bail unless they were rich, of course. And a trial could take forever.

"Justice, huh?" Bret crossed his arms. "How much time is your gut telling you it's going to take to get this justice?"

"Are you offering to help her?" Tabor probed. "Or are you looking for a way to not get involved?"

"Not get involved?" Ladonis attempted unsuccessfully to control the volume in her voice. "I don't see how we cannot be involved." Even though Bunnie was a thorn in her side, she was a fellow woman working in a man's world. And she had no family to lean on. No mama to nag her about right and wrong; or to put her back on track when life happened while she wasn't looking and scared the shit out of her.

"Sorry if I don't sound empathetic," Bret said to Tabor, taking his terse, arrogant, CEO tone. "Based on what Bunnie told you, and the evidence against her, do you believe she did it?"

"That's none of your business," Tabor said in a flat pitch.

Ladonis lifted a brow. Tabor sounded neither impressed nor intimidated by Bret, just reticent to discuss his conversation with Bunnie.

Bret squinted, his lips formed a pout with attitude. "I understand. Some legal code of ethics or the other says you're supposed to believe in your client's innocence no matter what. Well, I'm not bound by that."

"What?" Ladonis blurted out. She'd suspected that Bret would distance himself, thereby, the company, from Bunnie, but to hear him practically say it took her aback. "Are you saying you think she could've done this?"

"Calm down, Donnie," Tabor urged. "Whether she did it or not, Bret, here, has a product to sell, a company to run. My guess is he'd prefer not to get caught up in the legal grind." He turned to Bret. "I believe you're referring to the constitutional edict that states every suspect is entitled to legal representation regardless of guilt or innocence. Am I right?"

"Yes, that's what I'm getting at."

Bret stood up, walked toward the door. He rubbed his hand across his chin. Ladonis wondered what had provoked that dark expression he was trying to hide. Was he so put off by Bunnie that he wanted no part of the help Tabor could offer her?

"Ladonis, when you're done visiting with your friend, we need to work out a few more details on those charters." Bret broke eye contact. "That weather guy, Bob Breck, says that if Katrina hits—that's what they've named the storm, you know—it could be a big one." He stepped just outside the door before turning. "Nice to meet you, Tabor."

Tabor nodded. Ladonis shot her old friend an emotionally loaded look. She needed him to commit.

"You do believe Bunnie didn't do it, don't you?" she asked. If he thought Bunnie had gone off the deep end and taken a life, then how could he be sure? Had a seed of doubt been planted in her?

"Let's just say the cards are stacked against her," Tabor noted.

"That's why she needs you." Ladonis's voice fell deep into her throat. "Remember the promise you made when you graduated from Loyola? You said, and I quote, 'I'm going to spend my entire career keeping justice just.' Un-quote."

"I was right." A slight grin showed on Tabor's face. "You haven't changed a bit. You are still as bossy as ever."

"Does that mean you'll do it?"

"No, it doesn't," Tabor told her. This was getting too cat and mouse.

"Then tell me what Bunnie told you."

"I'm afraid I can't do that." Tabor rubbed his brow. "And frankly, I'm surprised you'd ask me to. What gives?"

"What gives?" She threw up her hands. "If Bunnie told you anything that could stop the media drama a trial will create, I need to know. It would make my job and my life a helluva lot easier. That's what gives." Just like her brother, Tabor refused to see how important it was for her to succeed on the path she had chosen for her life even if it was in a different world than the one they'd grown up in.

"I see." Tabor watched her through slanted eyes.

"She must've said something," Ladonis demanded. "There has to be a way to get to the bottom of this without putting everyone through a trial."

"If there is," Tabor's mouth formed a tight, stubborn slit, "her lawyer will make it happen."

"But if you were her lawyer—"

"Tell me again," Tabor said, "why this is so important to you?"

"Why?" She had to think fast. "I've just been assigned to complete two major charter deals that Bunnie set in motion. Deals that are critical to the company's profit margins this year. Seems to me, I'm being set up to take the fall if business takes a dive during a trial. If that happens, I may never get another job on this level again. I've worked hard and long to get here."

"Corporate politics." Tabor shook his head. "A woman's life is on the line, and the goal is to spare the company's profit margin."

"No," Ladonis said in an unsteady voice. "The goal is to get this over with as quickly as possible."

Tabor paused and focused an examining stare on her. "What are you willing to do to get this over with without a trial?"

"What do you mean, what am I willing to do? What did Bunnie tell you?" Had Bunnie told Tabor something that could save her?

"That I can't say without harming her defense. You know how it is."

Tabor's reproach loosened a trapped butterfly in her stomach. Bunnie may have made million-dollar corporate deals, but the girl was an operator not unlike HeartTrouble. So, what had she told Tabor? What had happened between Bunnie and Maynard? And what was Tabor now after?

"How?" Ladonis asked. "How can we end this? And to what 'we' are you referring?"

"What we need," Tabor said, "is to hire a private investigator. But Bunnie can't afford that. And judging from your boss's attitude, I can see this company won't give her any financial help. That leaves you to be our sleuth."

"Me?" Ladonis exclaimed. "Why me?"

"Remember that time the police arrested your mother's cousin for rape?" Tabor didn't wait for her to respond. "You believed him when he said he didn't do it and was determined to prove he was innocent. So, you got me, HeartTrouble, and Evalena all worked up to the point where we followed you into that Creole neighborhood in Gentilly. We canvassed that community until we found the girl and tricked her into confessing that she'd lied." He drew in a breath. Besides, no one else can be trusted," he stated as if this notion was true and reasonable, without question. "I can't risk being ratted out. The Maynards are powerful people."

"No shit?" Ladonis pushed up her sleeves. "And what exactly does ratted out mean to a hotshot defense attorney? Especially one that hates losing as much, or maybe more than injustice."

"It means," Tabor twisted the class ring on his finger. "I want to help. But I don't want my life's work put on the line."

It wasn't what he said that alarmed Ladonis. But acknowledging that her support for Bunnie was not because of her inclination to help others the way she'd been raised. The hard, self-truth running through her head now was how her natural goodness was in direct conflict with her need to self-preserve in the corporate world.

"You are not playing fair," Ladonis said, solemnly. You're a lawyer, I'm not a private investigator.

"And I'm not in the habit of representing people for friends against people who can destroy me," Tabor said. "But I am saying this could end before it begins if you did this."

Ladonis frowned as her anxiety lit up. Did she want to know? She tucked in her chin, thinking what it would mean to her career if she could get past this hurdle without the added burden of handling Bunnie's charters.

"Do what exactly?"

"Go to Bunnie's place and remove a laptop."

Chapter Seven
Working Against Law for the Law

LADONIS MADE HER way from the Magnolia Housing Project driving along Sixth and Loyola Streets. Unbeknown to Tabor, she'd decided that she did not want to go snooping around Bunnie's place alone, and drove to the old neighborhood on LaSalle Street, hoping to find HeartTrouble in the courtyard loitering on a cement bench with his no-account friends. But the courtyard and the bench were empty.

Now headed home, her ride was interrupted by a second line funeral marching into Lafayette Cemetery No.2, the black side of the sprawling, historic graveyard with its rundown cement-based stucco and granite rubble cladded tombs. The whites were buried in the well-kept side along Washington Avenue at Saratoga Street. Separate but equal. Past or present, Ladonis thought, the institutions in this town, even cemeteries, navigated the hardships of racial prejudice true to Jim Crow.

Waiting and anxious for the funeral to move along, Ladonis dialed her brother's phone number. He did not answer. Later, she pulled her Honda Accord into her uncovered carport exasperated. She'd spent way too much time looking for him and in a Sprint store while replacing her stolen cell phone, the service even more maddening than waiting in the long, slow-moving line. She expected rather than hoped, HeartTrouble would be waiting for her. But he wasn't. She'd agreed to play detective for Tabor, but hadn't mustered enough of that do-good feeling to overwhelm the apprehension that pumped through her veins. She needed her brother and his delinquent sensibilities for that.

She strode up to the front door to her condo, feeling disappointed HeartTrouble wasn't there, but grateful that Evalena wasn't. Her sisterfriend had met her at the Sprint office to retrieve her phone before heading home to have dinner with her mother. Tabor's plan to break-and-enter into Bunnie's apartment would find no approval with her longtime friend, already feeling put upon. She would, no doubt, hassle her about kowtowing to the operatives of what she called that slave-boat cruise line at the expense of her family and friends to get ahead.

She turned the key in the door lock and took one last look around outside for HeartTrouble. Clouds with patches of light shining through hovered over the oak trees lining her street. So much talk about the big, bad storm. It wouldn't be a surprise if the TV weather actors had over-reacted. Again.

"Geez, it's stuffy in here." Ladonis walked inside and slid the kitchen window open.

She made her way to the patio door off the kitchen and opened the doors to let in even more humid air. She heard acorns crackling in the tiny alley that separated her condo from the single-family home next door. No matter what time of day or night she arrived home, the neighbor's cat appeared, scratching around for the chance to pester her. She pivoted. Acorns crackled again. Too loud to be the neighbor's cat.

"HeartTrouble?" she called out. "Is that you?"

"Where the plywood?" HeartTrouble answered, making his way from the alley to the back patio. He entered the kitchen through the sliding door. "Ain't that why you wanted me to get here right away?"

"Ah—sure." Ladonis fibbed. How was she going to convince him to go to Bunnie's with her? What was she going to say to him? She'd better be prepared to keep her mouth shut and listen to his lecture on white-folk shit. "I need you to help me do something. For Tabor."

"For Tabor?" HeartTrouble stared at her through suspicious eyes.

"Yes." Ladonis wrinkled her nose.

HeartTrouble owed Tabor big time. If it weren't for Tabor, her younger brother would be rotting in Angola Prison by now. No way could he refuse to help the man who'd minimized his extensive arrest record over the years to a couple of misdemeanors. He'd want to repay him even if it meant doing something for her and her co-worker. But she couldn't tell HeartTrouble that Tabor had no idea she'd involve him.

"He's Bunnie's lawyer," Ladonis added.

"This about that girl from your job?" HeartTrouble twisted the shining gold-plated junk hanging around his neck. "You mean you done got Tabor mixed up in her shit? Well, I don't want nothin' to do with it."

An instant and emphatic no. Ladonis sighed with exasperation. Convincing him to go with her would be harder than she'd thought.

"Just think what it would do for Tabor's rep if he could get props for clearing Bunnie without going to trial." Tabor was still the key. "All he needs is for me—for us—to go to her place tonight and get a laptop."

"Looka-here, Donnie," HeartTrouble said, his tone firm and deliberate. "You can say what you want. I ain't goin' with you. Even if Tabor do say so."

"You'll be paying a debt to Tabor. Working for the law for a change."

Tabor had warned that this particular bit of sleuthing was a right/wrong issue dependent on interpretation. And that obstructing justice was definitely an interpretation of wrong. Still this one thing could free Bunnie and end any threat to the company's business dealings. Who knows? Helping Bunnie out of this jam just might give her a big, fat FPSC loyalty star to go on her window office door once she became a vice president.

"Workin' against the law for the law? Tell me somethin'. If it's so legal, why Tabor can't just go in to get what he need? How come you gotta sneak in at night?"

"It's complicated legal maneuvering." She tried to sound both professional and caring.

Tabor had told her that he could not be mentioned if she got caught. She was to say that she needed Bunnie's notes from her home computer for the company, an explanation that would also work with Bret. That was the plan.

"Besides," she added. "Tabor is expecting to have a long court night. Some high-profile money laundering case he's been working on for months."

"What that white girl case got to do with you, anyway?" HeartTrouble's swift, sideways glance dared her to speak. "I thought you ain't had nothin' to do with what she done. Wait. Maybe I ought to ask what you gonna lose if she go to trial?"

"What have I got to lose?" Ladonis snarled. Only her job is what.

"Then again, maybe I ought to be askin' what you gonna get if this girl get off," HeartTrouble demanded.

Why couldn't HeartTrouble wrap his head around what made her tick? Her dream? After all, her success was necessary for the good of her family, including him. Before buying her own condo, she'd helped her mother purchase her first home. It was her credit rating that enabled Mama to pay HeartTrouble's court fines to keep him out of jail.

She had to succeed. But at what cost to her soul, as well as her family's wellbeing? Times like this everything jumbled up.

"I know how you feel about cops," she said.

"It's not the cops I'm worried about." HeartTrouble's light brown eyes popped open. "It's Charmaine. I'm worried 'bout what Charmaine gonna do if I get in trouble right now. Remember Charmaine?"

"Yes." How could Ladonis forget the only time he'd volunteered any details about his love life with her? "She's the girl you broke it off with because she wanted to get married."

Ladonis had even praised HeartTrouble for having the good sense not to trap some girl in a marriage when he had so little going for him at the time. He'd done the right thing. And he'd done it without any coaxing from her.

"Well, come to find out, I shoulda married her." He stared directly into her eyes. "She had my kid. I got a daughter."

What? Oh my God. HeartTrouble is somebody's daddy? Ladonis wheeled backward, grabbed the countertop to steady herself.

"A daughter? You? Are you sure she's yours?"

"I saw her, Donnie." HeartTrouble took a deep breath. "I know she mine all right. I know she mine 'cause she look just like you."

"What?"

"Remember that baby picture Mama got of me where I'm wearin' one of Grandpa Tommie's big cowboy hats with just a diaper on? You know the one I mean. Mama always showin' that picture to people. She say it's her favorite picture of me. She said when we were babies, we looked like twins."

Ladonis nodded, lost for words. The thought of a child looking like her brought up feelings, maternal feelings she believed she didn't have. HeartTrouble reached into his shirt pocket, pulled out a photograph, and handed it to her. The chubby little girl had the same pug nose that she and HeartTrouble had, their mother's brow, and the liveliest hazel eyes she'd ever seen, same color as Ladonis's.

"How old is she?" Ladonis canvassed the photo shaking in her hand.

"Ten months," HeartTrouble told her, smiling.

How in the world had this happened? Hadn't anyone told this girl—this Charmaine—about contraceptive protection? Lena's mother used to tell the two of them all the time, "see the tax return before you go adding to the population." Ladonis rubbed her forehead to calm the ache thumping in her head. How could any woman allow someone who lived off the streets get her pregnant no matter how good looking he was or how exciting the sex?

"I don't get women sometimes." HeartTrouble's tone was as melancholy as it was intense. "She never told me nothin', you know."

"How did you find out?" Ladonis plopped down on a stool behind her as if a rug had been pulled out from under her.

"She came lookin' for me in the Magnolia to rub my nose in it." Anger crept into HeartTrouble's voice. "She went to one of them get-off-the welfare trainin' programs and got herself a computer job all the way in Atlanta." He sat down on the stool beside her. "So, she come to tell me she had my kid, and I ain't never gonna see her. Then she threw that picture at me and walked off."

"Oh, my God." Ladonis looked up from the photo of her baby niece. "That's cold blooded."

"I felt like killin' the bitch." HeartTrouble kneaded his hands. "But I collected myself. Then I went to the Calliope where she live with her mama."

The Calliope? Charmaine was not from the Magnolia. No wonder it took HeartTrouble so long to find out about the baby. And why Ladonis didn't know Charmaine. Projects were like little towns separated by long bus rides. Without personal transportation, an inter-project relationship was doomed the same as a transcontinental love affair could be.

"Took me all morning to ride the three buses to get over there. But I wanted to see my kid, you know. I bought her a little brown bear. I wanted to play with her. Maybe hold her. And I wanted to talk things out with Charmaine."

HeartTrouble stood up and paced like an expectant father in a hospital waiting room. Ladonis jumped when he punched his palm. Something he did all the time when he was angry and didn't want to hurt anyone. But this time she saw more than anger on his face. She saw pain, too.

"But Charmaine started yellin' at me," he said. "And I screamed back at her. We was arguin' like cats and dogs while my lil girl was lookin' at us, scared and cryin'. I know she just a baby and all, but I felt like shit, you know. Then Charmaine had the nerve to tell me she gonna tell my kid I'm dead. Said I might as well be."

Ladonis had never heard him sound so lost. She knew he wasn't insensitive. Just that, on the outside, he always showed that ghetto, tough-guy brand of inner strength. She'd grown up in the same environment, and had that same toughness instilled in her. Otherwise, she couldn't have survived the Magnolia. But it was especially hard for her brother. For a guy growing up in the projects, sensitivity was another word for "sissy." The worst name a black man can be called in HeartTrouble's world is sissy.

"Thank goodness Charmaine's mama got some sense," HeartTrouble incanted as if the mention of Charmaine's mother was magical. "She stuck up for me. She told Charmaine that I have a right to know my own daughter. That I got responsibilities."

"Lord, have mercy."

Ladonis wanted to tell him that his baby was beautiful. But her misgivings and fear of parenthood wouldn't allow her to say anything positive. Charmaine's mother was right. He did have responsibilities. And the most important was not financial. As hard as feeding and clothing a child could be, nothing was harder than sticking around to protect and help another human being grow up stable and productive in a dangerous world that's expecting her to fail. That's what scared her the most about having kids. She believed it should scare HeartTrouble too.

"I never planned on bein' nobody's daddy," HeartTrouble said. "But that's the luck of the draw I guess."

The luck of the draw? Why could a man, any man, get away with saying that? What if it was she, a woman who didn't have plans to be anyone's mama? It would come down to a hell of lot more than the luck of the draw if she accidentally got pregnant.

"When I told Mama, she was glad," HeartTrouble reflected. "But when I told her everythin' else, she called Tabor. She said she'd seen how grown-folk hatefulness can destroy a kid, and she wasn't havin' it. She said no son of hers was gonna be a deadbeat dad, and that she'd fed

Tabor enough when he was a boy for him to make sure Charmaine don't make me out to be one."

"Tabor?" What the hell? She'd been with Tabor all morning and he'd said nothing. Then again, he wouldn't. Tabor was big on lawyer/client confidentiality. But, this was her family. Did he think he could run her family like he did his practice? If he owed Mama and HeartTrouble, he owed her too.

"Yeah," HeartTrouble told her. "He's gonna file papers in court so I can fight for partial custody. Tabor say I can't stop Charmaine from movin' to Atlanta, but I can stop her from separatin' me from my lil girl and tellin' her I'm dead. Or worse."

"What's worse than telling a kid that her alive father is dead?" The words came up and out before Ladonis could suppress the hurt feeling they evoked.

"What's worse?" HeartTrouble's voice was practically a whimper. "Tellin' her that her daddy don't care 'bout her. That her daddy don't want her. That she ain't good enough to have a daddy."

That's worse all right. Their own dad had walked out and she didn't have a clue where he was. Would it have been easier to say that he was dead? Would that have changed the fact that he'd left her and her brother? That she felt she wasn't good enough? Ladonis realized that she and HeartTrouble had spent a lifetime denying, but mostly, hiding this shared pain from each other. Now Charmaine was making it real again.

"I gotta make sure," HeartTrouble said so softly, she could barely make out his words. "I have a chance to be a daddy to my kid."

"You think you can be somebody's daddy?" Ladonis's words spilled out. Why was it so hard for her to be empathetic toward her brother and his situation? Another indication that she'd lost the natural goodness her mama said everyone had before fear and the want of stuff got in the way.

"I been thinkin' on that long and hard." HeartTrouble rolled his eyes and snatched the picture from his sister's hand. "To tell you the truth, I don't know. I ain't no look-up-to kinda dude. And I sure as hell don't want no kid of mine to live like I do. At the same time, I don't want no kid of mine growin' up thinkin' I don't give a damn. If I turn out to be a good daddy or a bad daddy, my kid's gonna have a daddy. I'm gonna be around."

"But Charmaine doesn't want you around," Ladonis said.

"Who know what Charmaine want," HeartTrouble said. "All I know is she pissed at me from way back. And she got the upper hand."

And what an upper hand. The former welfare mom had a kid with a hustler father. A hustler who happened to be her brother. For crying out loud, Ladonis was the baby's aunt.

"To a dude like me," HeartTrouble said, "when a kid's in the picture, ain't nothin' worse than a pissed-off baby mama."

"I'll say," Ladonis mumbled.

What in the world was she supposed to say? To do? She had never seen this grown-up side of her brother. But she knew women like Charmaine. Women who'd play that kid like a slot machine just to brag to her friends how she was making the baby daddy suffer.

"I'm glad you want to do the right thing." Ladonis's deference rang in her soft tone. "And I plan to help you however I can. Meanwhile—" She held her hands along her sides in the calm-down position. She had to get back to Bunnie. "You've got to come with me to Bunnie's place."

"Didn't you hear me, Donnie? I can't afford to get in no trouble."

"I promise it won't take long. And we won't get into trouble."

"Is it legal or illegal? Goin' in that woman's house like that?"

"Don't worry," Ladonis proclaimed. "I'll take responsibility. Me and Tabor. I promise."

She clasped and squeezed her hands. She'd just get that computer and that would be that. No need to suppose more would happen.

"You didn't answer my question," HeartTrouble countered. "Is it legal?"

"I've got keys." Ladonis turned away from him. "It won't be considered a break in."

"But is it against the law what you gonna do?" HeartTrouble didn't relent. "Once you get inside, I mean?"

"Legal, illegal." She could feel the perspiration dripping between her breasts. "Depends on who you ask."

"Suppose I ask the po-lice," HeartTrouble said, his chin in the air.

"Then I guess it's illegal," she snapped.

"Then I say, no way." HeartTrouble barreled toward her front door. "I ain't goin' with you and that's all there is to it." The finality in his voice hung around him like a suit of armor. "What you oughta be doin' is boardin' up this place before that storm come."

Anger filled her. Her strategy had failed. "Prick. You're a coward and a prick. No wonder Charmaine doesn't want her child to have any part of you."

"See." HeartTrouble dropped his shoulders then lifted them up again. "That's what I'm talkin' 'bout. Nobody matter to you except you and them stealin', killin' white folks you work with." He shook his baby's picture at her. "See this child. She matters to me. I ain't goin' to nobody's house to steal from the police."

"It is not stealing," Ladonis said.

How could she admit that confiscating evidence was indeed a criminal act, and still convince him that the job had to be done. How could she, in all fairness, expect him to disregard his new set of circumstances to obstruct justice for her? She experienced a fleeting moment of pride in her brother. However, she couldn't—no, she wouldn't—concede that HeartTrouble showed more guts, more courage, and was more in tune with his natural goodness than she was with hers.

Chapter Eight
Breaking and Entering

LADONIS GOT OFF the streetcar and walked six blocks to Faubourg Way, a block-long cul de sac with three cars parked curbside. One was Bunnie's red Toyota Camry sitting in front of a Spanish Colonial house that had been sub-divided into a two-story apartment building. Having refused every invitation Bunnie had ever extended to her to visit, Ladonis had no idea Bunnie's uptown address was so deep into this historic area, site of the city's first two suburbs, the American Section for whites and the Creole Section for free people of color. Bunnie occupied the lower apartment in the so-called American section.

It was eight o'clock at night, and the grayness of dusk swirled around like fog. She expected life on the streets. She'd read in some magazine that uptown yuppies jogged or power walked after a long day sitting in an office. Only people were not exercising, but loading suitcases and boxes into their cars and vans. Evidently, news of the incoming storm had Bunnie's neighbors preparing to escape.

Per Tabor's instructions, Ladonis was to retrieve the laptop in the front hall, then drive away in Bunnie's car. Tabor had offered to park it in his garage for safety. Bunnie had told him that on-street parking was often a tempting target for vandals and thieves.

While Ladonis was breaking and entering, Tabor said he'd check on that gun residue test. He said if it hadn't been administered, that might play better in Bunnie's defense than if it had. Something about having to take the test four to six hours after a shooting to get an accurate result. Ladonis wasn't exactly sure what that meant, but understood no one was more in tune to police shenanigans than Tabor.

Well, at least she didn't have to break in, literally. Thanks to one of Tabor's NOPD connections in the evidence room, she had keys to Bunnie's home and car. But, she worried whether the keys guaranteed that she would be in and out of a crime scene in a jiff as

Tabor suggested. Only HeartTrouble could do that. And he'd refused to join her.

Blooming jasmine covered the arches and columns all around Bunnie's lower-level apartment. A gust of wind blew leaves and scent into her face. However, the sound of the pre-storm wind whispered to her that she wasn't on her way to steal evidence in a murder case, but on a mission of mercy, instead of the weather warning it was indeed forecasting. She could not ignore, however, that it would only be merciful if Tabor was correct in his assumption and the cops had not found the laptop. He noted that if they had, one of his police snitchers would have told him, especially since Bunnie took time to hide it in a secret compartment in a file drawer.

Ladonis eased inside to adjust to the dark, not wanting to rush in and risk falling or knocking something over. A line of soft lights and a flowery scent from the deodorizer plug-ins along the floorboards greeted her. But, it was still too dark to see anything clearly above the floor. She closed the door behind her then reached into her waist pouch for the tiny flashlight she'd brought along despite Tabor's warning that a nosy neighbor might see her shadow and call the police citing a prowler on the property.

The flashlight cast a dim light around the room. Plants and pictures covered every nook and cranny. Ladonis made her way over to a row of framed photos on the mantle. Sadness swept over her. Bunnie had helped herself to the un-purchased snapshots of FPSC cruise passengers. How lonely did a person have to be to do that?

The only print that wasn't one of the boat's photographer, Mr. Pete, was a small beaded-edge brass frame with a pewter-colored finish. Held inside was an old faded picture of a woman with sandy brown hair, a creamy beige complexion, and an expression that filtered brightness like a sheer window curtain did the sun into a room. Bunnie's grandmother, perhaps? Ladonis put the photo into the pouch around her waist. If she were Bunnie and locked up with no family to visit her or to speak with, she'd want to see that smile.

The desk sat tucked in a corner of the hall between the living room and the bedroom. The usual stuff sat on top—a pencil box, telephone, dictionary, sealed as well as unsealed mail. She opened the file drawer, pulled out all the files, and pushed the plywood at the back. The thin wood panel slipped from its groove, but there was no hanging file and no laptop. Shit. Had the cops taken the damn thing? If so, why was the mail still stacked so neat?

Ladonis moved toward the sleigh-back bed filled with pillows of all shapes and sizes, situated under an un-curtained narrow sliding window. The quilted pink and green comforter hung perfectly, characteristic of the meticulous Bunnie. She envisioned her own bedroom, a classic clutter den, and suffered a flash of heat over her body forcing her to plop down on the edge of the bed. Bunnie's space could be a picture in magazine.

She tossed a few pillows around. Pulled at the comforter. A spiteful gesture meant to eliminate the visual in her head showing her what she'd internalized—everything about Bunnie Sinclair, including her neatness—was a put-down.

"Lord, girl, what are you doing here?" Ladonis asked out loud. She shined the flashlight on the closet door.

The police must have confiscated the computer. Whatever Bunnie had told Tabor about Maynard, the cops probably knew. Still, Ladonis wanted to help her work nemesis. She didn't believe Bunnie was guilty, rendering her own unkind thoughts measured by her desire for justice.

The closet door stood ajar. Ladonis stepped inside. Every skirt, every blouse and jacket hung perfectly on colored coordinated plastic hangers. The cops couldn't have searched here either.

Her right foot moved forward and she almost tripped on a loose piece of molding. She cast her flashlight down and spotted a pile of shoes under a shoe rack that had apparently fallen over. Then she noticed a flat box, the side flap poking out from the pile of shoes. Ladonis stooped down to investigate, pulled the box from under the shoes, and peeled back the open flap. There it was. The laptop stuffed haphazardly inside the box. Clutter in a mass of orderliness. Who'd do that? Not Bunnie.

Something crashed in the kitchen. Ladonis's heart rate raced. Was Bunnie being robbed? After all, the news of her arrest had been plastered all over the airwaves. Oh, God. She turned off the flashlight. Maybe someone saw the light and called the cops like Tabor had warned. Her fingers went numb and the box slipped from her hand, landing silently, but painfully on her feet. She thrust her hand over her mouth to hold in the scream pushing against her throat, leaned down, and jammed the box back under the pile of shoes. Getting caught holding that computer, whether it was a thief or the cops, would be the end of her.

"Shit, shit, shit," she mouthed, easing from the closet out into the bedroom, her eyes peeled to the floor and the path forged by night lights. She feared Detective Bad Ass himself was out there, but saw no feet. She tiptoed from the bedroom back through the hall to the living room. Thief or police—she could not get caught.

The nightlights along the floorboards guided her through the dark house to the front door. She spun around looking for the impossible—a different way out—and heard another crash. The light in the hall behind her flicked on and immediately off. Heavy footsteps moved toward her. If not the police, who would be searching Bunnie's house?

She flung the front door open and ran. What thief closes the door when about to get caught in the act? She ran like she was running from hell, thanking God that she was dressed for a chase in black athletic shorts with a matching, long-sleeved, hooded sweat shirt.

Some eight or so blocks later, she rounded a corner onto Magazine Street, the Garden District's border. She stopped running to walk briskly, checking every step of the way to make sure no one had followed her. To make sure she'd gotten away without the getaway car.

The mansions along the boulevard gave way to rows of Creole cottages that over decades had morphed into antique stores and quaint shops. She looked around. The streets had scatterings of pedestrians, but no one chased her. She leaned against a streetlight pole and called Tabor on her new cell phone.

"Tabor," she said, out of breath. "The laptop wasn't in the desk like you said."

"What do you mean?" Tabor asked through a heavy sigh. "Didn't you find it?"

"Yeah." Ladonis snapped. "I found it in the closet, but I had to leave it."

"Leave it?" Tabor said. "Why?"

"Somebody else was in that house, that's why." Ladonis could not contain her anger. "So, I left the damn computer and the car, too. I had to or I would've gotten caught."

"Calm down, Donnie." Ladonis cringed at the agitation wavering in his voice. "Where are you now? Were you followed?"

"No." Ladonis glanced around. She spotted a couple walking out of the coffee shop on the other side of the street. "I don't think I was followed."

"So, where are you?" Tabor asked again.

"Do you know where P.J.'s Coffee and Tea Company is? That hot spot on Magazine Street that's all the rave?"

"Yeah, I know the place. I'm on my way. Wait for me inside. We can talk and figure this out."

Ladonis took a moment before making her way to the coffee shop. A panting black woman, dressed all in black, was sure to draw attention. She surveyed the area once more before stepping inside, her thoughts on the run even if her feet had slowed. Who was that in Bunnie's place? Not the cops or there would have been a police car outside.

She sat in the empty booth facing the café entrance so that she could see Tabor when he arrived as well as the police or anyone else who might've followed her. Her mind couldn't get past the thought that she'd gone to Bunnie's house to steal a computer that may or may not prove Bunnie killed a man who happened to be the richest man in New Orleans. She took in a deep breath and let it out in a long exhale as she felt the impact of that reality.

"Lord have mercy," she whispered. Suppose it was the killer coming for the computer. "I could've been killed."

Chapter Nine
Glitch

A YOUNG, PALE white-skinned woman stood before Ladonis, menu in hand, and asked her what she wanted. Ladonis tilted her head up and stared. If she'd walked into a restaurant looking for work dressed in black with dyed, orange hair, wearing about fifty pairs of earrings on her body, three in her nose, she would've been shunned. Maybe even escorted out by security. No way would she have been given a job. Yet, this decorated girl offered Ladonis the menu.

"Oh, I'll just have a—" Ladonis looked at the menu. "I'll have a Java." How in the world did all those piercings not hurt?

She scanned the small crowd of men and women, young and old, milling around at the bar across the room, sipping beverages. Too busy discussing the possible severity of the approaching storm to notice her. The weather report on a small television sitting on the opposite edge of the bar fueled the loud and animated conversations.

"The national weather center expects tropical storm Katrina, recently upgraded to hurricane on some news outlets, to make landfall in Florida sometime tomorrow," a voice from the television said.

Tropical storm. Hurricane. Ladonis shook her head. Which is it? Should people pack up and leave, or place a bet on how bad it was or wasn't going to be? In a city accustomed to bad weather, why did storm warnings have to play out as melodramatic media-speculation fantasy?

Ladonis shrugged and turned her gaze back to the window. Tabor appeared in the doorway, hood and all, dressed way down from his lawyerly *GQ* look. Just then the body-pierced girl placed the hot Java on the table so hard, it spilled on her tattooed fingers. Tabor squeezed into the booth across from Ladonis while the waitress watched, shaking away the coffee from her hand.

"Hello," Tabor said to the girl. "Coffee, black, please. Thank you."

"There was an intruder at Bunnie's and it wasn't the police," Ladonis blurted out as soon as the girl was out of earshot. "I'm sure of it."

Tabor looked toward the entrance. What was he looking at? Ladonis glanced sideways and saw HeartTrouble. *Oh, my God.*

"What are you doing here?" she asked in a careful, controlled tone. "I thought your life had too much new meaning to be bothered with me." She turned on Tabor. "And why didn't you tell me about his baby?"

"It wasn't my place to tell you." Tabor pushed the hood from his head.

HeartTrouble scooted into the booth next to Tabor. Ladonis frowned. His mouth was set into the same stubborn slit as hers. She hated that they looked so much alike, that their expressions mirrored one another. It bothered her that her emotions, especially her negative attitude, could be compared to his by her looks.

"But it's okay for him to be all in my business?" Ladonis narrowed her eyes.

"He was in my office when you called. Heard us talking," Tabor declared. "Besides, you're the one who told him your business when you asked him to go with you to Bunnie's house. But, let's not discuss that now." He took a moment to inspect the room, a god-forbid-if-I'm-recognized look on his face. "An intruder? What makes you so sure the intruder wasn't the police?"

"Because—"

"Because what?" HeartTrouble and Tabor interrupted in unison.

"Because whoever it was sneaked in through the back door and rummaged around in the dark. Same as me. Then a light came on." Ladonis unloaded her anger. "I lay you odds that that light came on by mistake because he clicked it right off. He must've leaned up against it or something."

"Did you see him?" Tabor asked.

"How could I?" Ladonis barked. "I was busy getting out of there."

Taking that computer had been his bright idea. How was she supposed to know someone else might show up? She sighed. It wasn't her intention to come across as flippant and defensive.

"Sorry I had to leave the computer." Ladonis lowered her voice. "And the car. No way did I want to get hauled in for auto theft on top of everything else."

Tabor tilted his head, his jawbones clenched, but he said nothing. Was silence a tactic to hide his anger? If not, then why did he look as though she'd cost him a million-dollar lotto ticket?

"Yeah." Tabor pulled out his cell phone and just stared at it. "If it wasn't the police, then it's not a problem. If it was——"

"If it wasn't the police," Ladonis repeated, excited. "Who else would be looking for the computer?"

"Calm down, Donnie." Tabor looked at the cell phone again then placed it on the table in front of him.

"Expecting a call?" Ladonis snarled. She'd grown tired of him ordering her to be calm.

"I'm always expecting a call." Tabor matched her irritation with good humor. "Chances are it was the police thinking they'd interrupted a burglary or something without giving any thought to you."

"If it was or wasn't the police," HeartTrouble chimed in, "don't matter. Whoever it was probably said, 'I can take care of her later.'" He reached into his pocket and pulled out a couple of crumbled dollar bills. "Donnie, you shouldn't've gone to that woman's house, is all."

"None of this would've happened if you'd been with me," Ladonis snapped.

"Donnie." Tabor glanced around. His voice held the strain of impatience. "Please."

Ladonis picked up her cup then slammed it down on the table. Was he chastising her because he knew that she and her brother were headed for their usual war of words? Or was he upset because she'd left the computer? Neither gave him the right to speak to her as if he had control over her.

"Maybe we ought to report this to the police." She was more than a little peeved. "Like you said, I could tell them I was there to pick up some work, a few personal things for Bunnie and heard someone come in the back door. That I got——"

"No." Tabor laid his hand flat on the tabletop with controlled strength. "We can't do that."

"Why not?" She bristled at his gruff tone. "What's on that computer anyway? And don't tell me you can't break Bunnie's confidence. I deserve to know why I could end up in jail."

"I wish Bunnie had downloaded that information onto a flash drive," Tabor mumbled. "It would've been so much easier to retrieve."

He gave Ladonis a look that was both apologetic and foreboding. Ladonis clenched her jaw muscles. Was the computer proof that Bunnie hadn't killed Maynard or that she had?

"Bunnie told me that she could prove that she didn't kill Maynard. And that the proof was on her mother's laptop."

"And you believed her?" HeartTrouble sneered, smoothing out the bills with his hand. "You bad as Donnie if you believe everythin' white folks say." He rose from his seat. "I'm goin' to see if they have chicory in any of them fancy coffees they sell in this joint. The stronger the better."

HeartTrouble headed for the counter. Ladonis pushed her Java to the side. A spontaneous outburst of laughter from the bar made her look around. She turned back to Tabor and his eyes locked with hers.

"Look, Donnie," Tabor confessed, "when I came to see you this morning, I came to tell you I'd recommended my lawyer friend in Shreveport to take Bunnie's case, not to discuss the details of my conversation with her."

Tabor tucked in his chin. He picked up his cell phone, looked at it, then replaced it on the table in front of him. Ladonis tapped her foot.

"But," he continued, "when you told me how important it was to you not to have a trial, I changed my mind. Especially since Bunnie had told me her mother's computer could help locate some bejeweled fountain pen her mother owned. She believes that if we find the pen, we'll probably find the killer. She's pretty confident, and I believe her."

"What are you talking about?" Ladonis watched HeartTrouble head back, a cup in each hand.

"After my visit with Bunnie," Tabor stared down at his phone and tapped it, "I did some checking. Her mother owned an antique shop, and Maynard, a collector, had been a longtime customer. He collected limited-edition items."

"I know," Ladonis told him. "Bunnie told me that much."

"Well," Tabor said, "it seems that in 1997 the Parker Company manufactured two-hundred-and-fifty eighteen-carat gold fountain pens with snakes wrapped around the barrels. The snakes' eyes were made of emeralds. Each pen retailed for twelve thousand."

"Dollars?" HeartTrouble let out a low whistle. He put a cup of coffee in front of Tabor and fell into his seat. "For a ink pen?"

"You got it." Tabor rotated the cup between his fingers.

"So what?" Ladonis said. "What does it matter? It's an old pen. The old man collected old things."

"Maynard, with the help of Bunnie's mom," Tabor retorted, "had collected a hundred of these Parker pens. The one Bunnie's talking about is number 101."

"Wow," HeartTrouble said. "Do the cops know this?"

"They didn't when I came up with the idea of getting hold of Bunnie's mom's laptop." Tabor looked at Ladonis. "I figured that if the cops didn't have the laptop, that would hold them off the pen trail for a while. Long enough to get the drop on another suspect."

Ladonis sat quiet, listening to Tabor as well as her own thoughts. After Bunnie's mom died, the girl's mission in life was to raise enough money to re-launch her mother's business in New Orleans. Ladonis surmised that goal was Bunnie's way of dealing with the death and legacy of her last living relative. But what if Bunnie had found out about the pen and all the money it was worth? She jerked her head up and stared at Tabor.

"How," Ladonis implored, "could you be sure the police had no idea about the computer or the pen?"

"How you think?" HeartTrouble grinned boastfully. "Tabor got connections on the inside, right?"

"It's the only way to win a case against the NOPD, to be a step ahead." Tabor winked at HeartTrouble. "Only it wasn't in the file drawer like Bunnie said. That means somebody else found it first."

Ladonis watched their interaction. Neither was a hardened criminal. Yet, each in his own way was in touch with the innate intricacies of criminal behavior. She felt a chill.

Tabor's phone beeped. Had he finally gotten the call he'd been waiting for? Ladonis looked around the café when he answered. The crowd was down to two men sitting at the bar debating whether they should leave or stay during the storm. One had a mother-in-law in a nursing home too sick to move and the other said he was afraid that looters, not the storm, would ravage his tire shop. The body-pierced girl busied herself removing glass items from the shelves.

"That was one of my guys at NOPD," Tabor confided. "Seems Clifford Maynard, the old man's brother, claims that a very expensive fountain pen is missing from his brother's collection. He said Maynard had gotten hold of the pen the day he was killed. That the pen took a while to reach him because the dealer he'd bought it from on the Internet had died."

"The white girl's mama, right?" HeartTrouble said.

Tabor nodded.

"And of course the police think Bunnie stole it." A grip of fear strangled Ladonis's voice. What if her breaking-and-entering episode was perceived as complicit in the theft? "Did they find the pen at her house?"

"No," Tabor said in his assertive courtroom voice. "And they didn't mention the other hundred pens in that particular collection either."

"Good news?" Ladonis watched Tabor's expression. Her old friend wasn't beyond manipulating the truth. This better not be one of those times.

"Not when they get a hold of that computer," Tabor acknowledged, all but wagging his finger at her. "With Bunnie's broken heel caught in a brick on Maynard's walkway and a neighbor who says she saw Bunnie rushing to her car, they won't need the actual pen to have an open-and-shut case against her."

"Well, couldn't her connection to the pen prove she had a reason to kill Maynard?" Ladonis wrapped her fingers around the cool cup of Java.

"Yes," Tabor admitted. His lawyer demeanor lessened. "Because it proves that she knew about its value before she went to Maynard's. If they can also prove that she had money problems, and they will, that'll show why she had to get it back."

"And that's why you wanted to get hold of the computer first." Ladonis looked down at her hands. If the cops knew she was in Bunnie's apartment searching for that computer, not protecting her home against Hurricane Katrina would be the least of her problems.

"Yeah," Tabor answered. "I thought that since the police weren't looking for the pen, and if we got the computer before they zeroed in on it, we could buy time to locate the whereabouts of the pen, and perhaps someone other than Bunnie who had a reason to kill Maynard."

"Now the police can use the computer to prove why Bunnie killed him." Ladonis pinched her itching nose.

Tabor nodded. "Provided they have it."

If the police had the computer, Ladonis's fingerprints were all over it. And how would she explain why strangers saw her hauling ass on Magazine Street in the middle of the night after what could be called Bunnie's home invasion? In this town, that was more than enough reason to lock her up. The implications of what she'd done unfolded in her mind as familiar as a scene in a detective novel. The evidence could lead to her. The possibility sped through her thoughts long enough to process her fear.

"What about the test?" Ladonis asked Tabor, her tone anxious. "You know, the gun powder test?"

"No test," Tabor responded. "The chief said the storm has commandeered her manpower in all departments."

"Forensics too?"

"Especially forensics. She said it was a priority to make sure that all evidence already collected is accounted for before the storm to ensure the proper litigation of cases already on the dockets."

"Oh, my God, Tabor, speak English," Ladonis said. "I'm no lawyer, but isn't Bunnie's case, her arraignment, already on the docket?"

"It is. But evidence is not presented at an arraignment. That's why I wanted it on the record that it wasn't done. Not performing that test in a timely fashion does not mean that the smoking gun in this case will not be the gun. It just means they will have to go to the extreme to prove she pulled the trigger."

"Do you think that could've been what was going down in Bunnie's apartment?" Ladonis asked, her tone both timid and forbidding. "Someone could've been planting the murder weapon?"

Tabor said nothing, staring once again at his phone instead. It crossed Ladonis's mind that his silence meant he agreed with her. If so, then what was he planning to do about it?

"If you had half the brain you claim you got," HeartTrouble's voice filtered through the maze of her emotions and thoughts, "you could see the mess you in right now. If somebody else killed Old Man Maynard, and was over at that girl's house tonight, whoever it is, gonna figure you saw him. You could be next."

"No." Ladonis shook her head. "He wouldn't have let me get away. He would've followed me."

"That's what's wrong with you, Donnie," HeartTrouble said. "Sometimes you don't think. Did it cross your mind that whoever it was saw you, but decided to let you get away 'til he come up with a plan—a plan that won't tie him to Bunnie or to you? Why you think he was there in the first place?"

"Don't talk to me like I'm an idiot," she scolded. She hated that he'd made her look scattered, like what her grandmother, Lucille, called a dimwit. "I know he wasn't there to water the plants."

"Good you understand that," HeartTrouble said. "Because if that white girl ain't the killer, and whether the person who went to her house was there to plant evidence or find some, you done made yourself into a glitch."

"A what?" Ladonis frowned, turned to Tabor for clarification.

"What he's trying to say," Tabor said in a placid tone, "is that killers consider anyone who witnesses their crime a glitch, the way computer programmers think about bugs in the games or systems they create."

"Yeah," HeartTrouble said. "You understand that?"

"Yes, I do," she snapped. Her brother's belittling attitude frustrated her. "It's crystal clear."

Her lips twitched. Computer glitches were short-lived. Someone got tasked to eliminate them. Who would be charged with eliminating her?

Chapter Ten
God Ain't Studyin' On Me Right Now

LADONIS STALLED AT the living room door of her mother's house on Mirrabeau Avenue in Gentilly. She took in and let out a big gulp of air, bracing for one of their mother/daughter control battles. Last night's break-in drama and the draining re-hash with Tabor and HeartTrouble afterward had dropped her into a mental cloud. But Mama had called. Demanded to see her. Said she had concerns about HeartTrouble's baby that needed to be addressed right away.

After choosing to go to Phoenix instead of her mother's church concert, Ladonis didn't have the courage to admit she was in somewhat of a flux about the baby, nor could she tell her mother she had more pressing career-related issues to deal with rather than her being a grandmother.

Feeling the anxiety fluttering in her chest, Ladonis walked into the living room, struggling to turn off the negative and focus on the positive thoughts. A beautiful, healthy baby in the family had to take precedence over her fears and lack of confidence, both in her brother as well as herself when it came to caring for a child.

Once she crossed the threshold, it dawned on her that Mama wasn't waiting at the bay window. And where were the sugary, buttery smells that normally greeted her on these family pow-wows her mother often insisted upon? And why wasn't the television blasting? Surely her mother's hearing loss hadn't gone away.

Her mother was in the living room, lying on an oversized, sky-blue sofa, her cane on the floor. Ladonis's stomach did a flip-flop, partly because she hated that hideous piece of contemporary furniture awkwardly situated in an otherwise traditionally decorated space. But mostly because Mama looked small—forlorn—uncomfortable in her own skin, lying there without the familiar sights, sounds, and smells that identified her in her home.

"Hi, Ma." Ladonis struggled to keep alarm out of her voice. Then she noticed the cake box on the English-American classic cherry-wood dining table on the other side of the open space. "Since when is Mackenzie's coffee cake better than yours?"

"Been feelin' poorly lately." Her mother lifted her head. "Too poorly to be messin' 'round in the kitchen. My neighbor picked up that store-bought cake for us. You can scrape the icing off. I know you don't like it."

Ladonis picked up her mother's walking cane and leaned it against the arm of the sofa. She looked over at her mom. The flesh on her chin hung from her neck like a rooster's wattle. How much weight had Mama lost? How ill was she?

"Cut me a sliver." Her mother used her thumb and index finger to demonstrate the size of a sliver. She sat upright on the sofa. "I ain't that hungry this mornin'."

"Are you still taking that pain medicine the doctor gave you for your hip?" Ladonis walked over to the white and green cake box from one of the city's most famous bakeries. "You know, the ones that cut your appetite." She lifted the lid. "Have you spoken to your doctor about how you've been feeling?"

"No doctor can fix what's ailin' me." Her mother's low-peaking voice was too low to be normal. "Nobody know what's wrong with me but God. And He ain't studyin' on me right now. I reckon He'll get to me in due time."

Ladonis dropped the plastic lid off the cake box onto the table. The lack of passion in her mother's voice, usually eager to make her point, and to subdue everyone else's, especially her daughter's, made Ladonis's heart skip a beat. Had she been so self-absorbed that she'd missed the changes in her mother?

"Ma—" Ladonis decided to goad her mother into an argument to pick up her spirits.

Ever since her pubescent clock ticked on when she turned thirteen, she and her mother butted heads. And while love, understanding, and respect grew between them with maturity, the tone of their communication never did. For Ladonis, the bantering fueled her ability to speak her mind without holding back, while remaining respectful to her mother. She assumed her mother felt the same way.

"Why didn't you tell me about your granddaughter? How could you keep something as important as a child in the family a secret from me?"

"Baby, ain't nobody tryin' to keep no secret from you." Her mother's eyes pointed toward the kitchen. "And pour me a lil juice in my cup."

Why wasn't she griping at her? Calling her selfish? Telling her she wasn't the earth's axis?

"Okay." Ladonis rubbed the back of her neck. Something was wrong. Very wrong.

Ladonis strode into the kitchen, retrieved her mother's drinking cup that was always chilling on the second shelf of the refrigerator. She located the Minute Maid shelved behind a Tupperware bowl of God knows what. Her mother didn't drink anything but Minute Maid. Funny how that detail just popped into her thoughts. A detail she suddenly felt compelled to recall so as not to forget.

"Bring a couple of glasses out for your brother," her mother called out. "He'll be stragglin' in here d'rectly. Him and Tabor."

Him and Tabor, huh? Ladonis heaved a sigh. For months, no Tabor. Now, too much Tabor.

"Your brother visitin' here, in this house, next week with his baby girl." There was pride in her mother's voice where energy had failed. "I want you here. And I don't want to hear nothin' 'bout that job of yours, either."

So that's why HeartTrouble and Tabor were coming over. Normally, it was mother and daughter sitting around eating homemade coffee cake, discussing what her mother needed and wanted. Not to mention arguing about anything Ladonis said or about why she was still single.

"So, the baby is coming here." Ladonis walked back into the living room, wondering if Charmaine had a change of heart. "I'm going to take my cake with me." She was not up to a face-to-face with HeartTrouble and Tabor after last night, let alone talk about the baby.

It was hard for her to think about HeartTrouble's baby. Perhaps because she didn't feel her brother was father material and felt guilty for having that sentiment. Or, perhaps it was because she harbored what her mother would call unnatural feelings about not wanting children of her own, and felt even guiltier about that. Especially since her mother and brother were so happy about the child.

"I really should be getting to the office," she said. "What time is the baby coming?"

"Lunch time on Tuesday," her mother responded. "Her other grandma said she gonna bring her 'round twelve o'clock."

"I'll see if I can make it." Ladonis placed a tray with the juice and cake on the end table next to where her mother sat. "Here, Mama."

"You better do more than see if you can." Her mother's demanding tone sounded more natural. "You better be here. I don't see why you can't stay and wait for your brother and Tabor now."

"I can't is all."

Her mother stretched out on the blue sofa.

Ladonis walked to the front door. "But I'll stop by later today to check in on you. We'll talk about the baby's visit then."

Ladonis tromped heavily down the walk. Though overcast, no storm clouds hovered in the early-morning sky. Filled with a strange sense of awareness, however, she noticed that the shrubs that lined the path to the front door were tall and uneven with what looked like patches of burnt-colored twigs. Limp, brown zinnia blooms hung from the overhang trellis. And weeds were thriving while the white peace lilies in her mother's cherished garden were not. What was going on? Her mother tended her yard like it was the promised land.

Ladonis got into her car, trying to collect her thoughts about HeartTrouble and his baby; about why being a parent scared the living daylights out of her; but most of all, about her mother's flowers. How could an avid gardener like her mother, despite her ailments and disability, allow her prize blooms to deteriorate so quickly? How sick did Mama have to be not to freak out about the condition of her yard?

First, there was the ordeal in Phoenix, followed by Bunnie's arrest for Maynard's murder, then the arrival of HeartTrouble's baby. Now, her mother. Instead of clearing the air in her head, this visit with Mama had only spiked her emotional discomfort. Made her feel even more disconnected from her own life.

Chapter Eleven
One Drop

LADONIS APPROACHED THE tall, dark wood information desk, her stare unfocused like her thoughts.

"Jeez Louise, Ladonis." Shelia, the receptionist, placed her hand on her chest. "You scared me. I didn't see you."

The bug-eyed look on the receptionist's face reminded Ladonis that just last evening, surprise and fright had kept her from becoming a thief and an obstructionist.

"I wasn't expecting you either," Ladonis said, thinking she had never seen the robust woman with the bleached-blonde short dreads in before eight a.m. And she had never admitted to anyone that she had issues with how a proud black woman could be shallow enough to bleach her kinks blonde. In her opinion, that trend, along with the drooping baggy pants young black men wore, took black rebellion to the point of ridiculous.

"You want to get an early start today, huh?" Ladonis, who prided herself on avoiding office gossip, sneered. No doubt Shelia wanted to be all in the Bunnie drama to get first dibs on what got into the rumor mill.

"You bet." Shelia's frankness was the one thing Ladonis liked about the woman. "When I saw the paper this morning with Bunnie on the front page, I got here as fast as I could."

"What?" Ladonis rubbed her itching nose. The sweet smell of cut flowers fought with the strong odor of Shelia's signature Oscar de la Renta perfume. "Bunnie's picture is in the paper? On the front page?"

"You mean you ain't, I mean, you haven't seen it yet?" Cynicism laced Shelia's sly smile.

Ladonis lifted an eyebrow. Would the clerical workers ever stop giving her grief for the company mandating that they participate in training on the importance of good verbal and written communication skills in the workplace? The way she saw it, if a telephone operator couldn't speak the universal English language correctly, then the Floating Palace's image suffered. Hence, her job performance as PR director was undermined.

"See." Shelia reached down into her oversized purse and pulled out a copy of the *Times Picayune* and thrust the front page with Bunnie's picture into Ladonis's face. "See, *Did She Kill Her Dad?* That's the headline."

"Her dad? That can't be true," Ladonis squeaked out.

Ladonis grabbed the paper from Shelia's hand, pissed at the excitement Bunnie's scandal seemed to give her. Sure enough, "did she kill her dad" were the words printed boldly below Bunnie's photo. No wonder Bunnie had made the front page.

The column's byline was Allison Spinner. A reporter's dream was to catch the world off guard with a story like Bunnie's, especially if it was true. Hell, it could be a reporter's career coup even if it wasn't true in this twenty-four-hour, reactionary, melodramatic news cycle. But in highly competitive corporate America with its coded bias toward women and people of color, that kind of surprise could derail a career, marginalize a business deal, even end a life.

Ladonis read on. The first sentence acknowledged that the story had been broken by none other than WDSU's star reporter, Monique LaFaye. She scowled. Her reaction a snapshot of confusion wrapped in disappointment and anger.

Why hadn't her old high-school chum come to her with the story before going to broadcast? Then again, the last thing Ladonis needed was to get caught up in the never-ending saga of Monique's quest for a CNN anchor job.

> As someone once wrote, "History is slippery and restless in New Orleans. As inescapable as it is elusive. So goes the tale of Bunnie Sinclair, accused of murdering Jarvis Maynard, the man some have described as the patriarch of New Orleans royalty."
>
> Born Bernadette Senare to Poupon Senare, October 21, 1974, at Charity Hospital, Miss Bunnie Sinclair returned to the city of her birth four years ago from Cincinnati as an employee of the Floating Palace Steamboat Company.

*Poupon Senare, a New Orleans Creole and the daughter
of a Norma Wallace, a former prostitute, had been Jarvis
Maynard's mistress. Shortly before the birth of their child, Ms.
Senare moved to Vermont, changed her name to Sinclair, and
lived as a white woman, owner and operator of a successful
antique business until her death two months ago.*

Where in the world had Monique latched onto this bombshell?
Ladonis envisioned Monique, microphone in hand, standing on the
dock in front of the *Magnolia Belle*. Quite the backdrop for a story about
a passé' blanc accused of killing her rich, long-lost white daddy.

"Something, huh?" Shelia said. "Bunnie's mama was a passer. You
suppose she ever told Bunnie she was part black?"

Who isn't part black? Ladonis wanted to say. Those DNA tests
people are taking is proving that. But, here, part black is not considered
in any shape or form, an ethnic identity. In this town, Bunnie and her
mother were black, plain and simple. That's how things have worked
since slavery. One drop of black blood made you black in these parts.
None of that multi-cultural bull here. Bunnie's mother must have
known that.

"By the way." Shelia held out her hand. "Here are your messages."

Ladonis took several pink message slips from Shelia, her hand
trembling. She passed the slips through shaking fingers, checking to see
if there was something from Monique. Nothing.

"You all right, Ladonis?" Shelia asked, her brow furrowed.

"Fine." Ladonis returned Shelia's newspaper. "Let me know the
minute Angela Hill gets here, will you?"

"Angela Hill?" Shelia gasped. "The TV reporter?"

Ladonis nodded. Bret had called before she'd left for her mother's,
telling her he'd set up the meeting. Angela Hill was the media diva that
drove her old classmate, Monique, to fatuous heights of competition.
Ladonis dreaded the interview and wished Bret had waited on talking
to the press. Suppose she made a mistake and mentioned that pen? Or
Bunnie's computer? She had to make sure that she didn't give any of that
away. Even if provoked.

And where was Bret, anyway? Had he seen the newspaper? If so,
how did he want her to handle this development in the interview with

Angela Hill? Or was she on her own, like she was with Bunnie's charter contracts?

"Bret in?" Ladonis asked.

"No," Shelia responded, annoyed. "Not yet. I mean I don't know. I just got here a minute before you did myself."

Ladonis trotted down the corridor to her office. How much did Bret know about Bunnie and when had he learned it? And was that why he'd given her the save-the-charter task? The nerve of Bunnie to drag her to Phoenix on what turned out to be a life-threatening mission and not mention that her half-Black mother had been Maynard's mistress. In jail or not, she had to talk to Miss Thang. Tabor had to arrange it.

Ladonis plopped down onto her desk chair. She had to think. She couldn't imagine things getting any easier as the account of Bunnie and Jarvis Maynard's relationship evolved. Questions mounted. Why was Bunnie so anxious to have her daddy imprisoned for stealing her jade? And what about Monique? How did she get to be the one to break the story about Bunnie without so much as a nod to Ladonis?

This puzzle required some work, her attention. And she'd start with Monique, the reporter's source. Perhaps the person who told Monique about Bunnie and her mother knew about the pen and could help Tabor zero in on the real killer. Despite the emotional stress and anger Bunnie had to experience after learning about her father, she still did not believe that Bunnie could be a murderer.

Ladonis flipped through her messages. It would irk Monique to learn about the interview Bret had arranged for Ladonis with his buddy, Angela Hill, from the other network WWL, and not her. No doubt the media darling would accuse Ladonis of selling her out for the white girl. She frowned. It was unfair to be called a sellout for doing her job.

The phone on the desk buzzed. Ladonis picked up the headset. It was Shelia, panting.

"Angela Hill ain't coming," Shelia blurted. "She said that storm, Katrina, supposed to make landfall in Florida sometime this evening, so she on her way there."

"Thanks," Ladonis responded, glad she had time to do some digging to find out just what was going on with Bunnie and the Maynards. She dialed Monique's telephone number, knowing she was an insomniac who poked around all night and slept all morning. She was sure to be home.

"Oops, I'm sorry, "Ladonis quipped when Monique answered. "Did I wake you? I forgot."

"Forgot what?" Monique asked, a sleepy frog in her throat.

"That according to you, a nocturnal reporter in a twenty-four/hour cable news cycle is a star reporter," Ladonis said in her condescending judgmental soapbox voice. Her tone whenever she talked about the media. "Or, shouldn't you be on the morning talk-show circuit after coming up with such breaking news?"

"I guess you heard about the story I uncovered about your co-worker, huh?" Monique's voice was measured, teasing.

"Who fed you that garbage?" Ladonis asked.

"I got a tip that Ms. Sinclair had demanded the police arrest Jarvis Maynard," Monique explained, "and I decided to find out why, is all. Thanks to my tipster, the Internet, my reporter credentials, and my police connections, digging up the facts and someone who could attest to the whole thing wasn't that hard."

Monique was lying. Had to be. No one could keep a secret like that for a minute, let alone for years. Ladonis felt her face flush, hot with anger. But at whom? Monique for doing her job? Bunnie, for holding out on her? Or at herself for being so damn gullible?

Okay." Ladonis softened her tone to control the muscles quivering inside her. "So why didn't you run it by me before you went blabbing it to the press? In the past if someone from the Floating Palace so much as stomped a toe, you'd be all over me for confirmation."

"Where is it written that I have to call you before I submit a story?" Monique coughed. "Wait a minute. On second thought, I can't talk to you now. I have to go."

"Since when do you even stir in your sleep before noon?" Ladonis shook her head, tossing her hair back.

"Since right now," Monique said. "Your call disturbed my bladder."

The phone went dead. Ladonis slammed her receiver into its cradle. "Bitch."

Chapter Twelve
Cold Hearted

NOTHING COULD'VE prepared Ladonis for her reaction when she caught sight of Bunnie sitting behind the bullet-proof glass wall in Orleans Parish Prison wearing orange and no make-up. She stopped walking and her heart pounded in her chest. She dragged her leaden feet to the steel-framed, puke-green chair at the window, sat down, and glanced back at the big female sheriff standing guard on the other side of the door. The guard's disheveled red crop was visible through the tiny square pane in the door.

After Angela Hill cancelled and after Monique flaked out on her, Ladonis asked Tabor to arrange what's called "lawyer's clearance" for her to visit Bunnie in jail. She'd told him that she needed a one-on-one with Bunnie to clear up some work details. That wasn't a lie, but if the whole truth was told, she wanted the details she didn't get from Monique, and she had to break ties. She couldn't afford to get caught up any further in Bunnie's world or murder and mayhem.

She picked up the black phone. The handset felt cool and damp on her sweaty palms. Bunnie already had hers to her ear.

"Ladonis." Bunnie's face was a portrait of fear. "I'm so glad to see you. I was afraid you wouldn't want anything to do with me."

"Why?" Ladonis said, her voice full of anger. "Because you're a liar?"

"I know what you must think of me." Bunnie lowered her head.

"Look, Bunnie, or Babette, or whatever your name is," Ladonis said in a biting tone. "I don't like being played."

"But I—"

"You deliberately misled me is all," Ladonis said.

"I should've told you about my mama and Jarvis Maynard, I know," Bunnie confessed. "And I'm sorry that I didn't. But I couldn't. Learning about him the way I did, upset me in ways I couldn't imagine. I was glad. I was mad. I was scared. All that made me feel like a stranger to

myself. I didn't know how to share that with anyone. Even if I wanted
to."

Ladonis blinked. She wanted to force back into her head any thought
that made her relate to this girl's dysfunction in any way. But it was too
late. It stood out in her mind that growing up fatherless could very well
be the reason she often felt lacking no matter her achievements.

"And," Bunnie said, "I didn't have my mother, or my grandmother
to help me come to grips with how I'd lived my entire life thinking my
father had to be dead, otherwise he would've searched the world until
he'd found me."

She looked Ladonis straight in the eyes. Ladonis looked away. This
girl's situation was turning her inside out. There were many times over
the years when she thought about her own absent father and experienced
those very emotions—anger, sadness, resignation. Evidently, so did
HeartTrouble, which would explain why he felt so strongly about having
a relationship with his baby girl. But was her brother up to the task of
giving his child a sense of fulfillment that his father had not given him?
Was she?

"When I found out that my father was alive, and who he was,"
Bunnie said, "my first thought was how great it was to finally know
where I came from. Then I thought maybe he doesn't want me. And that
angered me. But I did not kill him."

"You didn't think it was important to share that information before
dragging me off to a strange place to peddle jewelry? I could've been
killed?" Ladonis let out her fury.

"I'm sorry." Bunnie's eyes grew teary. "I had no idea of the danger
when we went to Phoenix." Fat water beads dropped down her cheeks.
"Do you really believe I would've gone if I had, let alone take you with
me?"

Ladonis gritted her teeth, unwilling to acknowledge the pain in
Bunnie's eyes. "Girl, I don't know what you'd do, and I don't want to
know."

The truth was she had to know. She had to know what had gone down
at Maynard's house between the old man and his long-lost daughter. She
had to know every sordid detail that could put this girl at the mercy of
New Orleans-style injustice, and FPSC in a media free fall.

"How are Bret and Velcroy handling all of this?" Bunnie asked.

Ladonis could feel her muscles tightening. The girl had more sad going on in her eyes than a sick puppy. She couldn't help thinking how she would feel if the situation were reversed and she was forfeiting her signature accomplishment.

"Actually, Bret has asked me to finalize your charter deals."

"I see." Bunnie's mouth twisted, her expression grave. "They are going to publicly disassociate the Floating Palace from me and my troubles. If you close the deals right away, the company will not look as though it's in a tailspin about whether I'm guilty or innocent."

"I agreed to do it," Ladonis said.

She flipped her briefcase over, opened it, and retrieved a file folder. "I see in your files that Keyes will be in town day after tomorrow." She opened the folder.

"He's coming for some other meeting." Bunnie shook her head. "But since the *Magnolia Belle* is scheduled to be docked here at the time, I convinced him to tour the boat to get a mental picture about how things might unfold during his company's retreat cruise."

"Good," Ladonis said. "I think it might help to secure the deal right away if he also met with the head of the Tourist Commission and the group that represents French Quarter restauranteurs during his visit. Particularly since so many cruisers plan for layovers before and after the cruise in the city. I have enough pull with those guys to get it done last minute."

"Yeah," Bunnie said, her tone melancholy. "That's a good idea."

"I think so." Ladonis pursed her lips in thought. "It makes the charters a city project that positions FPSC positively in the community. That's the sort of thing that plays well in advertising these days, and will up the ante for Keyes to sign off on the charter sooner rather than later."

"Smart move," Bunnie said, "to take advantage of his visit and get him to cinch the deal."

Ladonis took note of Bunnie's swollen eyes and the gloom they cast. She was unsure which Bunnie she was speaking to. The scared Bunnie accused of killing her father, or the deal-making manipulator.

"Wait." Ladonis had a revelation. "A mental picture? Why would the president of a Fortune 500 company need a mental picture of a business retreat? Doesn't he have someone to handle details like that for him?"

"Yes, he does." Bunnie sharpened her tone. "But according to his meeting planner, Keyes was concerned that the cruise provided a setting that might be too captive. That his people might get bored with no place to go after business to unwind for the next business day. So, I suggested that it be a theme trip to give attendees a fun focus after meetings."

"A theme trip, huh?" Ladonis fingered the pearl necklace around her neck.

"Yes." Bunnie's effort to sound enthusiastic came across as strained. "That way the attendees can have some fun dressing up for social events. They won't feel so locked down with work and get bored with what the younger employees might consider mundane, historic riverboat cruise activity."

"Okay." Ladonis faked an upbeat response, never losing sight of the fact that this was the sort of housekeeping detail that could, if neglected, depict her either as resolute and competent, or as inexperienced. Especially since the age demographic for traditional steamboaters was fifty and older. She perused the pages in the folder. "Have the theme or themes been chosen? I don't see any references in your notes."

"It's all on my computer. I didn't get the chance to download it before our trip to Phoenix."

"Which computer?" Ladonis enunciated to emphasize she meant her words to be hurtful. "If it's your office computer, the police have it. You couldn't mean the laptop. God only knows who has that."

Bunnie stared at Ladonis with the same scared, pleading expression on her face. Was she silent because Tabor had told her what had happened or was HeartTrouble right and Bunnie was playing her again?

"I've already made the arrangements with the boat's staff for the tour," Bunnie said. "You can have the captain fax you the logistics so that you can present a knock-out overview."

"Fine." Ladonis placed the folder back in the briefcase. "Too bad the rumors about you and Velcroy aren't true. Otherwise he and Bret might be more inclined to help you to get out of here."

Bunnie gasped. So did Ladonis. Everyone knew that success at the Floating Palace depended on being tuned in to, yet pretending to avoid, the rumor mill. The rumor was that Bunnie and Velcroy were an item. Bunnie was a successful Floating Palace employee. This was one of those times she should've avoided the rumor mill.

"You're one to talk." Bunnie's eyes were as piercing as Ladonis's tone was sharp. "I see the way you and Bret ogle each other. You can't tell me that you two aren't getting it on."

Oh, my God. Who else thought that? Who else knew that, in addition to being a woman in pursuit of a career, she was also hot-blooded and had a thing for her boss? But the real disclosure here was that she'd been too busy making sure Bret never saw her giving him the eye to notice him "ogling" her as Bunnie described.

"I have to go," Ladonis mumbled. Nothing walloped like a revelation from a least expected source.

"Ladonis, please wait," Bunnie begged. "You've got to believe in me. I don't have anyone else."

There was no end to this girl's gall. Did she think that crack about Bret wouldn't infuriate and alienate her? To share space on earth with Bunnie Sinclair was like living with your brain attached to a detonator.

"You should've thought of that before you lied about you and Jarvis Maynard." Ladonis refused to contain her contempt.

"How could I tell you or anyone?" Bunnie asked in a tear-shaky voice. "I didn't know myself. It was the last thing my mama said to me. Can you imagine what it was like finding out that my entire life has been based on a secret? You have no idea what I've been through coping with this. How could I talk to you or anyone about it? I had no one to turn to."

Ladonis searched for a way to keep her heartstrings away from Bunnie's troubles. "Yeah, well, you should've told me before I broke into your place for that computer. That was a scary and dangerous act for me, you know."

"Would you have gone if I had? Would you have gotten your friend A. Tabor to help me? No. You would've convinced yourself not to trust me. All because my mother had been passing all those years."

Was this girl for real? Bunnie's chastising expression made Ladonis want to shatter that window and choke her. She acted as if breaking and entering was of little consequence. Did it not occur to her that it was that little consequence that could land her in a jail cell too?

"You don't know what I've been through," Bunnie whined. "Trying to figure out who I am and where I belong. I swear on my mother's grave that I did not kill Jarvis Maynard. I've come to realize that I was counting on him to help me figure myself out. To help me understand why my mother maintained a relationship with him all these years buying and selling fountain pens, and never told me anything about him or him about me until she was dying. Why she never told me she was black."

Hearing Bunnie speak of her bloodline with such bewilderment and anger pulled at Ladonis's ethnic sensibilities. She shifted her body weight.

Bunnie pounded the table. Ladonis jumped and the guard opened the door to check in on them. Who knew Bunnie had the energy to even make a fist.

"If I could get out of here, I could prove it," Bunnie said. "Oh, God. If I could get out here, I could prove that I didn't kill my own father."

"What are you talking about?" Ladonis asked. "How do you propose to end this and keep your lying ass out of jail?"

"There's going to be an estate auction for Children's Hospital," Bunnie told her, "at Audubon Place tomorrow night."

"Audubon Place?" Ladonis echoed. "That's in an exclusive community for the rich and famous. How can an auction at the home of the president of Tulane University help you?"

Bunnie's body stiffened as if rigor had set in. Sweat beads formed on her nose. Her eyes widened.

"An auction like that is the safest way for a thief to get rid of my mother's snake pen without arousing suspicion. That's how."

Her mother's snake pen? Clifford Maynard said the pen belonged to his dead brother. Ladonis put her hands together, entwined her fingers, and pressed. Just how calculating was Miss Bunnie Sinclair?

"So, what if the pen is there?" Ladonis sat back in her seat and cast a probing stare on Bunnie. "It belongs to Jarvis Maynard. Your mother sold it to him."

"Not according to my mother. She wrote me that the pen had not changed ownership. My mother and my . . . My mother and Jarvis Maynard agreed that he could keep the pen, as long as he willed the collection to me. Keeping that particular pen in her name was her way of making sure that he did."

"I see," Ladonis muttered.

"No, you don't see," Bunnie cried. "Whoever has the pen either killed or knows who killed Jarvis Maynard."

Ladonis stared stupefied at Bunnie. Bunnie took the phone from her ear and lowered her head. She held the receiver to her chest. Was she going to lose it?

The blades on the ceiling fan barely turned. No air circulated. Despite the jailhouse sounds—clanging doors, jingling keys, and loud voices, no life stirred. Only Bunnie's sadness and Ladonis's suspicions. What game was Bunnie playing?

"That pen is at that auction." Bunnie bit down on her bottom lip. "Along with proof of who killed Jarvis Maynard. I'm sure of it."

Ladonis had arrived at Parish Prison mad as hell at Bunnie. Now frustration sweated up her clothes. Whether she believed Bunnie or not, this girl's life story was poised to piss off some powerful people. And Ladonis knew she would have to get further involved if she was ever to be free of this mess.

Chapter Thirteen
She's Got This

LADONIS HURRIED TO talk to Bret. The responsibility he'd given her for Bunnie's charters, coupled with the fact that the infuriating girl was in serious trouble had her tied up in knots. But when she arrived at the opened door to Bret's office, she heard Chairman of the Board, Edward H. Velcroy, on speakerphone. She stopped before knocking and stepped aside.

She could see Bret's body slumped in the chair behind his desk through the tri-parted wall of windows overlooking the Mississippi River as if it was a mirror. She stepped further to the side so he couldn't spot her reflection.

"Why her?" Velcroy said. "Why not the marketing or sales VP? Washington may be smart and all, but she's no Sinclair."

Ladonis's jaws clenched; tightened her fists. What did he mean she was no Sinclair? She wanted to storm in there and demand Velcroy show her some respect.

"She can do it."

Ladonis shivered. She didn't like Bret's condescending, bill-collector tone when he requested the someone from maintenance replace a light bulb. And she didn't like it now.

"You sure?" Velcroy said. "You know, we're facing that takeover—that merger—with Old Norse. Those charters make FPSC a very compelling acquisition despite the current fiscal challenges."

"Yeah, so you keep reminding me." Bret didn't sound impressed. Possibly because anyone who'd studied Business 101 knew that after mergers or takeovers, CEO positions were first on the chopping block.

"That's why we must give the job to Ladonis," Bret said. "My gut tells me these charters should remain a woman's deal. Good for marketing and publicity since women are our biggest market. Besides, Bunnie left things pretty well organized—negotiation items outlined and time-lined to a 'T' in her files."

Wow, Ladonis thought. Looks like Bunnie's charters are what's keeping FPSC in the game.

Old Norse. Old Norse. The name floated through her thoughts like a trapped bird on the verge of a breakout. Old Norse was the world's largest river cruise lines. She'd read in some cruise trade publication a while back that the company wanted to add American river cruises, specifically riverboat cruises, to its European fleet. If FPSC merged with them, the company could gain access to even more charter business with Old Norse's international outreach. This could be the back-end plan FPSC needed to turn a takeover into a merger.

"I tell you, Ladonis has got this," Bret said.

Had Bret complimented her or advanced his plan to set her up to be the scapegoat if the charters fell through? She tapped on the door and stepped inside. Time to take a stand.

"I take it you got the message from Angela Hill cancelling the interview." Ladonis strode in like a proud peacock, as if she hadn't heard a word Bret and Velcroy had said about her. She had to come across as professional, and not the angry black woman.

"Yes, I heard," Bret said in a flat voice.

"Ladonis Washington? Is that you?" Velcroy's voice thundered through the speakerphone.

"Oh, yes." Ladonis feigned surprise. "Hello, Mr. Velcroy. I didn't realize Bret was on the phone."

She imagined the company's eccentric owner removing a white handkerchief from his customary white pants pocket and wiping his entire face. A quirky habit of his that she'd observed during his infrequent visits to the Big Easy and the Floating Palace.

"Have a seat." Bret beckoned her to a chair at the conference table.

He then stood and walked around the table to sit at its head, keeping her in his sight. Ladonis took a seat, placing Bunnie's charter files in front of her.

"So, you've been in charge of public relations for a year now." The hint of hoarseness in Velcroy's voice made the sixty-year old sound like a teenage boy on the cusp of manhood. "I hear the news down there is full of doom and gloom about gambling. How do you propose to make that a positive for FPSC?"

"Too many gambling boats and not enough new money," Bret said. "Or old money for that matter."

"What does that mean, exactly?" Velcroy questioned.

"It means," Ladonis interjected, determined not to shrink under Velcroy's cynical scrutiny and criticism, "that the old money—the big discretionary dollars in this town—is spent in Vail or Europe. Or the Caribbean someplace. And the tourists—that is the new money—come here to eat, listen to jazz, and to take pictures of cemeteries. Gambling hasn't caught on yet. To date, most gamblers are locals who are betting with more hope than dollars."

"I see," Velcroy stated, pensively. Was he impressed? "What is marketing and P.R. doing to change that dynamic? That perception?"

"I'll tell you what." Bret glanced at Ladonis, his furrowed brow saying that it was his turn to speak. "Experts say the only casino that's going to withstand this type of pressure and come out on top is a land-based gambling operation at the foot of Canal Street. Or someplace near the major hotels in the French Quarter. You know, tourist traps like Planet Hollywood and the Riverwalk."

Experts? Ladonis's mouth flew open. She couldn't believe her ears. That had been her suggestion. Was he calling her an expert?

"Go on," Velcroy said with a stilted interest.

Ladonis sat tall, crossing her arms. She'd learned to discern that show-me-the-money undertone from dealing with Bret and Bunnie these past couple of years. In Velcroy, however, his penchant for the bottom line felt more like a ticking time bomb than just an attitude. She sensed that if the big guy didn't get pleasing figures and data capable of stomping out his lit fuse, he would blow her and Bret to smithereens. Especially if one cent of his millions was threatened because of his affiliation with a failing company.

"I'm negotiating with city planners and the gaming commission right now." Bret scrunched down in his chair. "To make sure the permanent structure is our newest boat."

"Yes," Ladonis cut in, "we can corner the gambling market in this town if we dock that boat right here on the Mississippi."

No way was she going to come across as just a do-as-I-say employee without a brain. Not after hearing what the old guy really thought of her. It was her idea to dock the new boat. She wanted the credit.

"How do you plan to sell that plan without Edwin Edwards?" Velcroy sighed heavily.

The former governor had had a convincing statewide perspective which had included New Orleans. Not the case under its current governor whose contempt was evident every time he referred to the city as a jungle.

"Besides," Velcroy went on to explain. "Those so-called tourist traps at the foot of Canal Street, the French Quarter, are the city's bread and butter. Even Edwin Edwards would have a hard time persuading local leaders to gamble with the city's bread and butter."

"Exactly." Ladonis swallowed her enthusiasm. "And that's how we pitch the idea to city officials."

Bret gave her a grave look. She inched up, making her body taller in her seat. This was not the conversation she'd expected when she came to see him, but it was one she didn't mind having. This was about her business ideas. Not Bunnie's. This could be her chance to let Velcroy know what she could do. If she saved Bunnie's charters and kept the company afloat, then implemented her docked-boat idea to guarantee a prosperous steamboatin' future with or without a merger, her vice presidency would be assured.

"Gambling and riverboats have a long history in this part of the world," she explained. "The ambiance and nostalgia alone will be selling points, even to foreigners."

"Excuse me. Have I missed something?" Velcroy's mocking tone was more than pompous. It was offensive.

"Oh, didn't I tell you," Bret said. He glared at Ladonis, swiping at a stream of perspiration puddling on his forehead. "I told her, off the record, what we were up against with the merger and all. But—"

"I see," Velcroy said.

Judging from the Bret's throbbing temples, he'd heard Velcroy's displeasure as clearly as Ladonis had.

"Washington," Velcroy said. "Aren't we already selling nostalgia and ambiance?"

"Yes," Ladonis told him, "we are, but on the rivers. Not in historic New Orleans. Our authentic riverboat vessel will be a step back in time to when New Orleans was a major gambling center in this country. When gamblers were suave, well-dressed men bigger than life, and their women were gorgeous thrill-seekers out to claim them."

Bret leaned back, cupping the back of his head between his hands. His eyes fell on Ladonis. Was he ogling her like Bunnie suggested, or was he telling her to shut up?

"Dock the new boat in the heart of the city's fabulous downtown, amongst all the tradition and history this place has to offer," Ladonis said. "Gambling via the Floating Palace will become a New Orleans cultural staple much like Mardi Gras."

"There are too many political contingencies involved," Velcroy reminded her. "State as well as local. There's zoning, gaming policies and restrictions, and liquor licenses to get. Besides, as your own research indicates, outside of the locals, who's going to pay the price to gamble in the city on a riverboat that does not go anywhere?"

"Tourists, for starters, and our cruise passengers," Ladonis informed him. "We'll lengthen the Crescent City shore stop by one, maybe two nights and offer an authentic riverboat gambling experience in sin city with first-rate New Orleans-style entertainment for a slight increase in fare."

Wow, that came out well. She smiled. She'd actually come up with that argument in that moment. And in her excitement, didn't let it slip that Old Norse would probably pay through the teeth to add this to its American river cruise itinerary should the merger become reality. This was the perfect back end plan to give FPSC a negotiating edge in the merger.

"The boat," she continued, "will offer fine Victorian staterooms for vacationers, overnight or weekend guests, fine food and spirits, and concerts that our cruise passengers as well as our wealthy natives will pay through the teeth for."

"Humph," Velcroy grunted. "I'm afraid that without Edwin Edwards, or someone with his influence and attitude toward New Orleans in the governor's mansion, our legal and marketing departments will not be willing to get on board with this."

Velcroy and Bret had lobbied Edwin Edwards hard to get the gaming law passed. And since Edwards' subsequent indictment for racketeering, it was no secret that many politicians were second-guessing the law.

"Yes, but—" She had to get Velcroy to see her research data. "Rather than depending on the special interests of any one person or corporation to bully a business concept into action, why not show charts and graphs specific to projected earnings, spending, and tax trends that are designed to jumpstart any city project?"

"You know," Velcroy didn't give her a chance to ask if he'd review her research, "because riverboat gambling is not catching on, the board is looking to sell that new boat. In fact, negotiations are ongoing with a company out in California to buy it."

Sell the new boat? Ladonis gritted her teeth. That would blow her merger back-end plan and a possible career move out the window.

"Why sell now?" Bret trumpeted her thoughts.

"Well," Velcroy said, "despite the advanced marketing for the boat's first sail in two months, the new boat has what is equivalent to no sales. And the person responsible for the company's only chance of making money this period is charged with murder."

"New Orleans is a popular tourist town, and Canal Street is its hub." Bret's eyes jumped on Ladonis. "My focus group data shows that gambling on the river—a throwback in time in fun-city—will ignite that tourist scene more than a gambling cruise."

Ladonis could feel the blood vessels in her head pumping. He meant her focus group data. She knew she'd need facts and figures to support any suggestion she put forth and she had already done extensive research. Now Bret was using her data, passing it off as his.

"According to the papers," Velcroy said, "some of the city officials say gambling is in this bind because the licensing process was too political, manipulated to line the pockets of a few, and leaving the city out in the cold."

"The good news"—Ladonis couldn't be left out of the conversation at this point—"is that FPSC doesn't have to sleep with the entire state legislature like it did to get the riverboat gambling license in order to secure the real estate it needs on the port."

She didn't disguise the edge in her voice. Deep down she even wished to be called out so that she could unload her true feelings. She was determined not only to get that window office, but to earn respect for herself as well as her hometown,

"By going local with a plan to expand the city's economy by re-invigorating its idle port, we distance ourselves from what has failed. Including the indicted ex-governor."

Was Velcroy considering her landside docking idea? She looked down. She didn't want to react to Bret's expression while waiting for him or Velcroy to speak. The sight of the charter files jolted like a rock thrown at her head. Whether Velcroy had or hadn't warmed up to her idea, she couldn't let go of how disrespected she'd felt when she'd heard him say, "She's no Sinclair."

"I want the plan," Velcroy said. "Demographics, expenditures, port traffic studies, expected generated revenue, focus-group data, the works. And I want it in my hands within twenty-four hours."

"Done." Ladonis stood up, determined to make sure Velcroy knew it was her work to which he referred.

Bret rose, too and went to the wet bar. He poured himself a glass of water. Ladonis had to get out of there. Even though she'd stood up for herself and her ideas, the possibility that Bret had delegated the charter deals to her to set her up to fail nipped at her confidence.

Perhaps she should go to that auction in Audubon Place. Find pen #101, prove Bunnie's innocence, and remove this excess pressure off her career. But suppose she completed the charter deals successfully. That would be her biggest professional accomplishment, especially if FPSC merged with the largest river cruise line in the world. She sighed, rolling her neck. Do all corporate executives have to compromise who they are to get ahead? How often would she have to ignore warnings from her natural goodness to get to the top of the ladder?

"Where are the boats?" Velcroy asked.

"Upriver," Bret told him. "But they should be here this weekend."

"What happens to them if the storm hits?" Velcroy asked.

Ladonis had already crossed the door's threshold. Let Bret explain that the boats would be docked at Avondale Shipyard. That the passengers would be put up in the Dixieland with the overflow in other French Quarter hotels if and when Katrina hit. He could handle that with or without Bunnie or her.

Her cell phone buzzed as she turned down the corridor to her workspace.

"Donnie." It was Evalena. "Get to University Hospital Emergency right away. It's your mama."

Chapter Fourteen
Before the Storm Come

LADONIS RUSHED FROM the parking lot like a thunderbolt into Charity Hospital now called University Hospital. It had been built in 1938 to service the state's poor while educating students from Tulane and LSU Medical Schools. She entered the busy emergency room without a clue who to talk to or where to go. She looked to the left where every triage nurse in sight was engaged with patients. To the right, patients were lined up on gurneys, some behind curtains, others in the open were in visual distress. She took a step and nearly toppled over, her body heavy with the weight of it all.

"Donnie, Donnie."

Ladonis looked around for the direction of the familiar voice. She spotted Evalena standing outside a pea-green curtain beckoning to her. Then a slender, medium-built man, wearing a sky-blue jacket that identified him as an LSU medical intern, walked from behind the curtained cubicle. Tulane interns wore light green coats.

Ladonis had to force her feet to move. She stepped around a kid sucking from a pale-yellow plastic bottle. His little body lying on a tattered blanket that needed washing. She had to get closer to the medical student, his sky-blue jacket looming ahead of her like a mountain.

"What's wrong with my mama?" she sputtered. Something in her head spun round and round. Her legs twitched, ready to run, but she couldn't move.

"We had to drain fluid from your mother's abdomen," the young man said in a thick British-Indian accent. He brushed back a strand of straight, shiny black hair from his face. "Otherwise, it would've emptied into her heart. And her tests indicate that her liver has hardened."

"What are you talking about?" The muscles around Ladonis's own heart pulled so tight, she grabbed at her chest. "Do you know what you said even means?" She needed him to name a medical term, something she could look up on the Internet. "Exactly what does she have?" She glared at the intern. Unlike her, her mother had no qualms about being a medical guinea pig. In fact, her mother often said, "them student doctors at Charity gonna either cure me or kill me. And that's all right with me."

"Your mother has hepatitis C," the young doctor said. "It's in an advanced stage, which means the fluid build-up will continue to reoccur."

"Hepatitis? Isn't that an alcoholic's disease? Intravenous drug users? My mom doesn't drink anything stronger than beer."

"According to her records, your mother contracted the disease through a blood transfusion." The doctor flipped through pages of the chart he held. "An amputated finger, I believe."

He finally made eye contact. His dark and distant stare was as off-putting as his accented words. Wasn't her mother's condition serious enough to warrant some sort of emotional bedside connection with her daughter?

"That happened thirteen years ago." Ladonis's frustration roared through her. "All that time and no one bothered to tell her about her liver? I want to see the head doctor."

"Someone did tell her," the young intern said, his tone now soft, but authoritative. "I told her months ago. And when I did, the head doctor was at my side."

Months ago? No. Ladonis wanted to scream. That can't be true. Her mother would've told her.

"Haven't you noticed your mother's weakened condition?" the doctor asked, checking his watch. "Her swollen abdomen and ankles?"

Ladonis gasped. Lord help her. She had noticed, but it didn't concern her until this morning. Her body swayed. She looked at the doctor. Now his deep dark eyes showed an expression of empathy as well as confidence. She hadn't expected the compassion. She believed that the intern was a medical student who operated under the premise that a Charity patient like her mother wasn't a person, just a sickness to study. That a daughter's concern was not his problem to address, just a distraction to tolerate. Could she be wrong?

"Is my mama dying?" she whispered.

"I'm afraid so," the doctor stated. "We recommend hospice care, either at home or in a facility."

"Hospice?" Ladonis whispered. "What about a liver transplant?"

"At her age and the advanced stage of the disease, that's not likely. All we can do now is treat her pain and make her as comfortable as possible." He lowered his head and made a notation in her mother's chart. "Social Service is here to help you with the Medicare paperwork, that sort of thing. I'll check in on her later."

The young Indian gave her a weak smile, turned, and walked away. Ladonis leaned against an empty gurney to steady her knees. Beg. A voice screamed inside her. But the words didn't come out. Cry. She squeezed her eyes shut. But no tears came.

"Donnie," her mother called out from behind the curtain.

The distressed sound of her mother's voice jolted an electric heated spasm through her body. She parted the curtains and walked up to her mother's bed; inhaled her scent; touched the tiny moles on her cheek. Why hadn't she noticed how the flesh hung from her mother's body? Had she been so self-absorbed she couldn't see her vibrant mother's body deteriorating?

Evalena put her hand on Ladonis's shoulder. Ladonis jerked away.

Evalena, her oldest and dearest friend, had been with her mother when she'd fallen and broken her hip last year. Evalena drove her mother to her favorite garden shop once a month. And she was here today. Did Ladonis resent her friend? If so, for what? Being there? She glanced away from Evalena's flushed face and squinted, questioning eyes. She had no idea how to explain or confront the anger that had overtaken her.

"Donnie." Her mother's voice was soft and shaky. "This here is a social worker. Tell my daughter your name, baby. I forgot it already."

"Vanessa," the blonde-haired girl said. "Vanessa Brownsy."

Ladonis nodded, taking in her look. Plain, but not warm. Professional, yet nervous. And she held onto her clipboard as if it were a body part.

"Dr. Taj says it is time to arrange for your mother's hospice care," Vanessa said barely above a whisper. "In situations like this, you have a choice. She can, ah . . . ah . . . recuperate in a facility or in her home."

The word "recuperate" exploded in Ladonis's brain. The social worker made a notation on her clipboard. How dare some mousy white girl check off her mother's needs, her existence, from an inventory list? Ladonis wanted to throw that damn clipboard out the window.

"I want to die in my own house," her mother announced in a strong voice, sounding like her old bossy self.

"Then, I will have a hospital bed delivered to your home immediately," Vanessa said.

Chill bumps popped up on Ladonis's skin, a rush of icy cold all over. The image of a hospital bed in her mother's bedroom thrust her deep into sadness. She had to fight back the tears.

"That's okay by me," her mother said. "Long as you get it there before the storm come."

For Ladonis, the storm had already come. The force of high winds had shattered the foundation of her confidence. She felt as though she was drowning under water, weighted down by HeartTrouble, Bunnie, Tabor, and the end of her career dreams.

The urge to pee overtook her. She rushed off to find a restroom. It was the only place she could think of to hide and lament her current circumstances alone. When she turned the lock to the restroom door, it dawned on her that without her mama nudging and fussing, she would indeed be alone, like a patch of duckweed sitting in a swamp.

Chapter Fifteen
Above the Fray

LADONIS PARKED HER car in Tabor's driveway. She and her old friend had to settle on a plan of action to get that pen and clear Bunnie. Now.

If Bunnie's charters failed, it would follow her career like a felony charge. Then there was Mama's illness, and to top off her troubles, that good-for-nothing brother of hers had a baby, an outside child that needed to be taken care of. Like never before, her job and her family were entwined. She couldn't risk having Bunnie's problems and her desire for a window office impede her ability to focus on what her mama called—all-important family matters.

The scent of mildew greeted her the instant she crossed the doorsill to Tabor's dilapidated office building, his mother's old shotgun duplex on Gayosa Street at Tulane Avenue. Unlike his upscale workspace at One Shell Square on Poydras Street, there was no receptionist, and Ladonis could see straight through to the kitchen. A ceiling fan circulated the stifling air much the way her thoughts shifted in her head. Tabor stood at the sink, shirttail out, sleeves rolled up.

"What cleaning service do you use?" Ladonis maneuvered her way through the clutter on the floor.

"Justice," Tabor yelled out. "And the guarantee that what's said here, stays here." He turned and walked toward her. "But perhaps pro bono is the more appropriate word."

"Well, like they say"—Ladonis kicked aside a small stack of newspapers in her path—"you get what you pay for."

There was just enough light to see that the off-white walls at the baseboards were colored fungus, throw-up gray. Black duct tape patched the brown vinyl sofa and matching chair flushed against the sidewall. And a coffee table stacked high with dusty *Jet* and *Ebony* magazines sat in the middle of the room on the cracked-up brown asbestos tile floor. Just the type of secret place to come up with a scheme to crash an invitation-only auction that, in all likelihood, would prove to be unethical at best and illegal at worst.

"HeartTrouble told me about your mama." Tabor held out his arms to embrace her. "I want you to know that I'm here for you, the way your mama was there for me when my mom passed. I'm real sorry."

Ladonis felt sorry, too. And bewildered. What should she do, knowing that her mother was dying while she was mixed up in Bunnie's murder problems? If only she could stop everything, act as if she hadn't already done anything stupid to compromise her freedom.

Tabor picked up a remote from his desk and aimed it at the television sitting atop a rusting, gray, metal file cabinet. Ladonis's jaw dropped when she saw Monique's image on the screen. How much more damage could the media diva cause in one day?

The camera angle pulled back from Monique. Clifford Maynard, Jarvis's younger half-brother and heir apparent to the Maynard empire, appeared on a plush white chair, his scrawny, reedy body dressed in his trademark light-colored linen suit. His bald head glistened without the cover of the usual straw hat. His beady eyes squinted arrogance she'd seen a thousand times on the television commercial spots he and his brother did for their auto stores.

Like everyone in the city, Ladonis had seen the face on the screen a thousand times. But this time she was not just looking at Jarvis Maynard's half brother. She was also looking at Bunnie's uncle. She could see the resemblance around the eyes and forehead. Strange to be watching Clifford Maynard, the son of his father's mistress—the city's richest bastard, make nice on live television with Monique LaFaye—the city's first black media darling. All while Bunnie Sinclair, a mixed-race orphan, sat alone in prison for murdering her long-lost white father, the richest man in town. Who would've thought?

"I want swift justice," Clifford Maynard said, "to avenge my brother's death." His words came out slow—perhaps too disciplined to display grief. He let out a trio of quick, short sneezes as he eyed the various clumps of colorful lilies, gardenias, and magnolias all around, then looked at Monique. "Why people have to fill a room up with perfume flowers is beyond me. Nature belongs outside. That way people as well as the flowers can breathe naturally."

Monique moved the microphone away from him and wiped it with the hem of her blouse. The camera found Monique's face, her brow furrowed into a frown mixed with surprise and displeasure. Ladonis smiled, imagining Monique's reaction when she reviewed this tape and realized that everyone watching had seen her make that icky face.

"The police have a suspect," Clifford Maynard said.

Ladonis's body perked up. Had someone else confessed? Her shoulders dropped. Who was she kidding? The police had Bunnie, a made-to-order suspect.

"I pray that she confesses straight away so that this town can properly mourn the loss of my brother." Clifford looked into the camera, tilted his head, and rubbed at his dry eye with the knuckle of his index finger and continued his fake sad, vindictive spill. "And so that I can get closure and grieve in peace."

"But, Miss Sinclair could be your brother's only child," Monique asserted. "Don't you have any empathy for her? After all, your mother—"

"My mother," Clifford Maynard said, his eyes and veins protruding. "My mother was a genteel, white lady. Descendant of English royalty. Not some hooker, shop keeper."

"Yes, sir," Monique cooed. "However, that does not change the fact that your brother could be Bunnie Sinclair's father."

"If she is my half-brother's child, I am sure he never knew, or he would've told me. How dare you exploit my family's misfortune this way." Clifford Maynard removed his earpiece and stormed off the set.

"Looks like Maynard's brother is out for Bunnie's blood." Tabor sat up in the chair behind his desk.

"Everybody knows Jarvis Maynard didn't like his half-brother. Remember the court battle Clifford had to undergo in order to work in the family businesses?" Ladonis eased back onto the edge of Tabor's trashed desktop, still looking at the television.

"You can't believe everything people say." Tabor pressed the mute button.

"True." Ladonis shifted her position to look at Tabor. "But, I can believe what I see with my own eyes. With all the media attention these guys get, a blind person could see that the Maynard brothers could not stand one another."

"It's true." Tabor leaned forward. "They always looked mad at each other, didn't they? But a bazillion-dollar inheritance has a way of creating phantom brotherly love. Especially in the surviving brother and heir."

"Yeah," Ladonis rubbed her forehead. "But, Clifford is an outside child, too, like Bunnie. The offspring of an affair with the maid. Albeit, a white maid. He wouldn't even be in the picture if their daddy hadn't been stricken with a conscience on his death-bed and acknowledged him."

"You're right." Tabor placed his elbows on the desk. "And as the story goes, when their daddy did acknowledge him, he included him in his will."

"Yeah, and the fight began." Ladonis's tone hinted sarcasm. "And with Jarvis dead and childless, Clifford stands to inherit the entire family's bazillion-dollar fortune. Even if brother Jarvis didn't write him in his will. Especially if Bunnie is found guilty of killing him."

"That's right." Tabor cupped his chin. His tone grew more contemplative. "But if Bunnie was acknowledged by her daddy, Louisiana law protects the bloodline when it comes to inheritances. That's why she has to prove her innocence."

Ladonis sighed. She tossed the papers from a nearby folding chair onto the floor and slapped away lingering debris before sitting down. "Do you suppose Jarvis Maynard told his brother about his blood niece?"

"If the old man did know, he never told Bunnie." Tabor squirmed and the wooden chair on wheels squealed.

Tabor turned the sound up on the TV again. Ladonis swiveled to see. The setting of the news had switched to police headquarters. NOPD's first female chief, Twyla Goodin, made her way to the podium.

Twyla stood proud, dressed in her police blues, the pants version. Ladonis couldn't get over how the lady chief's basic look hadn't changed since her high school days at Booker T. Had she patented that god-awful ancient French-twist hairstyle? In fact, Ladonis had never seen the svelte woman without her trademark pearl earrings either. Geez.

"I don't want to jeopardize the DA's case by disclosing any information at this time," Twyla said. "We don't want our suspect tried in the media."

Twyla pinched her lips together. Tick or a smirk? More likely a smirk. The woman was NOPD, after all.

Twyla's eyes expanded then narrowed. "I will say, however, that we are confident we have Jarvis Maynard's killer in custody."

"But Bunnie swears she didn't do it," Ladonis hissed at Tabor. "And for some strange reason, I believe her."

"The problem is, not even reasonable doubt will get an acquittal. Not in this town." Tabor clicked off the television. "I can site at least a hundred cases where reasonable doubt was proved, yet a guilty verdict was rendered. And that's the norm for high-profile cases. We've got to prove who did the killing."

"What about that laptop?" Ladonis suggested. "Any word from the police if they have it?" Her hand flayed. "Do they even know it exists?"

Tabor fixed his gaze on her. "What worries me is that when the cops do find it, they might be able to use what's on it to manipulate the DA's case against Bunnie."

Tabor picked up his cell phone, a blank stare on his face. That habit had begun to annoy Ladonis. She puffed out her cheeks and blew.

"It's obvious there's something fishy about that pen."

"That pen?" Tabor looked up at her. "You mean Snake Pen Number 101?"

"Um, hum." Ladonis nodded. "The snake pen with the emeralds. Isn't it strange no one has said a word about it?" She frowned. "You'd think that if the cops had that laptop, they'd know about the pen."

She took a moment to steady her thoughts. Time to tell Tabor she was prepared to go to Audubon Place. She didn't like it, but she needed to clear Bunnie, care for her dying mother, prepare for HeartTrouble's baby, and ready her condo for that hurricane on the way.

"You know, Bunnie told me there's a way to prove she didn't do it," she said.

"The auction," Tabor stated, "in Audubon Place. According to Bunnie, an auction is the safest way to get rid of the pen and make a profit at the same time without arousing suspicion."

"She told you too? Of course, she told you." Did this mean that Tabor already had a plan in mind to get the pen?

"One thing is certain." Tabor stood up. "Planting that pen on Bunnie could tie up releasing it into the estate. Especially if there's some question of ownership. That would not bode well for the inheritor of the other 100."

"Meaning what exactly?" Ladonis asked, narrowing her eyes.

"Meaning that a regular run-of-the-mill thief would be looking to put a pen like that on the black market. Might even go for a pawn shop. Lots of trading for high-end collectibles happens behind closed doors in pawn shops."

"So, what you're saying is—" Ladonis felt her temple veins pulsate.

"I'm saying that if pen #101 shows up at a private auction, I'm fairly certain it will lead to Maynard's killer."

"How can you be so sure?"

"Because at a private auction, the thief could offer the pen up in mixed collections and officially buy it back for a pittance of what it's actually worth and secure proof of ownership paperwork."

"In other words, that would be a way for the inheritor, or the killer, to both get rid of incriminating evidence and snag that pen to add to the inherited collection where it's practically priceless." She found Tabor's eyes. "The inheritor is Clifford Maynard if Bunnie is out of the picture."

Lord, was Tabor really going to accuse Clifford Maynard of murdering his half-brother? It was one thing to transfer the blame to someone else, but to a Maynard? Surely, he couldn't—wouldn't take this step unless he had the goods on Clifford. And to think he hadn't wanted to represent Bunnie in the beginning because of the Maynard connection to New Orleans legal system. Then again, his ego was why she'd solicited his services in the first place. Nailing the real killer of Jarvis Maynard would give him prestige in this town no other defense attorney, black or white, had ever achieved. He couldn't possibly expect her to help him.

Ladonis held her head between her hands. How did her life get so mixed up with Bunnie's woes and now Tabor's ambition? With the pressure of her mama's health and hurricane Katrina's arrival, she felt herself slipping farther down into a dark hole.

"I was able to get in touch with Bunnie's mother's assistant." Tabor paced the short distance behind his desk. "Too bad he is unavailable. It would be so easy to send him to that auction. I've been doing some checking. It seems high-end collecting is intense. I have no doubt that pen will be in Audubon Place. I'd hate to miss the opportunity to get first dibs on it. Then, we could clear this up and nail the killer before Katrina hits."

Ladonis studied Tabor's face. His eyes shifted from side to side before landing on her. Indeed he did want her to go to the auction. Ironically, she'd come to him with that intention, but just to find the damn pen, not to entrap the richest man in the city.

Chapter Sixteen
Ease the Burden

"HEY, TABOR." HEARTTROUBLE'S nasal voice filtered in from the front room.

"By the way," Tabor said, looking at Ladonis, "I forgot to tell you that HeartTrouble is coming by. He wants to put a rush on his custody case." He inhaled. "Because of your mother, you know. He figures it might ease her burden."

Ladonis sat up tall in her seat and glared at Tabor. He had insinuated himself into a leadership role in her family's personal business, and she didn't like it. For years, she'd been her family's problem solver.

"I hope you got plumbin' in this shit hole." HeartTrouble entered the room doing the I've-got-to-pee dance. "I saw some skinny white dude nosin' around your porch. Said he was lost, but I got a funny feelin'."

"What?" Tabor rose from his chair and went to the window. "Why do you think he isn't lost?"

"He said he couldn't see the numbers from the street." HeartTrouble moved fast to the next room. "Except for you, ain't nothin' on this street but a jail, cops, and bail bondsmen. And it's lit up out there like it's day time."

"Slow down, dude, and tell me about this man." Tabor scrambled to the front door.

"Can't. Gotta go," HeartTrouble yelled back. He hurried past Ladonis sitting in front of Tabor's desk. "He's in a big, all-black Hummer."

"Who do you think it could be?" Ladonis walked behind Tabor to look out the window onto the empty street. "No one actually lives on this block anymore."

"Maybe"—Tabor turned to face her—"he's somebody in trouble looking for a criminal lawyer."

"How can you be so cavalier?" Ladonis chided. "Your world is dense with bad people."

"Because I am A. Tabor." Tabor beat his chest with his fists, Tarzan style. "A predator for justice, as well as Public Enemy Number One to a whole lot of people out to ramrod the innocent."

Ladonis walked back to her chair. "You know, it's dangerous to believe in your own bullshit."

"Ha, ha." Tabor followed Ladonis into his office and plopped his body onto his office chair. "Stay focused, Donnie. The sooner we get to Audubon Place and get the heads up on that pen, the quicker we figure out who did what and when. Then we can get this over with."

"Audubon Place?" HeartTrouble made his way into the room. "Whatever it is y'all talkin' 'bout, don't do it, bro." He put both hands flat on the desk and leaned down in Tabor's face. "The big one comin'. We got more important things to do before she get here."

"Don't worry." Tabor patted HeartTrouble's hand. "I plan to make sure your little girl gets your name and is in your life."

HeartTrouble snatched his hands off the desktop and stood up tall. He squared his shoulders like a soldier called to attention. "That's not what I mean, man. Don't let Donnie pull you in her white-folk shit. Let somebody else save that girl's hide."

"That's right," Ladonis blasted her brother. "Let somebody else take care of things. That's surely the way you deal with your life's messes."

"Stop it, you two." Tabor squinted at Ladonis. "I could send in a private investigator. But, everybody knows that private investigators are, in reality, off-duty or expelled NOPD. Getting one of them could backfire."

"I've watched Bunnie do her sales thing before, you know." Ladonis pursed her lips. She had to find that pen. "I haven't been to an auction, per se, but I think I understand how they operate."

"Have you considered . . ." Tabor took a deep breath. "Have you considered what could happen if whoever has that pen is the person who found you in Bunnie's house that night?"

Did you? The words were on the tip of her tongue, but she didn't say them. Otherwise she'd have to acknowledge his suspicions. That would add to her reasons to be afraid.

"That means you could be in danger," Tabor said.

Ladonis frowned. Tabor acted as if she wasn't his intellectual equal. Did he think she didn't know the danger? Furthermore, did he think her so clueless that she wouldn't realize that his asking her to get that pen, despite the danger, was his plan all along?

"She don't care about that, bro." HeartTrouble shook his head. He moved away from the desk and paced.

"Man, oh, man." Tabor sighed. "Dealing with you two—I need a drink." He headed for the kitchen.

"Me too," HeartTrouble called out to him. "A beer if you got one."

"What about your little girl?" Ladonis rose and walked up to her brother on the other side of the room. "I'm the only one in this family with a real job, you know. And considering what I've already done working this case, do you want the cops sniffing around until they find something to pin on me?"

HeartTrouble's stare bore into her. Ladonis stepped away, jarred by the anguish that flared in his eyes. He knew exactly what was at stake for him and exactly what they were up against.

Tabor strode back into the room carrying two beers. He tossed one to HeartTrouble, uncapped the other, and took a swallow. Ladonis made her way back to the folding chair and plopped back down. HeartTrouble gave her a dismissive shake of his head.

"If the police don't have the pen or the laptop"—Tabor stood in front of her—"then, whoever stole it may or may not use it to implicate you."

"Are you sure the pen will draw the real killer out?" Ladonis eyed her brother who paced and mumbled to himself.

Tabor sat in his chair. "I'm sure that if the cops get a line on that pen before I do, Bunnie Sinclair doesn't stand a chance in court. Clifford Maynard wants her head on the guillotine and her hands off the family fortune, whether she's the killer or not. As for the cops and the DA, they can't risk not getting a conviction. And God forbid they should tarnish Maynard's aristocratic legacy." He leaned back and casually crossed his arms. "That's just the kind of injustice that sets my blood boiling."

Ladonis flinched. What could she do but go to the auction? The longer Bunnie stayed accused, the more likely Ladonis would be implicated, perhaps in a conspiracy to cover up a murder. Not to mention being declared incompetent if those charter deals fell through. There was no way to sugarcoat her dilemma.

"I'll need back up." Ladonis sounded as cool as she could manage. "I cannot go to Audubon Place alone."

She looked at HeartTrouble. She needed him. Her experience dealing with bad people wasn't as refined as his. Though she had learned that high-society criminals could have more of a devastating long-term effect on their prey than those of two-bit street thugs like the ones she grew up with in the Magnolia. Her anxiety—her insecurity—came out too quickly around white-collar bad people.

"Audubon Place?" HeartTrouble threw up his hands. "No way I'm goin' there. People like me can get lynched hanging out in a neighborhood like that. Besides, I got my lil girl to think about, remember. And Mama." He walked over to face Ladonis. "Lord, girl, how come every time you get the urge to break the law, you gotta take me with you? Why can't you see how much trouble you get me and everybody else in tryin' to be white."

"And what about the trouble you've been getting us into all of your sorry life." Ladonis put her hands on her hips. "Getting you out jail umpteen times. Paying your gambling debts." Her body swayed like Mama's did when she scolded the children who littered her front yard with chip bags and soda cans.

HeartTrouble punched his palm. She felt ashamed. What gave her the right to make saving Bunnie's hide his life's priority?

"Look, bro," Tabor said. "The sooner this case is cleared up, the—"

"Don't do that, man. Don't play me like that." HeartTrouble scowled. "My grandma told me once that life is like a tragedy for people who got feelings, and ain't nothin' but a comedy for them who got nerve to think about stuff. Don't make me out to be no joke, man. Don't make me lose my respect for you."

"Hey, man," Tabor protested. "I didn't mean to belittle your situation. It's just that time is critical here. The only chance I've got to save that girl's life and to keep me and your sister out of legal hot water is to find that pen as soon as possible."

"Everything is happening at once," Ladonis said, reeling from her brother's memory of their grandmother, and from the blow her words took to her natural goodness. How could she make her brother understand that she was already too close to a felony charge for obstruction not to do this? "Mama's illness. Pressure on the job. Your custody hearing. If we help Bunnie, I can get on with what I have to do for Mama without worrying about my job. And with Mama the way she is and you trying to get custody of your baby, if I'm not working, or if I'm not around—"

"No matter what, when it comes down to it, it's all about you, huh, Donnie?" HeartTrouble looked over at Ladonis, defeat coiling around his eyes. "I wonder how come that is? How come it's always gotta be all about you?"

Ladonis couldn't dismiss that knee-jerk pang of guilt she felt at the accusation as well as dejection in her brother's voice. If making her feel small was his concession to her, then his reward was that she felt even smaller. The sad part was, there was nothing she could say to explain the big picture the way she saw it. The trick now was to clear the hurdles and get through this, or run the risk of neither of them feeling tall again.

Chapter Seventeen
Tough Smart-Ass Donnie

"AUDUBON PLACE. WE'RE here." HeartTrouble hung his head out the window on the passenger side of Tabor's sleek all black BMW. "The owner of the Saints, Tom Benson, live here, right?"

"Right." Ladonis felt a sudden chill. "But not where we're going. We're going to the big white house right there on the corner."

Audubon Place, a privately gated street, was not to be confused with Audubon Street or Audubon Boulevard. Ordinary folks wandered those streets. Her real estate buddies often boasted that the cheapest home in Audubon Place cost around five million. Good thing she and HeartTrouble didn't have to go beyond the gate. People like them were definitely out of the ordinary past the big, so called, White House just outside the gate.

"I hope you can do more than walk in them high heels." HeartTrouble sat back in his seat.

"Why?" Ladonis gripped the wheel of the car with both hands.

"'Cause we need to park across the way on St. Charles near Audubon Park." HeartTrouble touched his temple, then pointed out the window. "If we have to get out fast, you might have to run from the back of the house, hide along the shrubbery in the back yard, and get to the car without anybody seeing us leave."

"How do you know so much about this place?"

"Lots of big parties here," HeartTrouble told her. "Especially charity parties. Every now and then I get to work one."

"Work?" she asked, hiding her jealousy the way she often camouflaged her faults and vulnerabilities, with attitude. Even in the corporate world and society circles in which she found herself, she'd never been to an event at Audubon Place. "Doing what?"

"Valet. Dishwashing. Serving. Whatever."

Ladonis drove into a parking spot on St. Charles Avenue, feeling sorry for the disrespect her brother must have felt from her questions. She knew better than anyone how being turned down to play high school baseball because of his heart condition had affected him physically as well as psychologically, demeaning his personal drive and ambition. He couldn't find a reason to stay in school after that. To make a living, he became a hustler for jobs and money by any means necessary. Despite suggesting he make another bad life's choice, she didn't apologize.

She stepped up to the wrought iron gate and looked at the huge southern colonial revival-style house that was Audubon Place. Since the house was donated to Tulane University in 1961, the university president lived there. It was dubbed the White House after the red brick was painted white and became a hub for social and charitable community events. No doubt the perfect setting for a Children's Hospital Auction. Using children to pull on heartstrings was a sure way to get rich folks and poor people alike to open up their purse strings in a home dedicated to helping community causes.

Ladonis glanced HeartTrouble's way. Mama had bought him a suit from Wal-Mart for his custody hearing. He looked about as comfortable in it as a nun in a saloon. Was it wrong for her and Tabor to urge him to break it in on a risky mission of mercy? But, who better than HeartTrouble to recognize a crook, any crook, especially one disguised in sheep's clothing? She took a deep, loud breath. Hell, she was the one taking the real risk, going for the pen. All he had to do was make sure she didn't get caught.

Tabor had said that she was bound to cause a stir. That blacks were a novelty in this end of the collectable business. As far as he could find out, there was only one black woman from California operating in this circle of rich collectors and traders.

Her plan was simple. Go in, look for the Parker Durfold's and Waterman fountain pens, find the snake pen, but do not ask for it specifically. Check for the identification number etched on the barrel and be gone. A six-digit number that began with fifty-two and ended with nineteen according to Bunnie's distressed memory. According to Tabor, that number can trace the pen even if it goes underground. That number, he said, authenticates the pen, and who ever ends up with it could be the killer, or can lead to the killer.

"Don't look so glum." Ladonis walked up to HeartTrouble already standing at the mansion steps. "I hear that every Saints football player worth his millions for beating up on each other for a ball, will be here." She gave him her Kool-Aid fake smile. To her, American football was a barbaric sport reminiscent of the Roman Empire gladiator fights, and she never missed an opportunity to let her ball-loving brother know it.

"Donnie." HeartTrouble stared at the house. "Even with that proper education you got, you ain't got sense enough to know that everybody's shit stink. Even yours."

She hated to lose an argument with her brother. But the last thing she needed now was to engage in one of their streetwise-versus-college educated philosophical disagreements. Especially here where they both were considered low life.

A short, pimply faced, light-skinned young man wearing a gold and black vest jogged toward them. Black and gold were the Saints colors. Nothing was off limits when it came to promoting that football team.

"Valet parking," HeartTrouble whispered as they approached the home's entrance. "But street parking is better in case we have to get out quick."

"We were lucky, bro," HeartTrouble told the young man. "Found a nearby spot on the street. Thanks anyway."

HeartTrouble gave the young attendant a ten-dollar bill, change from the forty dollars Tabor had given him for gas. He thanked the kid and bounded up the steps, Ladonis in tow. That had gone smoothly. Hopefully, everything else would be just as easy. She checked her purse for the exact location of her keys. She didn't want to hang around for a second once she'd found that pen.

"Say, bro," the young man called out to HeartTrouble. "They got TVs set up all over to keep folks up on the storm. Except ain't none out here. If you hear a weather report say it's time to get out of Dodge, would you let me know? The lil chump change I'm makin' at this gig ain't worth gettin' caught up out here in no-po'-black man's land in a storm. Know what I mean?"

"I hear ya, man." HeartTrouble nodded.

Ladonis pulled and patted her little black I'm-hot-and-I-know-it spaghetti-strap dress into place. Grandma Lucille had told her often that the only thing a tall, black woman had to do to be noticed was to strut into a room with her back straight and her head held up like a peacock. Today she wished she could weasel in without anyone seeing her.

"Whew." HeartTrouble whistled, taking in the view. "Is this a house or what?" He moved up alongside Ladonis. "This one room is about as big as the Blue Room in the Fairmont New Orleans Hotel where I used to work."

"Were you employed there long enough to even see the Blue Room? You worked there for what, two days?" She couldn't resist an opportunity to get under his skin after the "shit stinks" comment. Paintings, large and small, covered the walls. Floor rugs of varying sizes hung from rods just like in the Rug Depot. Rows of empty chairs faced a podium set up in front of the biggest fireplace she'd ever seen. She eased over to a row of tables used to display crystal vases, sculptures, and oriental pieces.

"Somebody givin' a speech? I thought we was to be in and out like a flash."

"Don't you know anything?" Ladonis told him. "The way an auction works is that people view all this stuff, decide what they want, then later they sit in the chairs and bid on it. The highest bidder gets to buy the item."

She eased further into the room, looking around, marveling at how old, yet modern everything looked. Where was everyone? She'd expected the almost-empty room to be packed.

"We gotta wait for someone to bid on that pen?" HeartTrouble was agitated. "How long that gonna take?"

"Not long," Ladonis said. "Because we're here for the viewing only. All I need to do is find the pen, check out the numbers, and we're out of here. Tabor is going to follow through. Easy."

"That's what's worrying me," HeartTrouble told her. "Remember what Grandma Lucille used to say? It's easy to do the wrong thing, and hard to do what's right."

She often thought of Grandma Lucille when she wasn't convinced she'd made the best choice. She had no idea HeartTrouble did as well. Funny how they'd heard the same lectures growing up and still turned out so differently. Or had they? Though initially it was a heart condition that stopped him from pursuing his dream, and not brick walls disguised as people, he had to feel as vulnerable and exploited as she did.

A crowd emerged from a side door like a puff of smoke entering the air. Ladonis stepped out of sight behind the rug display, HeartTrouble in tow.

"Uh-oh," HeartTrouble said. "White people attack."

Each person carried a champagne glass in one hand and a lit cigarette in the other. Ladonis frowned. Moving around unnoticed was going to be harder than she'd thought. Cigarette smoke triggered her allergies.

"We're sure to look out of place in this crowd," Ladonis whispered, her eyes on all the bright, expensive bling sparkling on the men as well as the women. Thank God HeartTrouble had removed his Zirconium stud earring and obnoxious gold chains. As it was, his off-the-rack suit and deep chocolate skin would make him stand out amongst the other tuxedo-wearing male guests.

"So we should leave, right?" HeartTrouble stepped back.

"Not yet." Ladonis scanned the area for someplace he wouldn't be noticed.

"I knew you was gonna say that," HeartTrouble mumbled.

Ladonis spotted what looked like an oversized copper pitcher sitting atop a tall Greek column to the left of HeartTrouble. A good spot for him to remain out of sight, yet a good vantage point to observe the happenings and to keep an eye on her. She motioned to him. HeartTrouble slipped behind the column just before the crowd ascended further into the room.

A cigar-smoking portly man walked toward her. She recognized him from his billboards. Zeno of Zeno Diamonds. She turned to look in the other direction, but he tapped her on the shoulder.

"Are you looking for anything in particular tonight? A diamond perhaps?"

"No." Ladonis smiled, presenting her best imitation of confidence. "Nothing in particular."

Why did he single her out? Did he think she was a thief? She could feel the lines of self-doubt crawling on her face.

"Well," Zeno cleared his throat, "had anyone bothered to tell me you would be here, I would've brought more of my great stones for you to check out."

She relaxed. Zeno thought she was the lone black dealer from the West Coast. She lifted her chest, determined to appear unruffled despite wishing the floor would open up and swallow her.

"No worries." Ladonis was unable to rid her voice of its shakiness. "I only decided to come this morning when the friends I was visiting informed me of the particulars."

Zeno coughed. His belly tugged at the buttons on his starched, white shirt. He covered his mouth with his hand, his jeweled pinkie extended. Seemed he wasn't afraid to show his feminine side.

She glanced over at HeartTrouble. His shoulders were hunched, his arms stretched out in questioning mode. His expression asked what the hell was she doing? Pretending, she wanted to answer. Playing a role and facing danger like a character in one of the novels she enjoyed reading.

"Allow me to show you what's available." Zeno took hold of her elbow.

Ladonis acquiesced and walked across the foyer with him. She turned her head ever so slightly and saw HeartTrouble sidestep a waiter carrying a tray of filled champagne glasses. He snatched two glasses before the waiter had a chance to see him. Uh-oh. HeartTrouble and booze did not mix.

"I understand," Zeno said, "that this is Napoleon's wife's pearl and diamond necklace."

He held up the antique jewelry for her to view. Ladonis oo'ed and ah'ed over the piece as if she knew what she was looking at. She fought the urge to look back for HeartTrouble, didn't want Zeno to see her searching for someone. She silently prayed that her brother was nearby watching and not off somewhere sucking up the free booze.

Next, Zeno drew her attention to a huge diamond. Ladonis pulled out the jeweler's loupe she'd gotten from Tabor to see the numbers on the snake pen. She decided to pretend to examine the diamond in the gaudiest necklace setting she'd ever seen.

"Very nice," she said. She had to ditch this guy before he asked her something technical. "Why don't I look around to see what finds I stumble upon? That's what makes these events fun, don't you think? Besides, I don't want to hog all your time."

Hog all your time? Would someone from the West Coast even say that?

"Sure thing, my dear." Zeno handed her a business card. "I'll be around if you need anything. And may I take this opportunity to invite you to my French Quarter store. I'll be happy to arrange a personal, private showing for you."

"Thank you. That's kind of you."

Zeno took a long draw on his cigar and turned away. Ladonis made a complete circle looking for her brother. Where was he? It didn't take much alcohol to set him off.

"Who you supposed to be?" HeartTrouble said from behind her.

"Zeno thinks I'm the one and only black lady dealer in this business." Ladonis exhaled her relief. "So, I figure, why not?"

"And the magnifying glass? If Tyler Perry saw you, he'd give you a part in one of his movies."

"Nice touch, huh? Tabor said it would help me see the small numbers on the pen. That Tabor. He thinks of everything." Ladonis didn't plan the edge she heard in her voice. Too bad the revered attorney was also a self-centered shit.

"Yeah." HeartTrouble gulped down what she hoped was only his second glass of champagne. "Everything."

"Boy, lay off the booze. You're here to watch my back, remember?"

HeartTrouble grunted. Ladonis smacked her lips, upset and afraid of what could happen if she goaded him into one of their sibling altercations. She needed him to be clear headed.

Ladonis picked up a small Japanese geometrically designed pottery piece. She turned it upside down and read "Y A Y O I." She had to look like a knowledgeable, albeit curious shopper, not like a nervous spy.

"What do you think you doin'?" HeartTrouble chided.

"Looking professional."

"Well, be professional and hurry up and find that God-damned pen so we can get out of here."

She guided HeartTrouble to another column with another giant vase, to another clear view of the massive space as well as the front door. Again, the sort of place Tabor had suggested he perch to watch her as well as the comings and goings of others.

"I'm going to check that table." Ladonis pointed to a spot a few feet away. "The items are small enough to be pens."

Ladonis pivoted to look for HeartTrouble and saw his eyes dart to the floor-to-ceiling windows that walled one side of the room. She followed his gaze, but a tall, thin woman approaching her blocked her view. She shrugged. HeartTrouble must have gotten excited to see some famous football player arrive.

Then, Ladonis saw HeartTrouble peeking around the column. He lifted the entire champagne tray, held it up waiter-style to hide his face and walked toward her. What was he up to?

Before she could get to him, a silver-haired woman draped in gold and diamonds bumped into her. Ladonis glanced around for HeartTrouble but he was no longer in sight. It would not be pretty if he went into one of his drunken meltdowns. She'd better hurry up and find that pen. No more time to lollygag.

"Do you think," Ladonis ignored Tabor's directive not to ask about the pen, "that the Maynard pen collection is going to be auctioned off here tonight?"

The bejeweled woman's eyes swept across her entire body. "The pens here tonight are set up in the upstairs foyer. Isn't it awful what happened to Jarvis Maynard?" The woman gasped. "Just awful."

"It is." Ladonis inched away. She had to discourage further dialogue or risk HeartTrouble ruining the plan.

"Why don't you ask Clifford about his brother's pen collection?" The woman touched her arm to get her attention again. "I hear he's expected shortly."

"He is?" Ladonis whispered, feeling the weight of those words in her knees. "That's good to know. Thank you for the information."

If Clifford was going to be here, she'd better get on with it. After he showed up, perhaps she could stick around and see if he bought the pen. Wow, that would be what they call in mysteries, a smoking gun.

Where was HeartTrouble? Had he seen Clifford and gotten spooked? Ladonis wrapped her fingers around the loupe and headed for the grand circular stairway. No time to waste. She had to find that damn number.

A small group of loud people arrived at the stairwell just ahead of Ladonis. And so did her brother. Ladonis almost yelled out to him but caught herself. He winked and tipped his head toward the front entrance, not once but twice. Ladonis looked across the room.

Two men in black hoods wearing masks and waving guns rushed in making their way into the crowd. Ladonis turned her shocked face toward her brother. HeartTrouble pointed, guiding her eyes back across the room. Two more hooded, masked men streamed in like a tidal wave.

"Party time," one of the masked men yelled out, pointing what looked like a machine gun in the air.

People scrambled in every direction. HeartTrouble eased his way over to a table near the stairway filled with empty glasses. He placed the tip of the tablecloth under his shoe and stepped away. The glasses crashed onto the floor. Everyone froze. HeartTrouble leapt over to Ladonis and pushed her under the stairway.

"Boy, are you crazy?" Ladonis cried.

"Get out of sight." HeartTrouble shoved her further under the stairwell. "You wanna get caught?"

Someone dressed in a King Rex Mardi Gras costume and wearing a whiteface mask made his way to the commotion at the foot of the stairwell. He fired a shot into the air from what sounded like a BB gun, or a fire cracker, not a car backfiring like a gun shot. She knew the sound. She'd been shot by a BB gun when she was ten on her first and last Girl Scout camping trip. The other man, dressed up like the pope, pulled a rifle (or was it a BB gun?) from beneath his red cape and pointed the long barrel toward the wall of paintings.

"I want all of you to line up over there," the pope said. "Move it."

Some guests were already tipsy, and could hardly walk. Others, so scared they couldn't move, their bodies trembled visibly. A few giggled as if they were watching a Carnival parade. Two more white-faced masked men, dressed like Santa Claus with guns descended the stairs, ushering down more guests. Thanks to HeartTrouble, Ladonis was safely out of sight, though her heartbeat raced.

"Give your cash and your Rolexes," King Rex ordered, "to the Father here."

"A robbery?" Ladonis whispered. "They're robbing Children's Hospital?"

"Be quiet." HeartTrouble looked past her.

Ladonis followed his gaze to a big and tall, slick-haired guy dressed in a white tux and a white-faced mask. The masked man made his way through the crowd to the stairwell. Ladonis shivered.

"Got any Tolliver paintings at this shindig?" the pope called out. "Now that's a brother who can paint a picture."

"He sounds like," HeartTrouble murmured, his face tightened into a question.

"Like who?" Ladonis hissed, snapping her head around to stare at him. "Somebody you know?" The combination of anger and fear rolled in her stomach.

King Rex eyed the big guy in the tux. The big man in the white tux nodded as he slipped something inside his coat. Was their plan coming together? Hers and Tabor's surely wasn't.

"Okay, folks," King Rex said. "Sorry to interrupt the festivities, but the charities we represent will appreciate your generosity." He scanned their faces, lingering a moment on Zeno. "Don't forget to have your accountants write off this little donation. Now lay face down."

The two Santa Claus and the masked men bolted out the door. Each carried a brown, paper grocery sack filled with the bling and wallets. The pope followed. King Rex tilted his gun upward and fired.

"Y'all have a good night, you hear?" he yelled as he ran out into the night.

"Jesus," Ladonis whispered, her legs and feet tingling with a cramping pain.

She tried to stand straight, but hit her head. Her knees buckled, and she fell onto her brother. She grabbed hold of his arm, her body shaking.

"We need to get out those gates before the cops get here." HeartTrouble grabbed Ladonis's hand.

She felt her body being pulled, but her feet were stuck. It was as though she were watching a silent movie. HeartTrouble yanked her arm, and she fell through the double doors opposite the staircase into the kitchen area.

Fires burned on the gas stove. Food sat on the counters and cooktops in preparation mode. The only thing missing from the picture was life.

"Help!" voices roared from a padlocked door. "Open up!"

Ladonis looked around. She was in this movie, but didn't know what to say. What should she do?

"Come on," HeartTrouble ordered, still holding her hand. "Someone will help them. Let's get out here."

HeartTrouble snatched the purse from her hand and dug in for the car keys. Ladonis didn't argue, didn't utter one word. She just stared at her brother. What the hell had happened? A boisterous crowd gathered near the broken glass. Through it all, Ladonis could see the big man, the robber, in the white tux staring at HeartTrouble, at her. Had he winked? Did HeartTrouble know the robbers? And if he did, did she?

"Tough, smart-ass Donnie," HeartTrouble said, grabbing her hand again, dragging her like dead weight behind him. "Come on."

As if he were following a blueprint, HeartTrouble guided her outside past the pool, through the tall hedges surrounding the garden to a big oak tree parallel to the entrance on St. Charles Avenue. Hidden by the massive tree trunk, they climbed over the three-foot fence careful not to get poked by the spear points. Ladonis looked back and saw that they'd barely crossed the street before the cops rushed inside past the bewildered valet.

HeartTrouble pushed her into the car and closed the door. Ladonis couldn't get a word or scream out, her throat clogged with anger, confusion, and fear. Did he know? Did HeartTrouble know this was going to happen? If he did, her brother would never get to know his kid. She and HeartTrouble were in big trouble now. And it was all her fault.

Chapter Eighteen
Pawns in the Pawnshop

LADONIS STARED OUT the window of Tabor's BMW. "Why here?" she asked in a whisper. "The plan was to go directly back to Tabor's office."

"I want to take off this monkey suit," HeartTrouble said. "Besides, we didn't get what we went for. You can't be in a hurry to tell Tabor that."

No, she didn't want to tell Tabor that. She shifted her body to glance out at her mother's neglected yard, images that stalked her thoughts. The assault in Phoenix, the frightful events at the auction, paled compared to the visual reminder of those overgrown weeds in Mama's yard. Her mother was going to die. Soon. Possibly alone, thanks to her and her dream of a window office.

HeartTrouble pulled Tabor's BMW in front of their mother's house. Someone walked up and down the porch. Evalena? A shadow sat in her mother's chaise, watching. Ladonis jumped out of the car before it made a full stop.

Evalena charged up to Ladonis. Her dreadlocks flapped in the wind, her face moist. How long had her friend been waiting?

"What's wrong? Is it my mama?"

"No," Evalena screamed. "It's you. I oughta punch your lights out."

"Keep your voice down." Ladonis looked around the quiet street. Her neighbors were rarely seen and almost never heard.

She spotted a large vehicle parked on the opposite side of the street before turning back to face Evalena. She tossed her hair. Evalena's ill-temper could be off putting sometimes, but her sister-friend had never threatened her with violence before.

"Did something happen at the pawnshop?"

"The pawnshop?" HeartTrouble rushed up to Evalena. "You sent her to a pawnshop lookin' for that goddamn pen?" He removed his clip-on tie and jammed it into his jacket pocket. "The cops picked you up, right?"

"You know it." Evalena glared at Ladonis. "I don't appreciate being hauled off to jail in handcuffs."

"What?" Ladonis's breaths were quick and loud. "Handcuffs? What are you talking about?"

Tabor stood up from the Wicker chaise lounge in the dark corner of the porch. Ladonis wasn't sure if she should be glad or sad to see him. She had a bad feeling about that robbery and a possible HeartTrouble connection. Now this dust up with Evalena. She was in no mood to be chastised by the likes of Tabor.

"What are you doing here?" Ladonis asked. "I thought you were at your place waiting for us."

"Well, I had to go to the police to represent Evalena. Afterward, she insisted the cab drop her here instead of picking up her abandoned car at the pawn shop. I didn't want to leave her alone, so here I am. Besides, I had a feeling HeartTrouble would want to get out of that suit before heading to my place. Either way, I figured that you or I could give her a ride later to pick up her car." Tabor looked down at Ladonis from the porch. "What were you thinking, Donnie? Didn't you realize Evalena would be a sitting duck once she described a jeweled Parker pen to the owner of a pawnshop?"

"Why?" Ladonis said, agitated. "Thieves do pawn what they steal and people do buy it, don't they?"

"Yes, they do," Tabor told her. "Didn't you think I'd check into that?"

"Well . . ." Ladonis sighed. "When I suggested it, you just went on about your theory, blah, blah, blah." She turned and Tabor followed her eyes to the loud humming sound of his car's engine. Tabor threw up his hands and walked toward the automobile HeartTrouble had left idling on the street.

"Don't you know the cops run the pawnshops?" HeartTrouble shook his finger in Ladonis's face. "That's how they keep a heads-up on the stuff brothers steal for 'em."

"Now how would I know that?" Ladonis snapped, her hands on her hips.

"You'd know if you didn't have your nose stuck up in white-folk shit all the time," HeartTrouble said. "Black folk know that a pawnshop in this town is like an off-site police property room."

"No surprise to you," Ladonis barked. "Since the NOPD is your field of expertise."

Had her brother gone completely over to the dark side and used his criminal connections to rob Children's Hospital? She dared not ask him if he knew about that robbery with Tabor and Evalena looking on. If he had, it was the kind of secret that should remain between them. Besides, what could Tabor do about the custody of his little girl if he's guilty?

If only she could stretch out on the ground and kick and holler away her frustration like a two-year-old toddler. She gritted her teeth instead and focused her attention on Evalena. She did not want to hear another word her brother had to say.

"What happened?" Ladonis asked Evalena.

"What happened?" Evalena gasped. "What happened is that I fell for that song and dance you gave me about losing your job if this girl went to jail at a time when your mama needed you most. I believed you when you said you'd be expected to do the work of two people, and would be under siege, set up to fail if there was a trial. So, I went to that pawnshop. That's what happened."

Ladonis lowered her head and rubbed her temples. The pounding on her brain was as intense as the thumping in her chest. At every turn, she got deeper and deeper into trouble, dragging her family and friends along for the ride.

"I'm sorry, okay," Ladonis said in a voice a little too loud to sound genuine. "I'm sorry."

"You oughta be." Evalena's annoyance glowered in her eyes.

HeartTrouble put his arms around Evalena. He looked at Ladonis, his face flushed with anger. Evalena laid her head on his chest, took a deep breath then pulled away.

"How did it go down?" HeartTrouble asked Evalena.

"I went to that pawnshop on Claiborne Avenue." Evalena kneaded her hands. "You know, where the Gallo Theater used to be. I asked about the pen. Described it just like Donnie told me. The owner said he thought he'd seen something like that. That he'd go check. I'm thinking, this is great. I won't have to go to the other two on the list."

She made two steps forward, turned, and walked three more steps, then turned again. "But before I knew it, the cops had me in cuffs. They took me to the station at Tulane and Broad Street. This detective came in like he was the hurricane they talkin' about all over the news. And that dirty-lookin' son-of-a-bitch tried to force me to tell him that you put me up to going to the pawnshop." She pointed at Ladonis.

Detective Travers. He had that son-of-a-bitch way about him. Ladonis felt like her skin had little black sugar ants crawling over her. Poor Evalena. Nobody deserved Travers's attention.

"He told the arresting cops that he'd been investigatin' that particular pawnshop for a long time." Evalena stepped closer to Ladonis. "And then he took me into a room and asked me a million questions about you, about that co-worker of yours, and that godforsaken pen. He said you'd told him that we were friends."

Ladonis sighed. No doubts now. The cops knew about the pen. Did they also know that she'd gone to Bunnie's apartment to steal a laptop?

"That detective guy scared the shit out of me and made me mad as hell at the same time." Evalena clenched her jaws. "I had my wits about me, though. I yelled, 'I want my phone call,' whenever I saw someone pass by. I stomped my feet and screamed at that detective that I wanted my lawyer present or I was gonna sue."

"I'm sure that didn't sit well with him," Ladonis whispered, irritated by the situation.

"You should've seen the way he slammed that phone down in front of me," Evalena said. "I think I should press some kind of harassment charges against him."

"That won't be necessary." Tabor reappeared from the street, pocketing the car key HeartTrouble had left in the ignition. "I cleared everything up."

"Come to think about it," Evalena said. "You did, didn't you? I couldn't believe it after you two talked and he told me that I could go home."

"That surprised me a bit, too," Tabor said in a reflective voice. "I was expecting a real dog fight, especially the way my contacts said you were behaving. But the detective said he didn't think you could help the case."

"I'm sorry that happened to you," Ladonis said, almost whispering.

"Not half as sorry as I am." Evalena stared straight into Ladonis's eyes. Ladonis reached out to hug Evalena, who stepped away from her. Ladonis looked to Tabor. "This is getting out of hand."

Tabor shook his head. "If you hadn't gone off half-cocked and gotten Evalena mixed up in this, we'd be home free. As it is now—"

"I'm sorry, all right?" Ladonis interrupted. "What do we do now?"

"From here on in," Tabor said in that commanding lawyerly voice of his, "we play this my way. Do you understand?"

Ladonis nodded.

"I hate to break it to you, bro," HeartTrouble said. "There was a robbery at that auction. We had to leave before finding that pen."

"I know," Tabor said, softly.

"You know?" Ladonis's throat tightened. "What do you mean, you know?"

"I thought I recognized Avery's voice," HeartTrouble said, slapping his hands together as if he'd correctly answered a *Jeopardy* question.

"Avery?" Ladonis said. "Big Dee's Avery?"

"Yeah," HeartTrouble told her. "He was the one dressed like the pope."

Cousin Big Dee, alias Deloise Washington, worked as the housekeeping dispatcher at the Floating Palace's land-based hotel, the Dixieland. And Avery, the Dixieland's big red-headed doorman, was more than her co-worker. He was her business partner as well as her lover.

No one knew their way around New Orleans underground better than Big Dee and Avery. They earned a small fortune enabling cops, government officials, as well as the city's richest high society who engage in clandestine activities to evade getting caught. Because some high-powered police and other more prominent law-enforcement personnel were among her best customers, the operation was successful. And because it provided an extra income to the maids, desk clerks, taxi drivers, telephone operators, etc. who switched hotel rooms, and/or mis-directed messages and private detectives in a flash, there was a code of silence that put the police blue wall to shame.

"What the hell is going on, Tabor?" Ladonis's temper rose. "Big Dee and her crew are not thieves. They're the good guys. We're the good guys. Remember?"

Tabor hesitated. He was on a cause and seemed to take Malcolm X's words, "by any means necessary," literally. But putting Big Dee's and Avery's underground operation in the spotlight was taking his ideology to the extreme.

"After all that has happened," Ladonis said, perturbed, "why would you get Big Dee and Avery involved in this?"

"I got a call from Travers," Tabor announced. "He told me he'd noticed a cord for a laptop on Bunnie's bed in a crime scene photo."

"What?" Ladonis said in shaky voice.

"He wanted to know if I knew anything about a laptop at Bunnie's."

"Jesus," Ladonis said. "That proves whoever broke into Bunnie's place must've stolen it."

"I told you not to go to that girl's house snoopin' around," HeartTrouble bellowed.

"What did you tell Travers about the laptop?" Ladonis asked Tabor. "Not the truth, I hope."

"Wait." Evalena covered her ears with her hands. "I don't want to hear. When the cops ask me about this, I want to honestly say I don't know nothin' about nothin'."

"I'm down with that." HeartTrouble went inside Mama's house.

"Can I bum a ride to pick up my car?" Evalena said to Tabor. "I don't want to call another cab."

Tabor nodded, reaching into his pocket. He tossed the keys to Evalena who caught them midair and walked toward the street.

"What did you tell him?" Ladonis asked.

"I told him that I needed to see that photo. I can't imagine the cops leaving a laptop behind if they had a cord and had searched the place. And if that's the case, then something isn't adding up."

"So you think he was lying to you?"

"Yes, I believe so." Tabor nodded. "My sources tell me there is no CSI recorded report on Bunnie's place. That the storm has delayed normal processes, including on Maynard's murder investigation. Could be he got a tip or something about the laptop and was feeling me out."

"And he bought that you needed to see the photo?" Ladonis asked.

"It's the law," Tabor said. "The defense has to see all evidence against the accused."

"So what about the laptop? Does he have it?"

"Don't know. He said he wanted to make sure I didn't have it before he went looking for it. Even suggested I bring it in. But my sources tell me the police does not have the laptop. That doesn't mean it isn't there. It could be kept under wraps until it's advantageous to their case to acknowledge." Tabor shrugged. "Assuming they do have it, and that they know about the pen, I had something more important to do."

"What?" Ladonis's body tensed, heat flushing throughout. "Arrange a robbery?" Her brother wasn't the culprit. It was his lawyer. Were unlawful acts the only way to get justice in this town? "Why did you do that?"

"I had to get you guys out of there," Tabor told her. "After you and HeartTrouble left, I found out that the auctioneers had arranged camera surveillance."

"Jesus, Tabor." Ladonis sighed. Every step she took to get out of this mess pulled her further into it. "How in the world did you find that out?"

"It was a fluke, really. The guy that set up the security is a grateful client, who just happened into my office to pay on his account. When I asked how he'd come by the money, he told me about his latest job for a Children's Hospital fundraiser at Audubon Place."

"Fluke is right," Ladonis said. "But how did you get Avery to pull off a robbery so fast?"

"You know how your cousin feels about you. She won't ever forget that you not only told her about the job at the hotel, you helped her fill out the application, you prepped her on what to wear, how to behave, and what to say on the interview," Tabor said. "Aside from that, she runs a first-class operation and has a top-notch crew."

He was right. Big Dee could run a scam between hotels on a dime, as in get the hotel workers to switch a guest from one hotel room to another. Or redirect phone calls and mail to avert media, the police, especially a suspicious significant other. Demonstrating once again that in order to stop wrongdoing, one had to commit wrongdoings. An impromptu robbery was probably a piece of cake. Only Dee and her crew had never engaged in robbery.

"You got Big Dee and Avery to go against what they stand for to stage a robbery?" Ladonis rubbed her sweaty palms on her dress. Her cousin and cohorts had built their empire on other people's sins and moral depravity, not by stealing. "That's lame, not to mention dangerous. We could've gotten caught."

"But you didn't," Tabor said. "Thanks to Avery and the guys, the cops won't have any surveillance tape to prove that you were the lone black woman collector there."

"To think that I was being taped prancing around that place acting like some hot-shot jeweler." Ladonis closed her eyes. Her head was going to explode.

"I'm afraid so," Tabor said.

"What about Avery?" Ladonis frowned at his condescending tone. "The robbery? Are you sure they're not on some tape?"

"Thanks to my client, I was able to tell Avery and the guys exactly how many cameras had been set up and where they were located," Tabor said. "They busted up the security room and the viewing equipment to be sure. That's gonna cost me, though. But you were completely fooled, right?"

"I was," Ladonis told him. "When HeartTrouble indicated that he recognized one of them, I thought he might be in on it." She lowered her head, ashamed. She'd thought the worst of her brother, again. "What about what they stole?"

"Don't worry." Tabor inched closer to her. "The plan was to drop the bags off at Children's Hospital."

"The plan?" Ladonis stepped away from Tabor. "And what about the pen? The cops picked up Evalena just for mentioning it. Suppose the laptop thief doesn't have it? Do you think he's going to come after me looking for the damn thing?"

Tabor looked down. Ladonis grabbed her head between her hands. What gall he had.

"That's what you want, isn't it?" she yelled at him. "You want the laptop thief to come after me."

"Trust me, Donnie," Tabor said.

"Trust you?" She choked on a scream. "Trust the guy who wants to stay above the fray to protect his career?"

"I know what I'm doing," Tabor said. "I'm playing the legal game by the only rules that can make me a winner."

A winner? She thought she knew Tabor and how far he'd go to win every case he took. But so far, he'd talked her into breaking and entering

Bunnie's place. He'd convinced HeartTrouble that it was in his best interest to go with her to crash that auction. And he'd staged a robbery at Audubon Place.

"I was never good at games, Tabor. Though it's obvious that you think you are." Funny how familiarity can breed contempt.

"Don't worry. I know cops. Tabor fiddled with his phone. "How they operate. How they think. Grant you, they've got a good hand against Bunnie this go round. But all I need is a little more time to flush out the thief that can help me build a case against someone else."

"What case?" Ladonis exclaimed. "You know as well as I do that the cops and the DA will do whatever to prove their case. The cops can manufacture a pen just like you did a band of thieves. I don't understand how you can be so bullheaded about this."

"I am not bullheaded." Tabor frowned. "Well, maybe I am. What I know is, someone wants Bunnie to take the fall. I aim to prove it, even if it's Clifford Maynard."

"Clifford Maynard was to be the special guest at that auction tonight," Ladonis spat. "Did you know that too?"

Tabor lowered his head "What I do know is that Clifford Maynard wants his alleged niece out of the picture."

"Why?" Ladonis threw up her hands. "For the money?"

"Listen," Tabor explained. "I did some checking. Seems old man Maynard had a conscience after all. Four months ago, he contacted his attorney about adding a codicil to his will."

"Four months ago?" Ladonis lifted her hair from her neck. "That's about the time Bunnie's mom died."

"Exactly," Tabor said. "Suppose Bunnie's mom had told Maynard about Bunnie before she passed on. After all, it was the pen collection that maintained the relationship between them all these years. What if at the very least, old man Maynard wanted to honor Bunnie's mother's request and give her that pen collection?"

"You know, right after Bunnie came back from her mama's funeral, she mentioned that some rich guy had gotten in touch with her. Said he was a friend of her mother's and had just learned of her death. He told her that she should feel free to call on him anytime if she needed anything."

"If Jarvis Maynard knew about Bunnie, that could be why Clifford wants Bunnie to take the fall," Tabor surmised. "Maybe the old man planned to acknowledge his daughter the way their father had acknowledged Clifford and left him in the will."

"Why would he be threatened by Bunnie's existence? He's in the will." How many billions can one man spend in a lifetime? "That's crazy. What's even crazier, though, is you looking to bring down a Maynard."

"That's not what I'm trying to do." Tabor's voice rose. "I want to save a woman's life."

The screen door creaked. HeartTrouble walked out onto the porch. He'd changed out of his custody suit into his trademark colorful polyester shirt and kakis. He carried a Dr. Pepper can in his hand.

"We never got to talk about my custody hearing," HeartTrouble said to Tabor.

"That's right." Tabor patted HeartTrouble on the shoulder. "We have a court date, Monday morning."

"Monday?" HeartTrouble asked. "You comin', Donnie?"

"I have to work Monday." The concern in his tone caught her off guard. "But who knows. The storm is supposed to hit on Monday."

"Your presence would certainly make a difference." Tabor walked toward his car. Ladonis trotted off after him. "Especially since your mother is too ill to be there." He turned and waved to HeartTrouble. "See you in court, Man," he called out. "Nine o'clock sharp, okay? The hearing is set for nine-fifteen."

"Yeah. Nine o'clock." HeartTrouble went back inside Mama's house. Ladonis followed Tabor to his car.

"I've got to go and check on Avery and the guys, and see what's on that surveillance tape." Tabor opened the door on the passenger side for Evalena who'd waited at the car. "And don't worry. I've got everything under control."

"Some control," Ladonis said.

Tabor slammed his car door.

"You're a cheeky s.o.b, you know that?" Ladonis called out to him as he turned the key in the ignition.

She looked up at the bright half-moon shining down on her as Tabor and Evalena drove off.

Before she headed into her mama's place, she spotted the dark Hummer parked on the other side of the avenue. For just a second, the man sitting behind the wheel locked eyes with Ladonis. Had he been watching the entire time?

Chapter Nineteen
The Storm's Really Coming

AT FIVE-THIRTY THE next morning, Ladonis gave up on sleep, got dressed, and went in to work. An hour later, Bret, wearing a faded pullover and worn jeans, appeared in her office doorway. He, too, looked as if he hadn't slept a wink.

"Glad you're here," Bret said, turning to walk away. He gestured for Ladonis to follow. "We need to get an early start. Governor Blanco has asked President Bush to declare a federal state of emergency."

Bret remained brisk steps ahead, talking as he walked. Ladonis had to strain to hear his words. She skipped to catch up, but couldn't.

"Jefferson and St. Bernard Parishes are recommending that all residents evacuate." Bret's voice picked up volume.

"What does that mean for FPSC?" Preparing for a storm in her world meant filling the tub with water, loading up on canned goods, and falling asleep because there was no power for television or no electricity by which to read.

"It means that the boats have to remain docked in Shreveport for God knows how long." He came across as confident, but worried. "It means we have passengers to put up or send home if possible. It means a logistical nightmare. Not to mention a revenue buster."

Ladonis sighed. God forbid FPSC should lose a buck. Hurricane and safety be damned.

She and HeartTrouble had agreed that she'd arrive at their mother's bedside around ten. That she'd spend the rest of the afternoon with Mama, and HeartTrouble would stay the night. That way Ladonis could use the late evening and early morning hours to prep her condo for the storm as well as work with Legal on the Keyes charter contract before hunkering down at Mama's to wait out the bad weather. That was her bottom line. She glared at the back of Bret's head.

Bret pushed through the double doors to his office. Ladonis followed. He picked up a remote from his desk, plopped down on the sofa, and turned on the television. Ladonis sat in a chair not far away.

The television, new to the office's décor, sat on the wet bar. Ladonis wanted to say something clever about having such a distraction in the workplace, but changed her mind. Whether the Maynard murder or hurricane Katrina, constant information was required.

"To cut down on calls from our passengers' families, I want you to instruct the media to announce that we're docking both boats in Shreveport until further notice." Bret picked began switching channels.

"Okay," Ladonis replied, thinking about all she had to do. "Refunds?"

"No," Bret told her. "But, customers have two years as opposed to the usual one year after a cancellation to take the trip."

"Okay." She brushed back a lock of hair from her face. She wanted to lighten her mood and spread her lips into a smile, but couldn't. "I hope you have a battery-operated radio on hand. In times like these, the radio is the most dependable."

"Our main goal has to be to make sure that the boats are safe." Bret lifted his head as if she'd said something wrong. "Radio, television. They are both dependable as long as we make sure passengers are out of the storm's path until the weather threat is over."

He found the Weather Channel and turned the volume up. Ladonis tuned into the forecaster describing the damage Katrina had perpetrated in Florida, too emotionally drained to respond to Bret. She hoped her mother, who had a long-time fear of storms, wasn't following this news. Otherwise she'd be in a panic as well as pain. Ladonis had to get her job done so that she could go to her.

"I'll put out a press release," Ladonis said in her best business voice. "That will inform relatives and others how to reach the passengers."

"Good." Bret got up and went to his desk, picked up two sheets of paper, and handed them to her. "Here is contact information for passengers and relatives including the location of the boats."

Ladonis perused the papers. "Have arrangements been made with the Shreveport airlines, buses, and so forth to accommodate our passengers?"

"That's also detailed there." Bret nodded toward the papers. "I've instructed the captains to contact you with updates."

"What about Keyes? According to Bunnie's notes, he's supposed to be in town Monday for a meeting onboard to hash out the last details for his company's cruise. I hope to get him to sign the contract and seal the deal. I've alerted Legal."

"Oh, that," Bret said. "Keyes won't be coming."

"The storm?"

"I'm not sure." Bret avoided her gaze. "Keyes told Velcroy that he'd been contacted by a reporter inquiring about his upcoming work retreat aboard the MAGNOLIA BELLE and his negotiations with Bunnie Sinclair at FPSC."

Ladonis felt relief despite knowing that this murder thing with Bunnie could go on for God knows how long. She was grateful, though, that the free time would make it easier for her to go to HeartTrouble's' custody hearing on Monday. That is, provided the storm didn't delay that too.

"I thought you had everything under control," Bret said.

"I do. I spoke with his personal assistant and scheduled the meeting. But if you're asking if I spoke with Keyes directly about Bunnie and told him I was taking over, I didn't. I thought that information should come from you."

Why should she let him off the hook? He was, after all, the president of the company. Why shouldn't he be held accountable? Especially for something as significant as a change in assignment as this was.

"Velcroy was able to convince Keyes to make arrangements to reschedule after the storm."

She wanted to ask how this would affect the takeover, but didn't.

"With you," Bret added.

"He did?" Ladonis asked. Velcory in her corner practically guaranteed her rise in the company.

Bret, on the other hand, had a strange, disappointed look on his face. He'd attempted to pass her ideas off as his, whereas Velcroy had used his influence to help Bunnie navigate her charter idea in the corporate world. Was he upset that Velcroy had showed faith in her the way he had with Bunnie? Some mentor he turned out to be.

"You know, I need to tell you something." Why couldn't he look at her? "I mean you should know . . ." He never looked away from the television.

"I should know what?" Ladonis asked with a deep breath of anticipation.

"You should know that I really trust you." Bret's voice had this lingering, soft tone. "And I really appreciate you working Bunnie's charters. If she hadn't gone over my head to Velcroy, and had followed the time line I'd worked up after she did, those deals would be signed by now." His eyes met and left Ladonis's in a flash. "I thought you should know is all."

"Thanks," Ladonis whispered through the frog in her throat.

His confession did not change the fact that she wanted Bunnie to handle her own charters. Nor did it kill her suspicion that he wanted to set her up to fail and was now trying to manipulate her. And just because he said he trusted her, she could not yet say that she trusted him.

Bret clicked the remote and returned his view to the television headline: "Suspect in Maynard murder is the Cruise Charter Sales Director at the Floating Palace Steamboat Company." He fell back onto the couch. Ladonis watched, replaying his words, *I trust you*, in her head. Jack, her last boyfriend, said he'd trusted her, too. He trusted that she'd give up her career and move to California to be kept by him. It crossed her mind that Bret trusted her to lay down and play grateful dead and let him walk away owning her hard work.

"Damn press," Bret stated to the television. "There is no such thing as timing with those people." He cradled his head between his clenched hands. "I need this deal wrapped up before Bunnie Sinclair and her distressful story drag FPSC into her worldwide tabloid headlines."

Ladonis needed Bunnie's case wrapped up also. That's why she'd gone to that auction. She had her own issues, her own dream to focus on.

"I'll be working from home on this," she said. "My mother is very ill."

"I'm sorry to hear that." Bret's voice dropped. "Anything I can do?" She shook her head.

"I'll be available if you do," Bret told her. "I'm not leaving town. And I'll get that radio, too," he added, his tone still quiet.

She stood up and headed for the door, a voice in her head reminding her there was a difference between trust and being used. She doubted his kindness was sincere.

Her cell phone rang. University hospital showed up on caller ID screen, so she answered. It was Vanessa, the social worker.

"Your mother's hospital bed will be delivered in an hour," Vanessa reported. "Will someone be there to receive it?"

"Yes, of course." Ladonis's thoughts had run way past the social worker's words.

The hospital wasn't wasting any time. Probably because the weather geniuses had predicted that Katrina would hit New Orleans late Sunday or early Monday. Or, it could be because the head doctor had told a news reporter that he wished there weren't so many patients on the hospital's wards. He'd said that he suspected the worker-patient ratio would drop dramatically because of transportation issues for employees combined with the inevitability of storm-related medical emergencies.

"What about my mama? When will she be discharged?"

"In about three hours. I'll arrange for her to arrive in an ambulance. Will you be riding with her?"

"Yes," Ladonis assured her. "My mother's house is about ten to fifteen minutes away from the hospital. I'll take a cab to the hospital as soon as the bed is delivered." If only her mother could stay in the hospital until that storm passed, or at least until she got the Bunnie monkey off her back.

Ladonis picked up the files, her purse, and briefcase and made her way to her car in FPSC's parking lot. The river air that flowed through the semi-dark parking lot should've been cool. But the New Orleans humidity and the ninety-one-degree temperature made steam of the breeze that dampened Ladonis's clothes. Still, the weather geeks had gone from calling the weather disturbance, which had begun in the Gulf, a low-pressure system, to naming it, to predicting its category status.

"Lady Katrina packs a wallop," a voice on the car radio said. "And looks like she's headed to the Big Easy. Mayor Nagin has issued a state of emergency and ordered voluntary evacuation. Don't wait until the last moment to head out, or you could end up at the Super Dome, the last-resort shelter."

Ladonis wheeled onto the wharf on Tchoupitulas Street. Why hadn't she listened to HeartTrouble and bought the plywood months ago to board up her glass doors and windows? Hurricane season, after all, was a given.

Ladonis looked through the rearview mirror and noticed the SUV truck behind her. She drove on, watching in her rearview mirror the reflection of the man driving. That head with the long chin shaped like a "v." Where had she seen that silhouette before? She pressed her foot down on the accelerator. She looked ahead just before plunging off the narrow dock's platform onto the railroad tracks below. Then she rammed her foot on the brake.

"Oh, my God," she cried, pulling on the emergency brake. The car on her tail rolled past. "The Hummer. It's the man in the Hummer."

Chapter Twenty
The Birds and Fish Are Gone

"WE NEED MORE bottled water and canned fruit cocktail," HeartTrouble shouted at Ladonis as she rushed to her car from her mother's porch. "Bring 'em when you come back in the mornin'."

"Okay." Ladonis looked around for the Hummer, fearing the driver was stalking her. She wondered if he could be the same man HeartTrouble had encountered outside Tabor's office.

After making sure Mama was settled and comfortable in that hospital bed, she'd spent most of the night staring out the living room window hoping to find out. Afraid he might be the real killer. One thing she knew for sure: She felt certain he wasn't a policeman. NOPD preferred in-your-face intimidation.

Ladonis heard the familiar clank and growl of Evalena's vintage Chevy Monte Carlo shutting off. The brakes set. After the last grunt of the engine, the brake lights went off. Evalena emerged carrying her overnight blue and white tote. Her dreadlocks and colorful clothes hung and flowed in perfect symmetry to her not-too-big and not-too-small body.

Earlier, Ladonis had called Tabor to tell him about Hummer Man, but he hadn't returned her call. She wanted to tell her brother about the man, but decided it was best he didn't know about this new predicament she'd gotten herself into. HeartTrouble had taken charge of the logistics to protect Mama from the storm, and that had lifted a burden off her. It would be wrong to repurpose his priorities again. Though it was worrisome to go anywhere without him at her side knowing someone was tailing her. But here was Evalena, her best friend in the whole world.

"Where you headed?" Evalena strapped the tote over her shoulder. "I thought you and Woodrow were stayin' here with your mama during the storm." Her voice softened. "I came to stay with you."

Evalena's affectionate tone and concern landed like a boulder on her conscience. Had she forgiven Ladonis for sending her to that pawnshop? Whether she had or had not, it was clear that Evalena didn't want to leave her alone to watch her mother die. Ladonis wished she could sprout wings and fly away.

"HeartTrouble staying," Ladonis said, holding her stomach. "I just figured I'd spend the night at my place. I need to take care of a few things in case the storm hits on Monday as hard as the weather reports say it will. HeartTrouble will be here with Mama." She opened the car door and tossed her purse on the seat. "I thought you'd be on your way to Houston by now. Didn't your mama say the birds and fish had left town already?"

"Don't make fun, Donnie. My mother has been more right than even the great weather god, Nash Roberts, used to be when it comes to predicting storms."

"I wasn't making fun," Ladonis lied. "But, you have to admit, that with the exception of a little rain, the weather has not been that unusual since the hurricane talk began."

"Maybe," Evalena said.

There was a time when Ladonis envied and tried to imitate Evalena's confidence and style. No matter how hard she tried, she could not pull off that carefree hippie sophistication and conviction that identified her sisterfriend. However, she'd grown to appreciate her tailored, business-chic appearance; her command for details and hard work. Heads turned when she entered a room, and people listened when she spoke.

"But," Evalena smiled, "Mother did say the birds and fish left yesterday. And today that lady Governor Blanco say no more tolls to get out. She even shut down the Interstate to all traffic comin' into town. She would not have done that if the weather gods hadn't warned her that Hurricane Katrina is going to be the big one." Her mouth drew upward to the left side in neither a smile nor a pout, but into a declaration.

Ladonis cast an examining stare upon the sky as well as Evalena.

"And I put Mother on the Greyhound to Houston this morning. If she's wrong about this storm, it'll be the first time."

"What about you? Aren't you going?"

"What for? All Mother and Aunt Teresa gonna do is get drunk and reminisce about Daddy and Chris. I figured I'd sit this one out here."

Whenever there was migration of fish and birds, Evalena and her mother usually boarded up their Conti Street shotgun house as well as their next-door rental property and headed to Houston, often before the news of an upcoming storm broke. At one time, that trip meant an impromptu fun family vacation with Mr. Matthews' sister, Teresa. But when Evalena was fifteen, she'd found her seventeen-year-old brother's shot-up body on their front stoop. And when Mr. Matthews died of grief and colon cancer a few months later, her mother, who spread love around thick like kids hooked on peanut butter and jelly did on bread, began drinking.

Ladonis felt that double loss had to be why Evalena felt attached to HeartTrouble and why she clung to Ladonis's mama. Why, even though there wasn't one drop of blood that connected them, Evalena was her sister, a member of her family.

"Get in. HeartTrouble will be okay staying with Mama alone, but I could use some help at my place."

Ladonis wasn't proud of it, but thought that if HeartTrouble couldn't go with her, why not Evalena? With the possibility of someone out there gunning for her, wouldn't she be safer if she were not alone? She noticed flashing lights hurtling up the street. The police? Before she could blink, a police car skidded to a stop with its nose on her mother's lawn.

"Go inside. Tell HeartTrouble to call Tabor." Ladonis couldn't determine what came out faster, her guilt or her words. "Call Tabor until he answers. Tell him the police must've found the laptop."

"I swear, girl," Evalena spat out between gritted teeth. "When it comes to white folks, you give yourself too much credit."

Ladonis retrieved her purse off the seat, got out of the car, and locked the door. She sucked in a deep breath and took deliberate steps toward the two uniformed cops, terror tumbling around her innards. No doubt she'd been identified as the thief in the night at Bunnie's place. Would it matter that she didn't even take the damn laptop?

Chapter Twenty One
Loose End

LADONIS, HER NAVY sweats damp and grimy, sat still as a plank on an old-fashioned wooden school chair. Almost four hours had passed since she'd been brought into police headquarters to "answer a few questions." At least that was what the police officers said when they hauled her in. And now she was being terrorized by that grungy, mean-spirited Detective Travers. She stared up blankly at him perched like a hawk on the edge of his desk. His arms folded across his chest. He looked down at her. His dark eyes, lit with confidence, telegraphed his readiness to attack his cornered prey.

"Tell me," Travers's voice rose, "why I shouldn't lock you up?"

Her response to this oh, Lord!-what-do-I-do moment, had to be silence. She pinched her lips shut and prayed to God to hold her tongue. Or should she lash out like she always did when her back was up against a wall? Perhaps she should pout and cry like Bunnie would. No. She'd best be silent and wait for Tabor. Where in the world was Tabor?

She'd used her phone call to contact HeartTrouble two hours ago. He had told her that Tabor was on his way. Where was he on his way from? Mars?

Lines of anger formed across Travers's pale forehead. He uncrossed his arms and leaned forward, his long, joyless face inches away from hers. So close, she smelled coffee on his breath.

"Well?" he asked.

"I refuse to answer any questions whatsoever without my lawyer present," she said as defiantly as possible.

A uniformed female officer walked up to Travers and whispered in his ear. Travers took off across the large open space to the office with Captain Twyla Goodin's name plastered on the door. Ladonis released her tense shoulders with a thump. She didn't know how much longer she could maintain her fake resolve of strength before breaking down into a million-piece heap of whimper.

She watched Wellsburg open the blinds covering the glass walls of the lady chief's office, then walk out the door shortly after Travers had entered. Twyla Goodin leaned back in her chair twirling a pencil looking up at Travers. Ladonis's heartbeat pounded in her ears. What was Travers saying? Was Twyla ordering her arrest?

Wellsburg stepped into her space. According to every cop show she'd viewed on television, it was within her rights to leave since she hadn't been arrested. Yet, no one ever left. She didn't either.

"The chief wants to talk to you," Wellsburg said.

"And I want to talk to her." Ladonis sat up taller in her seat determined not to move. "Just as soon as my lawyer gets here."

Wellsburg lifted her up from the chair with his hand on her elbow. Ladonis pulled her arm away, careful not to let him feel her trembling body. Wellsburg nudged her shoulder, steering her forward. Ladonis fought the urge to cry out. She straightened, took a deep breath, and followed him into Twyla's office. The smirk on Travers' face told her that no matter who asked the questions, he owned this cat-and-mouse police game.

"Ladonis Washington." Twyla sounded as though she had come across a long lost friend at a high-school reunion. "Have a seat."

"I hope you're ready to apologize for treating me like a criminal," Ladonis said, ignoring the voice in her head telling her to shut up.

"I beg your pardon?" Twyla said.

It was foolish of her not to expect the same authoritarian attitude from the lady cop in charge that she'd gotten from Travers. She'd hoped that it meant something to her they both were women of color working in high-profile careers dominated by white men. Damn it. Where was Tabor?

"We need you to help us tie up a few loose ends." Twyla adjusted the hairpin in her trademark French twist. Her condescending tone made it clear to Ladonis that she did not consider them comrades.

"Loose ends?" Ladonis wanted to tell the chief to go find a real killer to torment, but couldn't disregard the warning in her head telling her that would not be a smart. "What loose ends are you talking about?"

"It appears," Travers sneered, "that this pen everyone is all up in arms about was shipped to Maynard."

"Pen?" Ladonis said in a soft voice. She glanced out the glass window, hoping to see Tabor rushing to her rescue, but all she saw were cops shuffling around like footballers on a field. She spotted a man pouring himself a cup of coffee, laughing it up with a few policemen and women. She bristled.

Sweet Jesus. It was Hummer Man. A sharp pain in her stomach traveled up to her head. Was Hummer Man a cop? Had NOPD been following her after all?

"Guess what?" Travers said. "We found the pen. The way we figure it. Bunnie accused Jarvis Maynard of robbing her twice. First with the jade she'd tried to unload in Phoenix, then with the pen."

According to Bunnie, her mother was still the owner of the pen. Had Bunnie lied or was she mistaken? She looked out the window to keep her fake calm from unraveling, and saw Hummer Man and Wellsburg chatting it up. Who was this guy?

"Bunnie was furious, so she bumped Jarvis Maynard off," Travers said.

"You can't believe Bunnie killed him?" Ladonis leveled a fiery look at Travers.

"Why can't we?" Twyla sat up like she expected Ladonis to confess or something.

"Ah, yes we can," Travers rushed to say. "We have the witness we need to prove Miss Sinclair's motive." He pointed in the direction of his partner and Hummer Man.

"Jesus H. Christ." Ladonis sighed. "Are you shitin' me? Just because the pen is valuable, doesn't mean—"

Uh-oh. She should've stuck to her plan and kept quiet.

"All of a sudden you seem to know about that pen," Twyla said. "How's that?"

"Isn't it valuable?" Ladonis snapped. "I mean, why else would Jarvis Maynard want it?"

Ladonis could feel Travers watching her. Surely now he'd bring up the computer and the pawnshop, a great plan to entrap her. If she weren't careful, she'd give them all the evidence they needed to hang Bunnie and her. She could end up looking out a prison peep hole instead a wall of windows facing the Mississippi.

A policeman stuck his bald head through the doorway. "Chief. The director at the National Hurricane center called Mayor Nagin. Said it's time to evacuate the lower areas, especially the Ninth Ward. They predict a four or five category hit on the city day after tomorrow, Monday morning."

Four or five category hit? Ladonis stiffened as she watched every muscle in Twyla's face expand. A category five hurricane was the big one everyone feared.

Twyla took in a breath loud enough for all to hear. On her exhale, she nodded to the bald-headed policeman. He nodded back, then closed the door behind him.

Ladonis had to get home. Spending even one night locked away while her mother suffered became even more threatening.

Twyla and Travers shared a look.

"Nothing changes the fact that according to the time of death and an eye witness," Travers said to Ladonis, his tone low, "Ms. Sinclair was the last person to see Maynard alive. Not to mention she had sworn before others, including you, to get even with him."

Travers was like a dog with a bone. Storm or no storm, he was after Ladonis. That realization splashed inside her like a rock tossed into a pit.

"She was upset," Ladonis said, softly. "She thought Jarvis Maynard had set her up."

"Precisely," Travers said. "And in her own words, she wanted him to pay."

"Making him pay didn't mean killing him. She just wanted him to go to jail. That's why she went to the police." She should've heeded her own advice and kept quiet.

Ladonis cast her sight once again on Twyla who was watching the detective. Did real-life good cops worry at all about evidence that fell too neatly into place? Had Travers invaded Twyla's space?

"That is—" Travers began.

"A wrap." Tabor bounded into the room, looking as though he'd just come off an African safari in his big pocket khakis and a wide-striped, brown and white collared pullover shirt.

"Tabor." Ladonis stood up. "Thank God. They brought me here with lights blazing. Allowed me one phone call and have been badgering me ever since."

"Arrest her or release her," Tabor told Twyla.

Arrest? Apprehension rushed over Ladonis like wind blowing through trees. She rubbed at the chill bumps that popped up on her arms.

"She's free to go," Twyla said, sternly. She leaned back, pinching her chin. Her confident-yet-incensed stare was dead set on Travers. Ladonis wondered if her brusque tone meant for him, or if the approaching Katrina was preying on her thoughts.

"What about—?" Ladonis wanted to know about the man who'd been following her.

"Donnie," Tabor frowned, looking annoyed, "that's enough."

Travers opened the door for them to pass through. "By the way, we'll be in touch. We have another loose end that I'm sure you can help us tie up."

The laptop. Ladonis felt a tightening in her stomach. Travers did have a plan to get her, after all.

All six feet and four inches of Tabor's entire body seemed to grow taller. "Storm's coming. The mayor has shut the town down. Contact my office when it's over."

Chapter Twenty-Two
Bad News

TABOR TOOK LADONIS'S hand and pulled her tired body outside the precinct. Ladonis yanked her hand away. He'd shut her down like a naughty child in front of Chief Goodin and that scary detective. She would not give him the satisfaction of humiliating her further.

"Where were you?" Ladonis wouldn't be in this mess if not for helping him find another suspect. "I tried and tried to call you. Why didn't you call me back?"

"I was in Slidell," Tabor said through his teeth. "A couple of days ago, I closed on a house I bought there. I had to board it up." He clicked the key in his hand twice and the doors to his BMW unlatched. "The house is far into the woods and my cell doesn't work well out there."

"Well, I could've been jailed," she snapped, getting into Tabor's BMW.

"Look, Donnie." Tabor narrowed his eyes. "It was a mistake to ask you to get that laptop and to go to that auction. I regret the position that has put you in."

What position? Was he preparing her to go to jail? She glanced his way. His despairing look triggered an emotion she didn't want to respond to—forgiveness. She pretended not to notice. She collapsed into the passenger seat. She turned on the radio to refocus on the storm, determined to stay mad. Katrina was the one calamity neither she nor Tabor had anything to do with.

"The more I learned about the girl and what happened," Tabor went on to explain, "the more convinced I became that she's innocent. I just want to prove it is all."

On the radio, the National Hurricane Center issued a warning: "Katrina is moving in a westerly direction to an area that includes New Orleans." If only she'd done more to protect her condo. Katrina could very well be "the big one" that had been forecast for years.

"You know," Tabor said in a soft voice, "it was the video."

"What video?" Ladonis whispered.

"The one Big Dee's crew took from the auction." Tabor turned down the volume on the radio. "Watching the goings on at that auction made me realize once again how deeply connected money and crime are in this town. I didn't just feel it, I actually saw in real time the depth of the injustice I'm up against. Brought me down to earth."

"Wait a minute." Ladonis sat upright. "Exactly what did you see on that video?"

"Nothing that could prove Bunnie didn't do it," Tabor acknowledged. "Just a look I picked up on between Clifford Maynard and Leon Bayley when Clifford came in and found himself in the middle of a robbery."

"Leon Bayley?" Ladonis drew in a breath then released it. "I believe I heard a policeman call the man in the Hummer who's been following me, Bayley."

"Following you?" Tabor's voice rose with disbelief. "Are you sure?"

"Yes, I'm sure," Ladonis said. "I just saw him at the police station talking with Detective Wellsburg. And Detective Travers led me to believe that he's a witness in the case. Who is he?"

"He's a private investigator. He used to be a cop before serving time for assault."

"That's it." Ladonis fell back. "The way cops protect and cover for each other, Bayley must really be a bad guy. I believe Clifford Maynard hired him."

"Hired him to follow you?" Tabor didn't sound convinced. Why?"

"Because . . ." Ladonis glared at Tabor. Did he think he had the only working brain between them? "I was with Bunnie at the police station and I went to visit her in jail. He believes I know about the connection between the computer and the pen." She swallowed. "You say Bayley was at the auction?"

"Yeah." Tabor braked at a red light. "And that's odd. The cops I know—NOPD as well as private—say the guy's bad news. If they're correct about him, he's too broke and uncouth to be a part of the antique-collector, art-buying crowd. So it's fair to wonder who invited him to that auction."

"Clifford Maynard. That's who invited him. And he hired the bad news private eye to kill his brother and frame his niece."

"Careful," Tabor cautioned, shifting the engine into gear. "Black conspiracy theories tend to get laughed out of court."

"What are you talking about?" Ladonis rolled her eyes. "Conspiracy theory? A few hours ago, you were certain Clifford did it."

"As Bunnie's attorney, I can't be sure about anything without one, a confession, and two, proof, namely that laptop." The skin bunched up on Tabor's forehead. "What's on it will prove that Bunnie knew the pen existed, but it may or may not prove that Clifford and/or the private investigator, for that matter, had anything to do with the murder or that pen."

"If we've proved anything," Ladonis hissed, "it's that that pen has everything to do with the murder."

"At the moment, I can't prove that Clifford even knew about the computer," Tabor said, losing conviction with every syllable.

Ladonis's mind hopped on a speed bike and chased one thought after the other. She looked over at Tabor. Had he deliberately sent her on a fool's mission to get the laptop and that pen? He'd said if he had them, he could prove that someone else, namely Clifford Maynard, had murdered his brother. And now that she believed he had a way to prove it, he wasn't sure that he could anymore?

"The private eye is the killer." Ladonis touched her chest. Dealing with Tabor had become painful. "And Clifford Maynard paid him to do it. Why won't you come up with a plan to nail the bastards?"

"Listen to me, Ladonis Washington." Tabor's eyes darted back and forth from her to the road. "I agree that there's something going on between Clifford Maynard and Bayley that needs to see the light of day. But I'll handle it." He hit the steering wheel, his tone commanding. "Do you hear me?"

He'd handle it? When? He'd told Travers and the lady chief he'd be in touch after the storm. Well, she didn't want anything to do with the cops after the storm. She had to get off this road to prison tonight so when this storm was over, she could give her full attention to her dying mother.

Her thoughts reeled backward to Travers's last words: "there's a loose end you can help with." She frowned. So far, Tabor had dismissed her as a twit in front of the police even though she'd taken risks to make him a star as much as help Bunnie. As a result, she could end up either the prosecution's star witness, Bunnie's cellmate, or both if the real killer wasn't exposed immediately. She couldn't escape that reality even if Tabor could. Lord, how in the world was she going to prove Clifford knew about Bunnie, the computer, and that damn pen? How was she going to tie up that loose end before the storm hit?

Chapter Twenty-Three
Gut Feeling

THE SCENT OF jasmine from a trellis overhang greeted Ladonis on Bunnie's porch. She inhaled the smell, then opened Bunnie's door with the key she'd gotten from Tabor and never gave back after the computer retrieval fiasco. Too bad she'd left the flashlight. When she thought about it, she was a block away from her mother's house, and didn't want to risk going back and possibly waking up HeartTrouble. There was no way she could explain to him where she was headed.

"This is as wrong as it is stupid," Ladonis told herself as she entered the apartment, channeling her brother's disapproval.

She'd already taken some risky chances to help Tabor free Bunnie. Now, the need to do so wouldn't let go of her brain and drew her back to Bunnie's apartment like a magnet. Suppose there was something in Bunnie's place to prove Clifford had lied about knowing his niece. Rarely did an overlooked clue at the scene of the crime in a mystery novel not reveal a smoking gun.

Jarvis Maynard had made it clear in his press over the years that his half-brother's stepchildren would never inherit the Maynard fortune. That they could never because Louisiana law prohibits such transference if a blood relative exists. Knowing that his beloved wife's son and daughter would be overlooked for the likes of a stranger with a half-black mama, had to have driven Clifford as nuts as Bunnie's arrest had made Ladonis desperate.

Ladonis clicked on Bunnie's hall light. She prayed the neighbors, as well as the police, were too busy retreating from Katrina to notice a tall black woman entering the home of a jailed suspected murderer.

She sniffed the scented, suffocating air. The fragrance from the blooms and plug-in deodorizers were as strong as her conviction that the laptop had to be the so-called loose end that that evil Detective Travers had mentioned. But she'd been at police headquarters for hours and not once did the detectives or anyone say a word to her about the laptop even though Travers had asked Tabor about it. Why was that?

She blew out air of exasperation, making a blubbery sound with her lips. The more she thought about it, the more perplexed she became. Didn't the DA need that computer to prove that pen was Bunnie's motive for murder? Surely they needed it to make an obstructionist case against Ladonis. Was the damn thing still on the closet floor? And why hadn't the cops talked about it?

If Clifford Maynard knew Bunnie was his niece, it stood to reason that he knew about the computer. Otherwise, how did he know about the pen? He must've stolen them. Ladonis walked further into the living room, reeling from her unanswered questions. The facts just didn't add up. You'd think now that the police were involved, the whole thing would be getting clearer, but instead it was getting murkier.

"I visited a friend whose flowers aroused my allergies." Ladonis mimicked Clifford Maynard's interview apology for sneezing all over the television newsroom. "You visited a friend all right. You were in this house. That's why your allergies flared up."

She clicked on a table lamp and looked up into a man's eyes. She jumped back into the table and knocked over the lamp, clutching at her chest to stop the pounding.

"You're a regular Nancy Drew, aren't you?" Travers said.

"Damn it, Detective." Ladonis gasped for air. She looked around for the good cop, the partner, Wellsburg. "You could've let me know ya'll were here."

"What?" Travers widened his stance, his face partially hidden by Bunnie's bamboo plant. "And spoil the surprise?"

"What are you—? I mean—" How much deeper could she dig herself into the murder accomplice hole?

"What am I doing here?" Travers stepped from behind the bamboo tree. "I'm here because you are. Seems it turned out to be a stroke of genius having you followed. You know that? Whatever goes on with that steamboat crew you work with, you're always smack dab in the middle of it." His words weren't nearly as frightening as that menacing, edgy tone in his voice. Not even his Cajun drawl and easygoing demeanor hid the evil she feared lived in him. "When I learned you were with

Maynard's daughter when she tried to press charges, I knew you would be an asset."

The hair stood on Ladonis's neck. She was right to be afraid of this guy. The way his shifty eyes bore into her; his taunting half grin. She did her best to hold in the scream pushing against her windpipe.

"Clifford Maynard did it." The words came up inside Ladonis and were out before her mind had a chance to silence her.

Travers just stood there. Ladonis could hear his teeth grinding.

"Are you saying Clifford Maynard killed his brother?" Travers shifted something from under his left arm to the right, pulled out a hankie, and blew his nose.

"Or had him killed." Ladonis looked nervously around. Where was Detective Wellsburg? Weren't these guys supposed to travel in pairs?

Travers repositioned whatever was under his arm. Ladonis took in a full view of him. A laptop? Oh, God. He had the laptop.

Travers stepped forward. He wore his cockiness like a suit of armor, his body, his eyes—all of him covered with attitude and might.

"Take this?" Travers held out the laptop. Instead of a clean-cut, comforting, to-protect-and-to-serve image, he looked like a pauper ready to hit her in the head to steal her watch.

Ladonis struggled to control the panic pressing inside her. "What?" Her voice cracked.

"I don't have time to play around with you." Travers rushed up to her. "Take this computer. I want your prints on it. Then put it in the desk drawer where Clifford found it."

"In there?" Ladonis pointed to Bunnie's desk. "Not in the closet?" She'd found it in the closet.

"That's right. Put it under that piece of wood in the drawer so I can take a picture. You know, stage a crime-scene photo shoot." He grabbed her hand and dragged her to the desk. "Can't risk some crime-scene cop swearing that I didn't find this evidence where it was without a photo to prove it, now can I?"

Ladonis just nodded, too freaked to speak. How did Clifford know Bunnie's secret hiding place if he'd never been there? She was right; he did know about his niece.

She wanted to ask why Travers didn't plant the computer at her place if he wanted to tie the noose around her neck too. Oh, God, what if he hadn't wanted to put the noose around her neck. Now he had to.

She took the laptop with shaky hands, slid it into the drawer, and left the drawer open about an inch. Travers handcuffed her to the bamboo tree. He then pulled another gun from his sock, started to place it in the drawer, but slipped it back into his sock.

Ladonis assumed the revolver with the light-brown wood butt was not an official department issued piece. Therefore, it had to be the gun that killed Jarvis Maynard. Travis was planting it just as HeartTrouble and Tabor suspected the real killer would do to nail Bunnie for the crime. Then Travis took a camera from his inside jacket pocket and snapped a couple of pictures.

He rubbed his nose and frowned, never taking his eyes off her. The instant their stares clashed, Ladonis knew he wouldn't let her live to tell what she'd seen. How in the world was she going to get out of this?

"With this picture, I make sure the crime scene guys haven't overlooked a valuable piece of evidence." Travers put the camera safely back into his pocket. "Might be hard to do later. Right now, everybody at the precinct is preoccupied with Katrina. And we all know that in a court, a picture is worth a thousand words. Almost always guarantee conviction."

"Why?" Her brain flooded with HeartTrouble's warnings about corrupt police. "Why do you want to convict an innocent person?"

"Why do you think?" Travers unlocked the cuffs, stuck his gun in her ribs, and shoved her toward the kitchen.

Travers's exhausted tone and expression was at odds with his snappy response. Like he'd reached the top of a mountain just in time to catch his breath before jumping. She felt as if she were having a surreal moment in time. Who, or perhaps the better question, what was this man?

She found herself channeling HeartTrouble again. When it came to NOPD, her brother was a Billy Graham purist. "Police," HeartTrouble had said time and again, "murder people around here more than gangbangers do."

"You're one of them," Ladonis said, owning her brother's perspective. Of all the facts and speculations she'd gleaned and garnered in the Maynard murder, she was suddenly sure of one thing. HeartTrouble was right.

"One of them?" Travers squinted, and his lips sealed into a sneer. He flicked his nose as if he smelled something bad.

"You're one of NOPD's finest." Ladonis looked squarely at him. "Who kills for money."

Chapter Twenty-Four
One Shot

TRAVERS SHOVED LADONIS down the sun porch steps into Bunnie's small, dark back yard. Ladonis stumbled into the blackness, her hands held out to feel for something to hold up her quaking body. It should be dawn. Why was it so dark? Had the high winds blown out the streetlights? Or were the storm clouds already heavy enough to hide the rising sun? A blast of wind hit her sideways.

"Ever been to Woldenberg Park?" Travers asked in a tone that dared her to speak.

Ladonis loved the Woldenberg River Park. Some of her most intimate times with her ex, Jack, were walking and making out on the Woldenberg walking path, part of the sixteen-acre landscaped riverfront dock that stretched along the Mississippi from Canal Street to Jackson Square in the French Quarter. She felt alive there, in the hub of the city where she experienced the happy fun the city offered millions, while sharing romantic moments with her lover, with the ambiance of the Mississippi as the backdrop. An image of her and Jack holding hands flashed into her head. Her lower lip quivered.

Travers pushed her against a fence. Ladonis's chest bounced off the wire, joggling her mind and her body. Jesus. This diabolical detective from hell planned to bury her under the Woldenberg in the Mississippi River, possibly with the gun used to kill Jarvis Maynard. She heard the latch give on the gate and wrapped her fingers through the wire links.

"Let's go." Travers steered her into the back street with a gun pressed against her lower back.

Her body felt icky and hot. Not even hurricane-like winds and hard, stinging drizzle depressed the effect of the Louisiana humidity. Not even the dark, cooling clouds hanging overhead could evaporate the heavy moisture in the air.

Travers pushed his gun into Ladonis's ribs so forcibly, she labored to catch her breath. She looked around for a place to run, to hide, and noticed patches of light in the windows of the neighboring homes. Could she alert someone behind those lighted windows and get away alive?

If she yelled, Travers would either knock her out or shoot her, depending on how long he could avoid detection. She had to stall. HeartTrouble said she could talk her way out of hell. Could she?

"Why did you call Tabor and pretend you'd seen that computer at Bunnie's place on a crime-scene photo?" Ladonis battled her nerves and a rush brisk wind to stay on her feet.

"It's called protecting your ass." Travers poked her. "I had to make sure that there is no question at the Sinclair trial about where that computer was found. Can't afford to have the police report that it had been found in the closet if the Sinclair broad confessed she'd left it in a hidden compartment in her desk."

No, Ladonis rationalized, what he couldn't risk was Tabor proving Bunnie is innocent before he has a chance to complete his frame. Otherwise, Clifford would be two attempts out of two to get her out of the Maynard fortune-receiving line.

Travers snickered. "I'm here to see to it that the computer shows up where our girl hid it now that I've made sure the information on it shakes my client's way. Genius plan if I say so myself."

"And that pistol in your sock? Where are you going to plant the murder weapon? In the Mississippi?" Ladonis asked. "You're a genius, all right. And a killer."

Travers grabbed hold of her arm and yanked it so hard, she slid into him. Had she gone too far?

Ladonis felt her bladder loosening and pressed her thighs together. A stale whiskey odor blasted her nostrils through his clothes and his warm breath. She turned her head, and tripped on the uneven concrete sidewalk. She fell against the trunk of a huge Magnolia tree before stepping into a patch of smelly, wet grass and defoliated magnolia blooms.

She hadn't expected such intense Katrina winds so soon. The storm wasn't supposed to hit until Monday, a day away. She thought of Mama. Could see her pacing, checking the weather every other minute, then realized that her mama was lying in a hospital bed, too weak to speak, let alone complain about her fear of storms.

Travers went into a sneezing frenzy. Ladonis struggled to get free. How strong could a drunk with allergies be in a pollen pit? Travers tightened his grip, dragged her onto the street, and pushed her toward a Chevy pick-up parked a few feet away from her car.

Ladonis tuned into the quiet around her, praying for at least one of Bunnie's neighbors to have a barking guard dog lurking behind the tall backyard fences. If only she could crash into that row of garbage cans in front of the fence surrounding the house next to Bunnie's.

She heard a chirping noise followed by a familiar crunched-crackling sound that always made her skin crawl. Cockroaches. Any New Orleans native would recognize that sound. Someone moved around behind those hedges and had stepped on a bed of cockroaches. Ladonis closed her eyes and thanked God for the unconquerable, nasty flying insect that could be found caravanning in and around homes in rich as well as poor neighborhoods.

Jesus. Had Travers heard cockroaches? Her body swayed, dizzy from panic.

Travers kept moving, never looking around.

Her heartbeat raced. She had to keep him talking.

"I can't imagine wanting money so badly I'd kill my brother to get it," Ladonis said, thinking of HeartTrouble.

"That would be something now, wouldn't it?" Travers said. "Do you think that's why Clifford did it?"

"You mean, it's not?" Ladonis stopped walking and turned around. "Are you saying that he didn't have his brother killed to make sure that his precious stepchildren inherited the Maynard fortune?"

"You'd make a good cop, you know that." Travers pointed the gun at her head. "I respect that. And since I know how important it is for a good cop to prove why shit happens—well, that's why you're still alive and talking.

Ladonis resisted rushing out a response and saying something that would incite Travers and trip up his trigger finger. Travers grabbed her shoulder, turned her around, and used the gun to shove her forward. "From one good cop to another, just so you know, Clifford wanted to take the company's steel business global. But old-man Jarvis said he didn't want foreigners all in his shit. But the last straw was that damned Bunnie Sinclair. Jarvis Maynard knew she was all alone after her mom died, and wanted to tell her who he was. He even mentioned putting her in his will. Clifford didn't want to share the family fortune with a nigger." He gave Ladonis a sidelong look. "His words, not mine."

"So, you knew Jarvis Maynard was Bunnie's daddy the night she came into the police station. And Clifford knew."

"As soon as I heard about the woman demanding that Jarvis be arrested, yeah, I knew who she was." Travers chuckled.

A combination of alcohol, sweat, and something new, a liniment that scented her senses with an aura of danger and expectation hung in the air. Someone had to be watching. She had to keep Travers talking.

"You knew." Ladonis slowed her gait. "So, what did you do? Rush off to tell Jarvis Maynard that his daughter was gunning for him."

"No, Smart Ass. I called Clifford."

"Clifford. Yes, of course," Ladonis said in a soft tone.

"And when I told Clifford what had happened in Phoenix, about his niece's accusation against his beloved brother, Jarvis, he paid me to kill the old man that night," Travers said. "You see, the timing was perfect to make your friend the perfect fall guy."

"Sorry to hear that." Wellsburg, the good cop, stepped forward, gun hoisted with both hands.

Ladonis sucked in a breath, frozen in place.

Travers aimed the gun at Wellsburg.

Ladonis forced her leaded feet to stumble behind the cab of the Chevy pick-up truck.

"I knew the day we met," Travers said, his gun aimed at Wellsburg's head, "that your goody-goody crap policing attitude was going to get in my way." He spat on the ground. "It was Bayley, wasn't it? It was Bayley that clued you in. That son-of-snitch never knew when to keep his trap shut. That blabber mouth of his is what got his ass locked up for assault, conspiracy, and fraud last year."

Wellsburg nodded. Ladonis, shielded by the truck, gasped. Sounded like the Bayley guy saved her life.

"When I saw you two talking after we'd picked up Miss PR over there"—Detective Travers nodded her way—"I knew trouble brewed." He pinched his eyes as he focused his aim.

"You were right," Wellsburg said. "Bayley told me Clifford Maynard had hired him to get that pen. But the robbery went down before Clifford could locate it."

Ladonis's heart sank deeper into her soul than her fear had dared to tread. She'd tried to get that pen too. To commit the crime of obstructing justice. Had she become one of those selfish people out of touch with her natural goodness? Was this who she had to become to survive in the business world?

"He did, however, offer to help us solve the Audubon Place robbery."

Say, what? Sounded like Wellsburg was using her strategy and keeping Travers verbally engaged while waiting for backup. Ladonis bit her lower lip, looked around. She saw no signs of backup.

"Said he was there, but knew we couldn't go after suspects until the Sinclair case was all sewed up because A. Tabor was involved," Wellsburg explained. "He told me it was one of Tabor's clients who'd accused him of the fraud that landed him in jail. He made it clear that he'd be happy to help put that uppity lawyer in his place. That's when I knew. You are the only cop on the force always—and I mean always—talking about putting A. Tabor in his place."

Oh, my God, No wonder Tabor was hesitant to take this case at first. Helping poor black folks who'd been wronged by police was one thing, but exposing the upstanding funders and participants in the city's institutionalized criminalities, made him far more threatening.

"Since you were the only one who figured Tabor might know something about that robbery, I knew Bayley had to have had a direct conversation with you. I know because we decided not mention our suspicions about Tabor to the chief or anyone until we had more to go on. You agreed because you wanted to use it against him someday, somehow, and me, because—well, you know—I wanted to find out what inconvenient truths his antics had uncovered."

Did the cops know about Big Dee's involvement too? That Ladonis and Big Dee were first cousins? Ladonis released a loud throaty cry.

"Shut up," Travers yelled at her.

Wellsburg stepped forward. Travers took two steps backward, never losing his aim. Ladonis, contemplated getting in her car and driving home. But feared she'd get shot.

"I'd planned to take care of motor-mouth Bayley after I put that computer back," Travers told him. "Sinclair had no idea that the Maynard's own the building she lives in and had access. Clifford went snooping around when he learned from Jarvis about her trip to Phoenix. He's the one who found her hiding spot, and had me remove the damn thing."

"I'm guessing, then, that Clifford set up the robbery in Phoenix," Wellsburg said.

"You're guessing right, but when I told him that the daughter came into headquarters accusing her daddy of stealing from her, he knew his plan hadn't worked. She was still alive, so he hatched a new plan."

What a scumbag.

"But then Miss PR over there gets A. Tabor, of all the lawyers in town, to represent Jarvis's bastard, and she and Tabor start nosing around."

Ladonis wiped her face on her sleeve. This would be the point in a mystery novel where the pieces would begin to fall into place. Piece one: Thanks to Clifford, Travers had a key and was the other person in Bunnie's house the night she went to get the computer. Piece two: Clifford had already searched her home, found the computer, and knew what was on it, but evidently didn't know how to retrieve and change it to go against Bunnie.

"Clifford left the computer, but had to make sure there was proof on it that Sinclair knew about that pen," Ladonis heard Travers say through the fog swirling in her head. "But not about Jarvis's plan to change his will." He eyed Ladonis, then coiled and re-coiled his fingers around the butt of his gun. "I thought you'd beaten me to it when I saw you high tailing it out of there the other night."

"So, if I'd gotten to that computer the night I came looking—" Ladonis gasped, sagging against the truck.

"You would've found proof that the pen belongs to Bunnie," Travers said. "That Jarvis Maynard had emailed the mother to inform her that he was going to will the entire collection to their daughter."

Ladonis swallowed as something stirred inside her. Bunnie hadn't used her after all.

"Put the gun down," Wellsburg ordered. "You have no way out of this."

"Who says? How did you know I'd be here, anyway?"

"Frank came looking for you," Wellsburg told him. "He was wondering if you'd seen a camera he'd misplaced. Said he'd last seen it when you came into his office to find out what evidence had been collected at the Maynard crime scene. That's when I realized that you'd left in the middle of the National Weather Service's urgent weather briefing."

"Yeah," Travers said. "Frank's team had just returned from the Sinclair apartment when the chief called that briefing. If CSI had found her hiding spot without the laptop, it would be on the record. That briefing gave me the chance to get a photo of Sinclair's hiding spot on a CSI camera before the storm hit in case Tabor asked to see it. No telling if or when I'd get another opportunity before or after the storm."

Travers lifted his shoulder to wipe the sweat off his brow and re-aimed his gun. A tiny branch from the tree above the truck slapped Ladonis in the face as the winds picked up speed. She grabbed her cheek with one hand and the truck's door handle with the other.

"Now what?" Wellsburg asked. "Are you planning to kill me, too?"

"I could, you know. And blame all of this on you, the Sinclair girl, and your girlfriend accomplice over there. You'll be just another corrupt, dead, black cop."

Ladonis fisted her hand so tight, her nails bore into her palm. She winced in pain. Being black was the only reason needed to be blamed and convicted of a crime. HeartTrouble was right again.

"You won't do that," Wellsburg said in a confident tone. "You know me. I operate by the book. I wouldn't be here if I hadn't called for back-up. Now hand me the gun."

Wellsburg took one hand off his pistol and reached out. Ladonis slumped against the truck. Was the nightmare finally over?

"Give yourself up," Wellsburg urged. "Think of your wife and kid."

"You're joking, right?" Travers said. "How's my wife and daughter supposed to live in this town if I'm in jail? They'll be forever reminded that I'm a killer cop for hire."

"What, then? Are you suggesting that I let you go? You know I can't do that." A hard wind blew, and Wellsburg's body swayed backward. He planted his feet to keep the swift breeze from disturbing his aim.

"Yeah," Travers said. "I know. You're a chicken shit cop not loyal to the code."

"Chicken shit, huh?" Wellsburg tightened his grip.

"Yeah, chicken shit." Travers leaned forward. "Not man enough to stand up for the police brotherhood."

"Brotherhood?" Wellsburg cocked his head. "But, you're a cold-blooded killer, my brother."

Travers made two steps to the side, his gun still hoisted and pointed at Wellsburg. His hands shook as he struggled against another forceful breeze. "Let's say, you agree that if I retire and left the force that you'd forget I had anything to do with Maynard's death."

Ladonis stared at him. What about her? How would Mr. Good Cop keep her from talking?

"Sorry," Wellsburg said. "I can't do that. Besides, it's not just you and me here. What about Miss, how you say, Miss PR over there? She knows what you did. If you kill her, I wouldn't just be helping you get away with Maynard's murder, I'd become your accomplice in hers."

Ladonis felt the blood thumping through her body like a pile driver. "He's got the gun," she yelled. "He's got the gun that killed Maynard in his left sock."

"I won't stand by and watch you murder someone," Wellsburg promised.

"That settles it then," Travers said in a calm voice, his gun still pointed at Wellsburg. "One of us has to die here right now."

What madness did Travers's peaceful look camouflage? And why couldn't Ladonis move?

"It doesn't have to be that way," Wellsburg said.

Travers swung his arms around and pointed the gun at Ladonis. Her brain screamed at her to move, but her body, her feet refused to listen.

"Duck," Wellsburg yelled at Ladonis, moving toward Travers. "Put the gun down, Travers, or I'll shoot."

Travers pulled back the trigger. The sound of the click detonated like a bomb in her ears. She stumbled to her car, fumbled with the handle with shaking hands, and flung open the door. She threw herself inside, pushed the passenger seat back, and forced her lanky body into a knot on the floor.

She closed her eyes. Salty tears squeezed through and flowed down her cheeks as fright, anger, and a host of other emotions flooded through her.

The shot exploded. Ladonis screamed. A gale of wind ripped through the car. Then silence for what felt like an eternity. She opened her eyes, rubbed away the bleariness, and peeked out the window. Light from windows and flashlights cast shadows around her.

Detective Travers, holding his gun smoking from the barrel, lay in a growing pool of blood in the street.

Chapter Twenty-Five
Turning Point

HEARTTROUBLE CHARGED through the screen door onto their mother's porch. Ladonis grabbed the back of her head. Deja vu. Bunnie had rushed her too, stripped of her prison orange, wearing the same raggedy jeans and bad hair as the day she'd been arrested, and bombarded her with thank you tears and a request for a ride home. All she could do was say, "Glad things worked out for you. My mama is really sick, and she's afraid of storms. I can't risk taking you to your apartment and getting stranded on that end of town." What drove HeartTrouble outside to greet her that way? How was she going to appease him?

"Is it Mama?" Ladonis cried, set to blast HeartTrouble for sucking down a Budweiser.

She'd witnessed a top NOPD cop commit suicide. And after waiting around for hours to tell what she'd seen, she was abruptly told that her statement could wait. Had her mother's life ended while she waited? Good thing she'd told Bunnie, "You'll just have to come with me."

HeartTrouble glared at Ladonis and the sadness in his eyes hit her like a sledgehammer. He saw Bunnie and his expression turned to discomfort. Ladonis realized not only could Bunnie get stranded with her, but with HeartTrouble and Evalena as well. She sighed as HeartTrouble stormed back inside, Ladonis on his heel.

"What about Mama?"

HeartTrouble opened the refrigerator door and pulled out a Budweiser.

"Don't talk to me." HeartTrouble pointed angrily at her. He snatched the cap from another Budweiser.

Ladonis hurled him a hateful look. How was he supposed to help her take care of their sick mama during the storm if he was drunk?

She threw up her hands and headed to her mother's room. She opened the door and listened. She let out a soft sigh at her mother's labored breaths.

"What's wrong with you?" Ladonis eased the door closed.

"What's wrong with me?" HeartTrouble snapped back. "What's wrong with you? Bad enough Charmaine's mama called to tell me they was leavin' and takin' my baby girl. Said they wasn't sure where they'd end up." He hung his head. "Why did you sneak off like that in the middle of a hurricane? You know how Mama feel about us being together when it's stormin'."

"What?" Ladonis tuned in to his fear.

"If that white dude you work with hadn't come here lookin' for you—" HeartTrouble said.

"White dude?" Ladonis asked. "What white dude?"

"What if Mama had took a turn for the worse?" HeartTrouble said, his voice, scratchy and low. He took a big swig of beer.

"What white dude was here looking for me?" Ladonis screamed at him. "Bret? Was his name Bret?"

"That's the dude you work for, ain't it?" HeartTrouble snapped. "I mean work with. He made sure I got that point clear when we was talkin'."

"Talking? What in the world were you talking about? What did Bret want?"

"I figured you'd gone off like you the police or somebody," HeartTrouble mumbled, ignoring her. "I thought you had went and got yourself killed."

"What did Bret want?" Ladonis asked.

"It's what he did." Evalena flowed into the kitchen, stopped next to HeartTrouble, and gently removed the beer from his hands.

"What did he do?" Ladonis insisted.

"When I told him what you been up to tryin' to save that Bunnie girl and all"—HeartTrouble looked past Ladonis at Bunnie watching television on the other side of the room—"He turned red and dialed your phone number, over and over. And when you didn't answer, you shoulda seen the look on his face."

"Ladonis." Bunnie walked into the kitchen. "Mayor Nagin's on television making an announcement. Want to listen?"

Ladonis nodded. She needed to find a safe place for her thoughts as well as her mama to get through the storm. She also needed to focus on another real situation—readying her own home. She went to the den and stood beside Evalena to hear what Nagin had to say.

"What's she doing here?" Evalena whispered to Ladonis. "Is there a way to get Miss Thang home before she gets too comfortable?"

"No." Ladonis turned up her nose. What gave her friend the right to judge who she associated with?

Besides, where would Bunnie go? Her mom and dad were dead. It's no wonder she latched onto Ladonis at the jail when she was set free.

Ladonis took a long stare at Bunnie. If that storm was closing in like the weather reporter predicted, there's no telling when she'd leave. Lord, this orphan could be around forever insinuating herself into her life.

"We're facing the storm most of us have feared," Mayor Nagin said. "This is going to be an unprecedented event."

Ladonis walked over to open a window and discovered it had been boarded up. She went to open the kitchen door. Still raining. Still hot and muggy. Thunder clapped. Her mother's treasured Mardi Gras Indian lithograph blew off the wall. She closed the door.

"I think we oughta leave." Evalena picked up the framed poster from the floor. "The London Avenue levee is a block away. Forget the winds. If that levee breaks, this house will be under water in no time flat."

"Has anyone said anything about levees breaking?" HeartTrouble asked.

"Not yet. But think about it," Evalena said. "Every time there is a major storm, there's talk about the levees."

"No way is the Corps of Engineers going to allow those levees to break," Ladonis said.

"Oh, no." Evalena sneered. "Remember that when we floatin' around out of here. Word is that the last time the government gave the Corps money to ready the levees for the so-called big one, the city built the Superdome."

"For crying out loud, Evalena. You and your conspiracy theories. You cannot be serious," Ladonis scolded. "And what irony that would be since the Superdome is the last resort shelter being offered to people."

"Humph," Evalena grunted.

"Where should we go?" Bunnie asked. "Should we go to the Superdome?"

"No," HeartTrouble blurted out. "We can't take Mama to the Superdome. Where she gonna lay down in there? We oughta use the hotel reservation that white dude made for us."

"Hotel reservation?" Ladonis muttered. "What reservation? You didn't say anything about any reservation."

"Yeah, he called Big Dee to get us rooms and she told him we needed three on account of you and me can't be around one another without fightin'."

"Oh, my God." Ladonis's face and body dripped sweat.

"I told him thanks for the rooms and that we'd take it." HeartTrouble rubbed the hair growing on his chin. "And he said he would get a hospital bed for Mama too. You need to call him to make sure he wasn't lyin'."

Call Bret about something other than the state of the Floating Palace's affairs? About something personal? The veins in her head pounded. She could not make this about her. Like Evalena had said, they probably could weather the storm. But how would her mother fare in her condition after the storm? That was always the true test of surviving a storm.

She pressed the contacts button on her phone and typed in the letter "B." Bret's name came up. Ladonis closed her eyes. Bret picked up on the first ring.

"Ladonis. God, Woman. Where are you?"

"I'm with my mama."

"Why didn't you tell me your mom was so, so, ill?"

Why? Ladonis's chest tightened. How could she tell him something she hadn't processed herself?

"Didn't you think I'd want to know that?" Bret asked. "And what's this about you acting like a private investigator to clear Bunnie? What's that all about?" He took a quick breath. "Well, say something."

"How can I? You won't stop talking." Once again she stood in that door of shame HeartTrouble had opened for her, still unwilling to walk through and admit out loud that she'd been selfish. "Did you locate a hospital bed for my mama? My brother said you offered to."

"Deloise did." It sounded strange to hear her cousin, Big Dee, referred to as Deloise. "And she's working on an ambulance to pick you guys up. It may take a while though."

"How long is a while."

Mama would want to weather the storm in her home, like they always did. But how could they take care of Mama after the storm without water and power for more than a couple of days? No. Mama would be safer and better cared for in a hotel that had an emergency generator.

"A couple of hours. Around three o'clock. There's a run on ambulances to help transport sick people from nursing homes and hospitals. Phone lines are on overload. So, we're on hold trying to make the connection." He cleared his throat. "But if we haven't gotten an ambulance after my conference call with Velcroy and the boats' captains at one-thirty, I'll drive over in a company van. I have the garage guys removing the back seats in one now just in case. It won't have emergency equipment, but at least your mother can lie down."

"I don't know what to say. There's no way we can transport her in my car."

"So, that's settled. I'll see you later."

She held onto the phone a moment after he'd hung up. His kindness felt like more than concern for a co-worker. Could Bunnie be right?

Chapter Twenty-Six
Yet to Hit

"BRET SAID BIG DEE is trying to find us an ambulance," Ladonis told HeartTrouble, Evalena, and Bunnie, all glued to the Weather Channel. "It won't be here until around three."

"That long, huh?" Evalena's intonation exposed real concern. "Waves already startin' to crash over that exercise path on the Lake Pontchatrain levee in Kenner."

"For real?" Ladonis held in her apprehension, processing what Evalena's words meant. "Kenner isn't even an hour away."

"Ladonis," Bunnie said. "Since we have to wait another hour or two, can I trouble you for a toothbrush, a change in clothes, and a shower?" Her eyes were pleading again. "Also, I'd like to ride this storm out with you guys if you don't mind, but without the jail grit."

"Why not?" Ladonis looked around at her brother and Evalena. What else could she say? Go home? "Hurry up, though. I want to be ready to walk out the door as soon as our ride gets here." She waited to hear some wisecrack from Evalena, but she stayed glued to the television.

Ladonis went to her mother's room where she found a toothbrush, still in the wrapper, in the bathroom medicine cabinet. Evalena trotted off to the guest bedroom. Ladonis returned to the family room at the same time as Evalena, who tossed a pair of her Capri jeans and a white, fitted Old-Navy tee-shirt at Bunnie. Ladonis handed her the toothbrush.

"When you finish showering," Evalena said, "refill the tub with water. If we get stuck here, we gonna need that water to flush the toilet."

"I've got my radio," HeartTrouble said, "but it needs batteries. Mama got any extra batteries 'round here somewhere?"

Ladonis pursed her lips. She went into the kitchen and retrieved the batteries from a drawer and handed them to HeartTrouble, who had followed her.

Afterward, she entered her mother's room. The welcoming ambiance had transformed into a hospital ward. The French pine bed had been dismantled and removed to make room for the metal hospital one. Her mother's prize eighteenth-century chest of drawers pushed to the side to clear a space for the portable toilet.

Ladonis sat down beside her mother, who was deep in a drug-induced sleep. Ladonis's weight didn't even dent the hospital bed mattress. She placed her mama's cool hand between hers hoping she'd stir so she could hear her voice. But the only sound she made came from her shallow breathing, her only movement her heaving chest.

Did Mama know that HeartTrouble had boarded the place up and that Evalena was making sure there was water to flush the toilet? And that Ladonis had made sure there were batteries and food in the house. If Mama was awake and aware, that was exactly what she would have made them do.

Ladonis walked past the bed into the bathroom. Mama's favorite perfume sat on her vanity. The pink bottle evoked emotion and memories like a magnet's pull on iron. No matter what other gift her mama requested on her birthday, she expected Ladonis, not HeartTrouble, to give her a bottle of Chantilly perfume. Ladonis always obliged, loving and cherishing it always made Mama smile.

She filled her mama's tub with water, uncapped the Chantilly, sniffed the powerful fragrance, then poured it in her bath. Ladonis's tears hit the water along with the perfume. What was she going to do without Mama to keep her grounded and focused on what her mama called the nuts and bolts of life—family and friends.

Ladonis languished in the tub aware of the time, how long she had to prepare before the storm hit. She showered off the oily perfume and shampooed away the sticky combination of rain and hair spray before cleaning and filling the bathtub with water. She dressed in gray sweat pants and a black New Orleans Saints short-sleeved jersey shirt. Funny how all of her relaxing clothes bore Saints logos despite the fact she thought football was a savage sport. Unable to ignore that the team was source of city pride that she felt obliged to share. She brushed her wet hair hard and smoothed it back with hair gel into a pony tail.

She collected the ominous brown bottle of morphine left by the hospice nurse, a couple of nightgowns, her mama's favorite picture album, and lined them up on the foot of the bed. Bret had a plan for her. A plan that made it possible for her to take care of her mama.

Her phone buzzed. "Can't believe I got through to you." It was Bret. "I've been trying for an hour. Deloise is having a hard time securing the ambulance." The phone line filled with static. "I'm—" was all she heard before the phone went completely dead.

"Bret?" Ladonis yelled into the receiver.

She opened the door and took a step through the doorway.

A loud gurgled erupted from the bed.

HeartTrouble jumped to his feet and rushed past Ladonis. A baby-rattle sound escaped Mama. Ladonis made giant steps to the bed.

"Oh, my God." Ladonis put her head next to her mother's chest. "She's not breathing."

Bunnie came in and stood next to Ladonis. She gently grabbed hold of Ladonis's shoulders. Ladonis broke loose and collapsed onto her mother, sensing more than seeing HeartTrouble at the foot of the bed.

Bunnie lifted up Ladonis's shaking body. Evalena came in, bent over Mama, and held her hand over her nose. She looked at Ladonis and shook her head. Ladonis spotted her mother's dentures in a jar on the nightstand and went to get them.

"Quick," Ladonis said to Evalena. "Open her mouth before we can't pry it open with a crowbar." Evalena hesitated. "Mama always said she wanted to be buried with her teeth in."

Evalena, aided by Bunnie, opened Mama's mouth while Ladonis pushed the dentures inside. Evalena closed her mouth and gently placed a sheet over her face. She walked over to HeartTrouble at the foot of the bed and pulled him into her arms. HeartTrouble broke loose, went to his mother's closet, brought out Mama's African dress and headpiece. A gift from a missionary friend who'd visited Namibia.

"Mama said she wanted to meet her maker in this dress." HeartTrouble held the outfit, unable to hold back his tears. "She made me take it to the cleaners about a week ago. Then she made sure I picked it up the next day."

"Here." Evalena handed Ladonis a blue spiral notebook. "This is from your mama. She made me promise to give it to you when she— when she—" She lowered her eyes.

Ladonis put her hand over her mouth to stop the emotion threatening to flow out of her. But she couldn't stop the ache, nor the agony. And she couldn't crawl in her mother's lap and cry like a baby.

She noted the time. 2:25 P.M., Sunday, August 28, 2005. Her mama had died, and Katrina had yet to hit.

Chapter Twenty-Seven
Mama's Got an Attic

LADONIS CALLED THE police and the coroner for the umpteenth time and was told that the lines were busy, to try back later. She also dialed Bret's number and got the same response. Every time she heard that recorded message, it became clearer to her the personal toll Katrina was poised to have on people's lives, on her life. And it wasn't just about the loss of property.

HeartTrouble had no clue about where to find his little girl. Mama had died, and Ladonis couldn't contact the police about getting her body to safety. And Bunnie and Evalena were also stuck. How long would she be haunted by the notion that if not for her being gung ho to outsmart the cops and to beat Tabor at his lawyerly strategies they all would've had time to get to safety?

"Donnie," HeartTrouble called out, "come hear this."

Ladonis entered the family room where HeartTrouble, Evalena, and Bunnie were watching the television. They'd been there all afternoon, having agreed to wait together until they contacted the coroner to pick up her mama's body. Because she was unable to reach Bret by telephone, she'd determined that he had probably gotten stuck in the massive traffic jam resulting from closed streets and people trying to get out. But what was she going to do if he managed to get through? Would she leave her mother's body?

"Approximately twenty thousand evacuees have already gathered at the Superdome with roughly thirty-six hours' worth of food on hand," a reporter said.

Ladonis sat on the arm of the sofa next to HeartTrouble. She clung to the spiral notebook containing her mother's last wishes as she grappled with how she could carry out her mama's plan despite Katrina.

"Meanwhile, the national weather service has issued this special hurricane warning—" Damon Singleton, the young black weatherman, interjected. "Devastating damage is expected from Katrina."

Ladonis shivered at the roar of thunder going on outside.

"Tell us something we don't know," Evalena shouted at the television.

"The majority of industrial buildings will become non-functional," Singleton said. "Partial to complete wall and roof failure is expected. High-rise office buildings and apartment buildings will sway, a few to the point of collapse. Windows will blow out. Power outages could last weeks. The vast majority of native trees will be snapped or uprooted."

Ladonis listened in a trance of disbelief. The weatherman's information seemed unheard of—surreal, even though hurricane threats and severe storms came and went every year. The big one had been forecast so often, it was almost a routine storm prediction. But today, the words "the big one" rolled around in her stomach. Could this actually be the big one?

"Once tropical storm and hurricane force winds onset," Singleton said, "do not venture outside."

"The winds are knocking down trees and power lines already." HeartTrouble jumped up, paced, and kneaded his hands.

"Yeah." Evalena never took her eyes off the television. "And people are outside, tryin' to get away."

"So what do you think we ought to do?" Bunnie asked, with a quiet emphasis on "we."

They all stopped and stared at her.

Ladonis cleared her throat, more ready to reflect than to respond. She, like Bunnie, was now motherless. Both left alone without the guidance and comfort of mothering to, first of all, weather the ramifications of this storm, then to navigate the ups and downs of their own lives.

She stared at Bunnie. Should she and HeartTrouble stay through the storm or leave their mother and return after Katrina to handle her remains? Her fingers lost feeling and she dropped the spiral notebook.

"Over a hundred-and-ten-mile-an-hour sustained winds are certain within the next twenty-four hours." Singleton's intense expression was as telling as the howling breeze outside. "Winds at that velocity could put the storm into the hurricane-four category."

Category four? The highest is five. Would her mother have been safer at the hospital? Ladonis sighed. How in the world could she leave her mother's body alone to weather Katrina?

"Donnie," HeartTrouble yelled.

"Huh?"

"I don't know about you"—HeartTrouble's brown eyes darted sparks—"but I'm gonna stay. Nothin' worried or scared Mama more than bein' alone durin' a storm."

Ladonis couldn't bear to look at HeartTrouble. That weatherman had said that category four and five hurricane winds could move stainless-steel refrigerators like dust. And God forbid if that levee broke like Evalena predicted. Her mother could end up in Lake Pontchatrain.

But what would happen if they stayed and the big one actually did hit? What could they do for Mama? The fear of her own death paralyzed her. But she felt compelled to listen to her heart. Her heart told her that her mother was afraid of storms and had gone to great lengths throughout their lives to make sure that her children weathered them with her.

"Chances are things will be like always and all we'll have to deal with is no power and no runnin' water afterwards," HeartTrouble said, his voice strong, his tone in command. "Then I will walk to the police or the fire station if I have to, to get them to come for Mama."

"Yeah," Evalena said, "and if we're lucky, the rains won't flood us out. It has flooded here before, you know. So you know how bad that can be."

Ladonis frowned at Evalena. Why couldn't she keep the positive tone going?

"Mama has an attic." Ladonis blinked, hoping to erase the image of her mama's body under water. "We can go up there if the street floods."

"She do?" HeartTrouble asked. "Good, 'cause the last thing I heard Nagin say is if you stay, he hope you have an ax to chop your way to the roof."

"Yeah. Fool," Ladonis said. "What do you think that hanging string is for in the hallway?"

She pointed to the area between the family room and the guest bathroom. HeartTrouble headed for the hallway, pulled on the string, walked up the ladder and crawled into the attic. Ladonis went to

Evalena. It was clear what she and HeartTrouble had to do. But what about Evalena and Bunnie? Evalena, who had stayed to help take care of Mama, could be safe in Texas with her mom. Bunnie was alone, but hung around to thank Ladonis for getting her out of jail. HeartTrouble had a little girl somewhere out there that he wanted—needed—in his life. And Lord knows where Bret had ended up trying to help her.

Would she ever forgive herself for the horrible place everyone had landed because of her? At least she'd saved Bunnie, proved Clifford was behind the murder of Jarvis Maynard, and seen the end of Travers's terror. None of that could begin to offer her consolation.

"According to the weatherman, the storm won't hit full force until the morning," Ladonis said to Evalena. "You and Bunnie should leave straight away for safer territory. Hopefully, the police and coroner will show up and take care of Mama before the storm hits in the morning. Then HeartTrouble and I will have time to get out, too."

"Donnie, Why do you think the coroner ain't here yet?" Evalena's words came out in a growl, but raw anxiety squeaked in her voice.

"I wish I could call and find out." Ladonis waited for Evalena to accuse the system of not caring about a dead black woman. "But considering the reports and pictures on the news, and that the phone lines are either down or busy, I'd say they're not here because the roads are gridlocked. Not to mention the rain and high winds that ordinarily slow up traffic."

"Yeah," Evalena added. "You know how it is, rain-slick roads and water-filled pot holes. Slows driving down to a crawl in this town. And they're probably backlogged to boot. Lots of sick, panicky people out there."

"She's right," Bunnie said. "And if the weather reports are half correct, none of that is going to get any better, just worse. I think what Evalena is saying is that if the coroner can't get in, what makes you think we can get out?"

"What are you guys telling me," Ladonis whispered, her eyes filling with tears.

"I'm sayin'," Evalena rose from the sofa, "let's check out that attic."

"That ain't no attic." HeartTrouble made his way over to them. "Just a crawl space for insulation and stuff."

"Well, can we store food and water up there at least?" Ladonis said, deflated. "You know, in case it floods?"

"I wouldn't." HeartTrouble brushed the pink insulation foam from his clothes. "It's hot as hell up there. The food could cook in the cans. And there ain't no window. Fresh air is out of the question."

Bunnie turned up the volume on the television for a weather update. Evalena gasped. Ladonis followed her eyes to the crawl line and saw the words "London Avenue Canal," followed by, "Location: Gentilly," roll across the foot of the television screen. Mama's house was in Gentilly and the London Avenue Canal was the levee just up the street.

"Storm-driven rain," the announcer said, "could lap over New Orleans levees when Hurricane Katrina winds, near category-five speed, push through the Crescent City early tomorrow morning."

The expression of horror that distorted HeartTrouble's face matched the dread that twisted around in Ladonis's gut. Her mother's house was close enough to the London Avenue Canal to go under with its first gush.

Chapter Twenty-Eight
Boom

"DONNIE." HEARTTROUBLE SHOOK Ladonis, her curled-up body a damp ball of dread. She'd dozed off on the family room carpet next to Evalena. "Get up. Katrina just hit hard in Plaquemines Parish at that . . . that . . . truck-stop city, you know, Buras-Triumph."

"What?" Ladonis reached around for the flashlight. The electricity had gone out hours ago. She sat up and leaned her back up against the sofa. "Where's that, about fifty-sixty miles away?"

"I believe so. They say the wind was about a hundred and twenty-five miles an hour."

"That hard, huh?" Evalena stretched out her limbs. She clicked on the battery-operated candles on the side table near her and tugged at the wet shirt sticking to her skin. "What's that, category three?"

"I guess." Ladonis blinked at the soft light.

She looked up at Bunnie, asleep on the sofa.

"Turn the radio up so we can hear what's going on too." Ladonis rubbed her eyes. In her entire life, she had never awakened before a storm was over. Never experienced the middle of the storm, just the prep time in the beginning and the inconvenience at the end. "And will you please open the kitchen door and let a little air in here? I'm suffocating."

"Okay." HeartTrouble placed the radio on the side table beside the sofa. "It is gettin' pretty ripe in here." He glanced toward his mother's room. "I un-boarded a window in mama's room, too."

Ladonis didn't say anything. According to her favorite forensic television show, it could take at least two days for a body to decompose. But in this heat, with the house boarded up and the air-conditioner off, decomposition accelerated? Still, she didn't want to acknowledge the good sense behind her brother's thoughtfulness. She didn't need nor want another reason to confront the pain of her mother's death.

"Power failure is preventing an accurate measurement of wind speed in New Orleans at this time," the radio announcer said. "However, it's been reported that Plaquemines Parish experienced winds of up to a hundred and forty miles an hour."

"That means it was category four." Ladonis couldn't recall ever having kept tabs on hurricane categories before.

"Because of the sustained winds," the announcer said, "we've been experiencing a category one and two hurricane winds in the Crescent City since yesterday."

Ladonis wiped her brow with one hand then used the other hand as a fan. She stood up and followed HeartTrouble into the kitchen. HeartTrouble opened the door. Something crashed. She rushed closer to HeartTrouble and stared through the locked screen door in disbelief.

"What was that?" Ladonis said.

"The tin top off the neighbor's carport," HeartTrouble told her. "It just rammed into the side of their house, now it's rollin' down the driveway."

Ladonis stood there watching Katrina take charge. The gray, wet darkness blazed down as if it were the sun. Trees swayed. Plants, shrubs, and branches blew up and down the drive like globes of hair. Her mother's two, full garbage cans bounced around the yard like soccer balls, contents flying.

"It's more than category one or two out there. That wind so strong out there, it's whistlin'. Hear it?" HeartTrouble paused. "Sound like a tea-kettle goin' off."

"Oh, my God." Ladonis pointed to the big black pole across the back yard. "That transformer just snapped in half. See the sparks?"

"What?" HeartTrouble said.

"That electric pole," Ladonis shouted. "Look at it. It's snapped in two."

A gush of wind whirled by thrusting rain pelted her skin. HeartTrouble tried to push the door shut. Ladonis pulled it open again. She stood in the doorway, inhaling and exhaling while the rain sprayed over her.

"I'll mop up the water." Ladonis had slept through storms in the past. Had that undermined her fear of them now? "I need the fresh air."

"The windows on the Hyatt Regency have blown out." Bunnie bounded into the kitchen, radio in hand. "They say beds are flying up and down Canal Street."

"I'm with you, Woodrow." Evalena made her way into the kitchen behind Bunnie. "That doesn't sound like ninety miles an hour, category one or two winds to me."

Was this the new norm? Bunnie and Evalena showing up in tandem? Would she be forever stuck between the opposing forces of her childhood and her adult world?

"No," Ladonis whispered. "It sounds like the weather geniuses really don't know how hard the wind is blowing."

She wondered whether or not the Dixieland, six blocks or so from the Hyatt, and only three floors high, could stand up to these hurricane storm winds. Perhaps it was best Bret hadn't been able to pick them up to stay at the hotel. In addition to the wind and rain, the promise of a flood put everyone there in imminent danger, especially those who sought refuge from raging wind and rain in the underground parking lot. The same danger they faced here if the levee broke.

"Most of the major roads traveling in and out of the city are damaged," the radio announcer said. "Large portions of the I-10 Twin Span Bridge have collapsed. However, the Lake Pontchartrain Causeway is open for emergency traffic only."

Ladonis strode into the den, using her flashlight to locate the notebook her mother had left her. She flipped through the pages. Mama wouldn't just die and leave her alone to experience the big one.

"Donnie," her mother had written. "Don't feel bad I didn't tell you how sick I was. I didn't tell you 'cause you been my mama long enough. I had to be in charge of this, so, I prepared my funeral. Picked out the songs and verses. Picked out the casket. Arranged to be buried next to my mama in Zachary. Thanks to you helping me out from time to time, it's all paid for."

Ladonis hunched over. How dare Mama keep her illness a secret.

"Don't make sadness a way of life after I'm gone, Donnie," her mama wrote. "I had a good life. Met some good people and did some pretty good things. I might be a little scared now, but I'm good to go."

Good to go. Lord, just like Mama to chastise and comfort her at the same time. Even if it was done in a notebook.

"All you have to do for me from now on," Ladonis read, "is keep an eye out for your brother and his baby girl. Don't sell this house. That way, no matter what, he can have a home for her to come to. And find yourself a man. It ain't natural for a woman to live her whole life without a man. Loving as well as losing your daddy taught me that."

It dawned on Ladonis that these were her mother's last demands of her. She dropped her hands to her sides and let out a sad, loud sigh. What was her life going to be like without Mama's nagging perspective? The notebook slipped through her fingers to the floor. She stooped to pick it up. She smiled. Mama had put her last lecture in writing for future reference, guidance, and comfort.

A loud thud erupted in the other room, followed by Evalena's screaming and feet scuffling. She ran into the kitchen. The wind had hurled Mama's treasured birdcage across the room. Ladonis felt a rock land on what had to be her heart.

Mama had bought the little, round, red, vintage birdcage on her first trip to the French Quarter in 1965. Blacks weren't allowed there until after the Civil Rights Bill in 1964. The cage was the only thing she could afford on her first-ever visit to an antique store, so she bought it to remind her. Ladonis pressed the notebook to her chest.

HeartTrouble, Evalena, and Bunnie struggled to close the door against the wind's push-back. The radio was on the floor. "The 17th Street canal levee has given way," the announcer said in an excited voice.

"That's the third one this morning." Evalena picked up the radio. "They say all you can see in the Ninth Ward right now is rooftops."

"We have to have a funeral." The words seemed to boom from Ladonis's lips. "Seems now that the storm has hit, we're in more danger of flooding. Suppose we can't get out in time." The thought had been percolating inside her brain since the last weather report.

"What you talkin' 'bout now, Donnie?" HeartTrouble asked.

Ladonis could only stare at her brother in response. Her hands shook. She tightened her grip on the notebook. Her mother had entrusted her send-off to her. How could she explain to her brother—to anyone—that she had to read the verses, sing the hymns that her mother believed would shepherd her into the heaven she believed in? And she had to do it now. She had to be the daughter her mother had written to.

"Evalena, you know that song Mama used to sing all the time? 'To God Be the Glory'?"

"Um, um." Evalena grunted.

"Then you can sing it. Mama requested it. Did you know that?"

"No." Evalena kneaded her hands. "She gave me the notebook the day I brought her to the hospital. She told me to give it to you and only you when she—when she, you know."

Ladonis looked down. It still didn't seem real that she'd never see or argue with her mother again. She turned to Bunnie. Would she and her family be any safer if she hadn't been so keen on helping this orphan beat a murder rap? She could hear her mother telling her, "You know you growing up when you have the good sense to regret stuff."

"I want you," she said to Bunnie, "to read this tribute my mama wrote for me and my brother." She flipped through the pages of the notebook, then handed it to Bunnie. She pointed the flashlight on the notebook. "Can you read her writing?"

"I held you close, with warm concern and care," Bunnie read. "With love and understanding that I pray will always be there."

"Good," Ladonis asserted.

She closed her eyes, took a deep breath, and led the way to her mother's room. Bunnie, followed by Evalena carrying the radio, entered the room. At the door, Ladonis called for HeartTrouble.

Wind and rain from a cracked window imposed the will of Katrina and blew out the candle the instant Bunnie crossed the doorsill. HeartTrouble slipped in and stood beside his mother.

"Sing, Evalena." Ladonis made her way to her mother's bed.

Evalena cleared her throat. The words poured out. Evalena's voice was strong, not sad and trembling. Ladonis could feel her mama's smile.

"To God be the glory," Evalena sang. "Great things he has done."

"There's a leak in the Superdome," the radio announcer interrupted.

"Great things He has taught us," Evalena sang louder, "great things He has done. And great our rejoicing through Jesus the Son—"

"But purer, and higher, and greater will be our wonder," Ladonis joined in, "our transport, when Jesus we see."

A deafening and forceful boom shook the house. The levee had breached. The unspoken realization weakened Ladonis's knees. She fell on top of her mother.

Chapter Twenty-Nine
Hope and Pray

"LET'S GET TO the roof," Ladonis commanded, walking behind HeartTrouble, Bunnie, and Evalena through flood waters just above her waist in her mother's living room. "I think we'll be safer on the roof."

"If we're on the roof,"—Bunnie held the portable radio up to her ear—"a helicopter will pick us up and take us to where Governor Blanco has ordered school buses to evacuate people."

"We've been stranded here for almost two days waiting for your boss, Big Dee, or someone to come for us. Do you really think the government gonna send helicopters out here?" Evalena's too-loud voice verbalized Ladonis's anxiety.

"They have to come now that the levee gave way." Once again Bunnie's words softened Evalena's aggressive tone and attitude that Ladonis loathed as much as she admired in her character. "That's what they are saying on the radio. That helicopters are out looking for survivors on rooftops trying to escape the flood waters."

"This is Gentilly. They're reporting on what's happening in the Ninth Ward. What if they don't come here? Suppose they think people in Gentilly had the good sense to evacuate before the storm," Evalena said. "Then what?"

"We hope and we pray." Bunnie's soft-spoken words overtook the space as if amplified. "That's what I did in jail. I hoped and prayed that something would happen to prove that I was innocent."

"Hope and pray," Ladonis said. "Sounds like something Mama would say."

She looked back and could barely see the silhouette of her mama's body on the hospital bed, water inches from the mattress. Oh, God. She couldn't let her mama get lost in the rising water.

"Go ahead." Ladonis turned around. There had to be something she could do to make sure that her mother didn't spend eternity floating out there somewhere without a way to identify her. "I've got to make sure I know Mama when this is over."

"Donnie," Evalena called out. "Come back. You did all you could. Believe me, your mama's spirit gone on to her glory. She'd be first to say her physical body does not matter now."

"Good to go. Mama said she was good to go," Ladonis whispered, ignoring Evalena. She used her hands and arms as oars to navigate through the flooded space that was her mother's home, looking aimlessly around for something—anything—that could identify her mama's corpse.

Her mother would never know what had happened to the home she'd worked hard to own. The home where she wanted HeartTrouble to raise his little girl. The furniture—slimy-wet chairs, sofa, tables—were buoyant and smelled like a dirty mop. The Magnavox color television Mama had saved up a year to purchase levitated over the flooded kitchen floor, never to show another episode of *Little House on the Prairie* or *The Guiding Light* again. Ladonis felt sad. She'd planned to surprise Mama with a new Sony for Christmas.

The little red birdcage glided past her headed to her mother's bedroom. "That bird cage," Mama would say, "is my personal proof that the Civil Rights Act is for real." Ladonis caught up to the hunk of junk her mother held dear. She twisted and pried loose a broken spoke from the cage's tiny steeple and paddled her way to her mother's bedside.

She lifted the sheet covering her mother's right arm and wrapped her fingers around her mother's hand only to snatch it back as though she'd touched hot ice. She took a deep breath and tried again, determined to get past the unusual feel of death.

"I hope and I pray." Ladonis forced the spoke between her mother's closed, rigor-mortis set fingers. "I hope and I pray that you can hang onto this until I can get you buried properly."

"Hurry up, Donnie," HeartTrouble shouted. "I think I hear a helicopter."

Ladonis plodded through the stinking water as fast as she could. HeartTrouble had leaned a ladder up against the front of the house and the lower part of the roof. Evalena was already on top, lying on her stomach reaching for the radio Bunnie held out to her.

"Watch out for that missing step," HeartTrouble warned Bunnie.

"Oh, God," Bunnie cried. She'd missed the step. The radio fell into the water. "What have I done?"

"Don't stop," Evalena said. "Keep movin' up."

Bunnie fought to get her balance, crying like a baby. She grabbed hold of Evalena's outstretched hand. At the top, she plopped down and bawled some more.

"Hurry, up, Donnie," HeartTrouble ordered.

He held on to the bottom of the ladder. Ladonis hesitated, looking back. HeartTrouble touched her arm.

"I hate like hell to leave Mama here, too," he told her, "but if a helicopter comin', I don't want to miss out. I gotta find my lil girl."

A blend of melancholy and affection swept over Ladonis. Her good-for-nothing brother had lost his mama same as her, but had found an important reason to move on. That window office she coveted, could be floating on the Mississippi for all she knew, along with her dreams and evidence of her hard work.

HeartTrouble had a purpose he could articulate and a will to press forward with clarity and freedom. She felt jealous. She—the college graduate, the homeowner—felt none of that lucidity, and was fearful that Katrina, not Bunnie's charters, or the takeover, had taken away her opportunity to be FPSC's first female vice president.

She stepped up the ladder to the roof and laid on her stomach to secure the ladder in place for HeartTrouble. The air was saturated with water vapor, the clouds dark gray. Hard to believe that the slippery shingle roof was the safest, driest spot available to them. Once HeartTrouble was on the roof, he dragged the ladder up behind him and placed it on the higher part of the roof.

"Just in case," he said. "Don't want a wind to sneak up and take it away."

HeartTrouble was in charge. Ladonis felt relieved that he was, thinking that perhaps the time had come for her to relax. To live her life without believing she was responsible for his.

Night loomed, though time was hard to measure without the sun or her waterproof watch. And without the radio, there was no way to get information. Everything about the situation frightened Ladonis, as much as the sound of the levee giving way had.

A waft of wind and a clap of thunder sailed over the roof. Someone unfamiliar let out a yelp full of fright. Ladonis trembled.

"Who's that?" Bunnie cried out. "Somebody down there?"

Ladonis spotted a thin woman wearing a pale blue ripped nightgown with matching robe making her way through the water. She held above her head the smallest television Ladonis had ever seen. There was absolutely not a second when that water rushed in when she'd thought to grab something. Even now she couldn't think what to salvage if there was time. What made this woman grab a television?

She glanced over at her brother and her closet friend and felt a sensation of warmth. Even the sight of Bunnie gave her comfort. Now she understood why Mama insisted they weather storms together. The replaceable stuff you lose in a storm can be devastating for sure, but the loss of memories and loved ones was life changing.

"You welcome to come up." HeartTrouble placed the ladder back in the water. "It ain't dry, and it's slippery, but sooner or later it's gonna get dark. It'll be better up here with us than down there in the water by yourself."

"Yeah," Evalena said. "And we heard on the radio that helicopters are rescuing people from rooftops."

"For real?" The woman's voice was so raspy, she sounded hoarse. She gripped the ladder with one hand and secured the television under the other arm. "I went to bed expectin' to wake up in the dark ready to eat Bluerunner red beans and rice from the can and to drink water out the bathtub for a few days. Instead I ended up floatin' through God knows what shit in my house." The woman handed Bunnie the television so that she could use both hands to give herself a final push up onto the roof.

"Good thing my TV was on the top shelf in the closet or it would be floatin', too."

"Is it one of them battery-operated televisions with a radio?" Evalena asked.

"Yeah," the woman said, taking a seat on the roof's edge beside Bunnie. She retrieved the television. "But it ain't worked in years."

"Then why are you hauling it around?" Bunnie said, disheartened.

"'Cause my old man gave it to me," the woman said. "He been dead for two years now. Died right after we scrimped and saved enough to buy what was the blue and white house on the corner. I figured if I'm gonna die too, I better take it with me." She chuckled. "Then we can have somethin' to watch the Saints on while we chillin' in heaven."

The woman hugged the tiny, broken, battery-operated television, a gift from her man and a symbol of love to last two life times—her man's and now hers. Ladonis felt a longing that flustered her to the bone. There was no longer a question in her mind why Mama was afraid of the so-called big one.

The rain started again, harder, steadier. As far as Ladonis could see, Mirabeau Avenue was flooded. The more it rained, the longer it would take to recede, and the longer they would be stranded. She looked up at the darkening sky and shuddered. If a helicopter was coming, it had better hurry up. It was scary to think how they could survive the night in the rain on the roof, especially if the winds gusted.

"I just thought of somethin'," HeartTrouble said. "Before it get too black out here, I'm gonna check to see if I can find Mama's neighbor around the corner, Mr. Wilson. He got a boat. Maybe I can find him or the boat and get us outta here."

Good. Her brother was still thinking and in charge. Without an utterance, Ladonis held the ladder steady for him to descend. She nodded when he reached the bottom. The less she said, the better he performed.

She looked away from HeartTrouble, drawn to Evalena, gnawing on her bottom lip, her face and dreads dripping wet. Ladonis scooted closer to her oldest friend sitting on the edge of the roof next to Bunnie and the woman, Miss Diane. Their legs dangled as they stared into the water with no protection from the steady showers.

"I'm sorry." Ladonis took hold of Evalena's hand. "I'm sorry you're not safe in Texas with your mama."

"You ain't got nothin' to be sorry for," Evalena said. "I'm here because of a choice I made."

Ladonis smiled, reminded of their discussions on freedom. She always said that to be free meant having choices. Evalena argued that to be free meant not only to have choices, but having the dignity to demand others respect your right to have those choices. She was all about the respect.

Taking in Katrina's devastation, Ladonis contemplated their predicament. Her mother's home was under water. They had no food. No clothes except for those they wore. When she looked into the faces of her companions, she saw shattered dreams, drowning hope, and human loss. The visual made parts of her body sting from numbness.

Ladonis examined the darkening sky. The sounds she imagined were helicopter engines were no more, and she questioned if there had ever been a helicopter out there. She vowed to God that if they were rescued, she'd never ignore a storm warning again.

Ladonis glanced at Bunnie sitting quietly on the other side of Evalena. To think her life almost ended because Bunnie wanted her dad jailed. She claimed she wanted him punished for setting her up to die. But in retrospect, Ladonis believed it was because she wanted him to pay for not being her daddy. The deep creases in Bunnie's forehead telegraphed her sadness as she huddled close to Evalena, a stranger who in the past, had nothing but contempt for her. Ladonis wondered how could a hurricane, a destructive act of nature, produce horror beyond belief, yet create such a coherent example of humanity.

"Donnie." HeartTrouble stood in the middle of the ladder, looking at her. "Mr. Wilson and his wife okay. I found out that him and some of his buddies goin' around in their fishin' boats pickin' up people who stranded. One of them got a bigger boat than Mr. Wilson. He said he got room for all of us. He right behind me."

"Praise the Lord," Evalena said. "Now we can get on a bus to Texas, and to my auntie's house." She looked at Bunnie. "You too if you don't have no place else to go."

"Praise the Lord," Ladonis repeated. She smiled at Evalena. "I sound like Mama."

"And you smell like her too. Even through all this stink." Evalena rubbed her nose. "What did you do? Drench yourself in her Chantilly?"

Ladonis broke down in tears that morphed into a fitful laugh. Now, she could think about her tomorrows. Mama's soul was safe in heaven with her beloved Jesus, and she was not alone. And even though NOPD thought she was a loose end to be tied up, she felt safe to begin her journey forward with HeartTrouble and Evalena. And Bunnie.

EPILOGUE

"TABOR." LADONIS OPENED the door to her condo. "You made it." The lines around her mouth and forehead magnified her tenseness. She knew the time had come for her to face the music about why and how Detective Travers had died. She was prepared, but she wasn't ready. Her mother's voice entered her thoughts, reminding her how important it was to face unpleasant things head on no matter how difficult. "Deal with it," Mama had instructed, "or it becomes an albatross forever."

"Let's talk outside," she said, closing the door behind her. "I don't have furniture or air yet, and it's pretty uncomfortable inside."

Tabor sat down on the edge of an empty planter on what used to be her covered carport. Seeing the cracked-up slab of concrete redirected her thoughts to the pain and hope she had lived through since Katrina. To the ghosts and joys that still loitered inside her head.

"I thought it strange Chief Goddin wanted to meet us here," Ladonis said, looking past Tabor. "But I thought I'd at least have a table and chairs when I said it was okay. I wished I'd mentioned that I don't have air, though."

"Me too." Tabor took off his jacket.

"Couldn't this conversation wait until the police get their act together?" Ladonis said with a tinge of sarcasm, knowing that the circumstances surrounding Detective Travers's death would forever be part of her life's story. "The news is filled with reports about NOPD's loss of command control and cops who've become car thieves, or have gone missing. Besides, I've got to find my mama so that I can properly bury her. And HeartTrouble still hasn't heard from Charmaine, or her mama, for that matter. He's worried sick about his little girl."

"That's exactly why I agreed to meet with the chief today. And why she wanted to meet someplace other than police headquarters." Tabor wiped the sweat from his forehead. "I learned something about the

Maynard case that can end your dealings with the cops once and for all. You have to trust me."

Trust him? The last time she'd done that, she'd ended up kidnapped and almost murdered.

"How are things?" Tabor asked, loosening his tie.

"Things are okay, I guess," she responded.

She was not ready to relegate Katrina to small talk. She'd spent that first week after Katrina in Houston, watching her hometown and its people disintegrate on television while stressing about the whereabouts of her mother's body, and her brother's baby girl. A week had passed before she'd heard from Bret that the boats were safe, but the New Orleans port was too ravaged from which to operate, and closed indefinitely. She was surprised when he'd called and asked her to report to work as soon as she could. She'd arrived in town a couple of days ago.

The FPSC building was still there, but the windows in the offices overlooking the river were all blown out. The furniture and equipment ruined. The Board hadn't determined if or when to reopen. She had to decide whether or not to apply someplace else or give them more time to figure it out. Either way, for her foreseeable future, that vice presidency, or any vice presidency, had to remain in her dreams.

"I talked to HeartTrouble earlier." Tabor scooted over so that she could sit beside him on the planter. The big, square flowerpot was forlorn and ugly without the colorful blooms her mother had planted, same as everything she'd seen in her home city since her return.

"He's going to stay in Texas with Evalena's aunt a while longer." Ladonis smoothed out the navy and white sun dress, designed and sewed by Miss Diane. Who knew that the woman walking through floodwaters with a broken television hoisted on her shoulders was a seamstress by profession? "One of his homeboys told him that he was on the same bus to Houston with Charmaine's mama and her granddaughter. My brother hopes to find that his little girl ended up at a shelter somewhere in Texas and not in Iowa or some other faraway place."

"I heard," Tabor said, "but I had to tell him that the Atlanta company that hired Charmaine informed me that she never showed up, even though she'd called to get confirmation on her start date and her housing arrangement two days before."

"What?" Ladonis asked. "And how do you know what company hired her? Besides, I thought she'd left long before the storm?"

"I don't know for sure when she left, but I know about her employer because she had to give the court an address and phone number where she'd be working in Atlanta as a matter for the court record." Tabor patted the briefcase on his lap. "Luckily, I had the file with me during the storm, or it would be floating in the Mississippi along with everything else in my mama's old house. But what has me more worried is that according to her Atlanta landlord, Charmaine hasn't picked up her keys even though her company paid the deposit and first month's rent."

"Oh, my God." Ladonis thought of all the stories about rapes, questionable deaths, and disappearances during the storm. "What do you suppose happened to her?"

"Don't know," Tabor proclaimed. "Hopefully, HeartTrouble will make headway at the shelters where the grandmother and baby might have been taken and find her with them."

Tabor looked at his cell phone. Ladonis frowned. How dare he act as if she were a nuisance. He'd asked her for this meeting.

"Much damage to your condo?" Tabor pocketed his cell.

"I wish I'd boarded the place up. The windows and glass patio door blew out. Looters took everything the rain and wind didn't destroy."

"Evalena told me your insurance company practically handed you a check on the spot."

Ladonis wanted to, but didn't ask what was going on between him and Evalena. Tabor had tracked her and HeartTrouble down at Evalena's aunt's. Afterward, he and Evalena had become daily phone pals.

"It's a cleanup rather than a rebuild. I suppose that's why."

Ladonis shifted her body weight. She looked forward to the fresh start—new furniture, fresh paint. And was especially anxious to finally have the funds to replace the carpet with hardwood floors. She'd come to agree with her mother who believed that carpet was unsanitary.

"Did Evalena tell you that she and her mom will stay here with me until they get back on their feet?"

"Yeah," Tabor answered. "The biggest repair they have is to the damage that was done by the tree that fell onto their lanai and part of their kitchen. She's hoping they get power soon since their duplex is so

close to the French Quarters. And hopefully because of that, the work
will be fast tracked, and you won't be inconvenienced for too long."

Tabor had all the details. Ladonis wondered if Tabor's and Evalena's
relationship was getting serious. If so, that would be a really nice outcome
for her sisterfriend. Tabor was a catch. That didn't change the fact that he
could be a chauvinistic asshole sometimes.

"Any word on your mother's remains since we talked yesterday?"

"I've called every operating agency in the city a thousand times
over," Ladonis told him. "Nobody knows for sure where to find fifteen
hundred-and-seventy-seven presumably dead missing bodies." She
lowered her head. "The water rose over ten feet on Mama's street. I'm
scared we won't ever find her."

Ladonis wanted to scream every time she endeavored to look for
Mama in a city with most of its data lost in un-workable agencies. Just
thinking about the search in a town without street signs or lights, and
sidewalks that had disappeared under water and dirt, with refrigerators
and stoves literally littering the roads, tore at her heartstrings

"You'll find her." Tabor sounded more like a caring old friend than a
strategizing attorney. "I hear the feds have joined up with the state and
the city to help. They've set up a headquarters in Harrah's Casino. Try
there. And it goes without saying that I'll help you maneuver through
the bureaucracy any way I can."

"Tabor." Twyla strode up to them. She eyed Ladonis. "Miss
Washington."

Twyla's pulled-back hairdo revealed her high forehead, speckled with
creases like a crumpled paper bag. New worry lines. The scuttlebutt
around town was the lady chief had a lot more than crime to deal with
since Katrina.

"Something has come up in the Maynard case," Twyla said. "Shall
we go inside?"

"No furniture," Ladonis responded. "Let's walk instead." No way
could the three of them sit on that planter.

"What's come up, Chief?" Tabor flung his coat over his shoulder.

"Clifford Maynard has disappeared," Twyla blurted out. "Seems
while the city battled with Katrina, Clifford was selling and re-locating
assets, and made a getaway."

Ladonis gazed at her with feelings hovering between alarm, anger, and relief. Detective Travers had killed Jarvis Maynard and himself, and Clifford, the person who paid him to do it, had left the country. Would he ever pay for killing Bunnie's daddy?

"Wasn't he in custody?" Tabor asked, coyly, in a voice Ladonis felt incapable of shyness.

"No," Twyla said. "We decided to arrest him after the storm."

Ladonis looked at Tabor. Got a view of that distinct suspicious smirk on his face. A look that could only mean that he already knew Clifford had left the country. What was he up to now?

"What does that mean for justice now that he's left? Who's going to pay for his brother's murder?" Tabor asked in his wounded, lawyer-of- the-underdog voice. "How will the orphan, Bunnie Sinclair, and my client here get closure and move on if law enforcement doesn't order the murder charge his crime of complicity deserves?"

"We don't. We can't." Chief Goodin's shoulders slumped, her head hung down. "The governor has decided that since the man who pulled the trigger is dead, and the city is figuratively and financially underwater, that we don't have the resources to go after the conspirator in this mess."

Ladonis studied Twyla. In the past, she had projected, despite her boring style, an exciting, provocative image with an air of un-touchability that was challenging. Today she did not.

"Surprise, surprise." Tabor's attitude escaped from that big box of arrogance he lived in. "Another rich guy gets off scot free."

"Why are you here then?" Ladonis tried to sound agitated, reluctant to admit how relieved she felt by all of this. "If Clifford Maynard is not going to be prosecuted and the killer cop is dead, what do you want from me?"

"I'd like you to give a deposition," Twyla told her.

"But, you said the case is closed," Ladonis stammered.

"The case against the actual killer, Detective Travers," Twyla said, "has been closed because he killed himself, which for all practical purposes is a confession." Her lips spread. If that was an attempt to smile and ease the tension, it failed. "But, the D.A. wasn't who called off the manhunt for Clifford Maynard. The governor did."

"This is about saving your ass down the road." Tabor's tone scolded yet overflowed with his self-righteousness.

"I beg your pardon." Twyla's jaws flexed.

"I know for a fact," Tabor said, "that the police department produced an elaborate hurricane plan in 2004 that would've spared the evidence and property rooms from Katrina. Aren't you afraid that another governor who is not on the Maynard payroll, and a new D.A. might want to know why there is no evidence to seek the justice murder deserves?"

"Get to your point, Tabor." Twyla lifted her eyebrows.

"The point is," Tabor said, "that plan was funded but never implemented because it sat on a bookshelf in your office. God forbid a law maker should go after Clifford Maynard. Katrina took away all the evidence in the property and evidence rooms along with those plans." He was on his soapbox. Ladonis felt sorry for Twyla. "Even if the case goes cold, they'll need evidence. And because Katrina somehow absconded with the photos, the fingerprints, and any DNA that had been collected, Miss Washington's statement and testimony are all that's left."

"She can be subpoenaed," Twyla said, "forced to testify, statement or no statement. And don't forget there is some question about her presence at that Children's Hospital fundraiser that resulted in a burglary."

"A question? Perhaps," Tabor stated. His tone so matter-of-fact and cold. "But no proof."

Twyla stepped into a puddle of mud that used to be a sidewalk and just stood there looking down at her muddy pumps. Ladonis side-stepped that puddle, thinking she'd lived next to Tabor in that arrogant box of his since she was a teenager. Had he always been so cutthroat?

"If that happens," Tabor went on to say, "you don't want some lawyer to get Clifford off because your officers neglected, mistreated, and released a prime witness without securing her statement in a high-profile case that resulted in the death of an officer. You know as well as I do that in the current state of the NOPD, your career cannot withstand any more negative publicity. Nor the administrative scrutiny, should that information be leaked to the press."

Twyla's left hand folded into a fist. Her jaws clenched. Ladonis couldn't believe how fast her body language shifted from congenial to angry.

"Let's say . . ." Tabor amplified his lawyerly tone. "Let's say that I advise my client to give this deposition to at least shield you from incompetency charges in case some reporter starts yapping about those upgrades that you never got around to fulfilling."

"What are you proposing?" Twyla said to the sound of her wet, muddy shoes sloshing as she walked.

"I want the Audubon Place robbery case closed," Tabor said. "I want your word that your people will not come up with any evidence, any witnesses, and that no charges are ever filed against anyone you suspect is involved. Besides, I can prove that what was taken was donated to Children's Hospital as planned."

No institution in the country used the you-scratch-my-back-and-I'll-scratch-yours more effectively than those in New Orleans law enforcement, including A. Tabor. On the other hand, she'd learned that it would've been impossible for him to acquire any degree of justice if he were not willing to take some serious, possibly borderline criminal risks.

"And," Tabor went on to say, "I want all solicitation charges dropped against the five women your people locked up and abandoned in male holding during the storm."

Ladonis couldn't believe her ears. He had an insurance plan. How did every human being with a problem find him? And how could five hookers hurt Twyla more than the current corrupt state of the NOPD?

"What?" Twyla sputtered. "How do you know about them? There's been no report filed on them."

"Believe me, Chief," Tabor's disdain couldn't be missed or contained, "if those women get anywhere near a court, I can assure you that word will get out about how two men working on storm cleanup found them starving in your lockup days after everyone else had been evacuated. About how the workers had to use welding equipment to get them out." He cleared his throat. "And how you got some preacher to put them up until you can figure out what to do with them."

"Again, what do you propose?" Twyla looked squarely into his face, eyes glaring.

"That you dismiss the charges and connect the ladies with social services for counseling and transportation to wherever their families are. In return, my client will stand by anything you say about that deposition. That it was given before the storm, and repeated after the storm—whatever. And the five women will not sue you and the NOPD for deserting them during the worst storm in the city's history."

"And if I don't agree?" Twyla said. Her brooding eyes expressed how serious Tabor's threats were to her. Didn't she know that to Tabor, this bribe was a card he had to play in order to win in the game of Big Easy justice?

"I will see to it that you become the media scapegoat for everything wrong with the NOPD, especially during and after the storm," Tabor advised.

Considering all of this, Ladonis swallowed a bitter taste in her mouth that often follows reflection. Tabor was ambitious, same as her. But, was he honorable? Was she?

"And the old money behind the power in this town that hand-picked you to be the city's first African-American female police chief can gloat about your failure in secret and continue to support you publicly." Tabor was on a roll. "God willing that will be enough to keep the stain on your name from denying another woman or leader of color the opportunity to succeed in this city's law enforcement."

Ladonis breathed in a long, deep gulp of air and let it out slowly. Like Bunnie, the lady Chief of Police had been set up. Is that why Tabor had put the squeeze on her? If so, then the next question had to be what would happen if and when Tabor stopped plotting against the so-called "man" to overcome the bias and fear that plagued them all, the oppressors as well as the oppressed? Was his attitude—his ideology—a good thing or a bad thing?

What Ladonis did know was that she'd trusted her old friend, A. Tabor, and even though she'd be haunted by memories of what went down to free Bunnie, she had closure. She was free to start over. Free to search for and hopefully bury her mother one day. Free to help her brother locate his daughter. Free to pursue her life without that NOPD albatross.

A native of New Orleans, Alice Wilson-Fried attended Tulane University and later worked in Public Relations at the Delta Queen Steamboat Company. For the past thirty years, Alice has lived in California, first in Alameda County then moving to Vacaville in Solano County after the death of her husband, Frank Fried, in 2016. She is the mother of two, the stepmother of two, and the grandmother of nine. She has two published works, a nonfiction entitled *Menopause, Sisterhood, and Tennis*, and the first of a mystery trilogy called *Outside Child*, set in New Orleans. *One Drop*, is the second trilogy installment and has the main characters caught in the middle of murder and mayhem while struggling to escape Hurricane Katrina.

www.ingramcontent.com/pod-product-compliance
Lightning Source LLC
Chambersburg PA
CBHW021701260626
47154CB00022B/1311